THE
DRAGON'S
GATE

ALSO BY BARRY WOLVERTON
Neversink

THE CHRONICLES OF THE BLACK TULIP:

THE
DRAGON'S
GATE

Being **VOLUME TWO** *of*
**THE CHRONICLES OF
the BLACK TULIP**

BARRY WOLVERTON

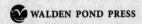 WALDEN POND PRESS

An Imprint of HarperCollins*Publishers*

Walden Pond Press is an imprint of HarperCollins Publishers.
Walden Pond Press and the skipping stone logo are trademarks
and registered trademarks of Walden Media, LLC.

Library of Congress Control Number: 2016936631
ISBN 978-0-06-222194-0

Typography by Carla Weise
17 18 19 20 21   CG/BVG   10 9 8 7 6 5 4 3 2 1
❖
First paperback edition, 2017

For Brit, the most magical potter I know

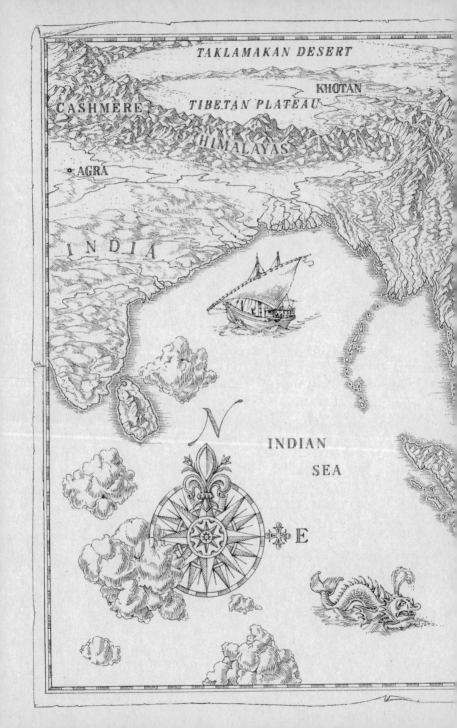

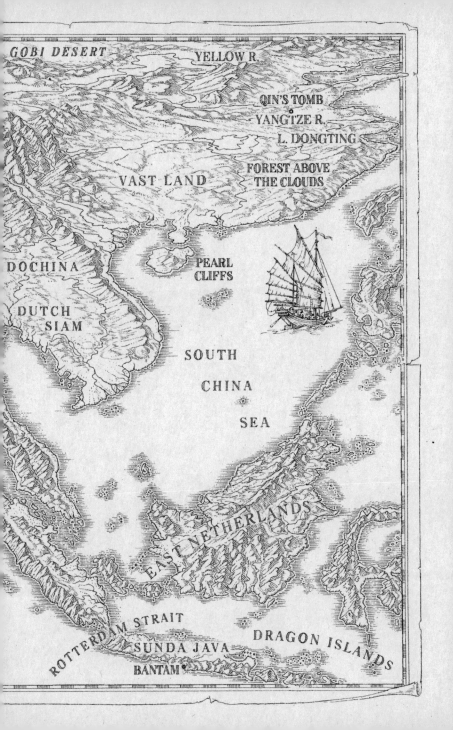

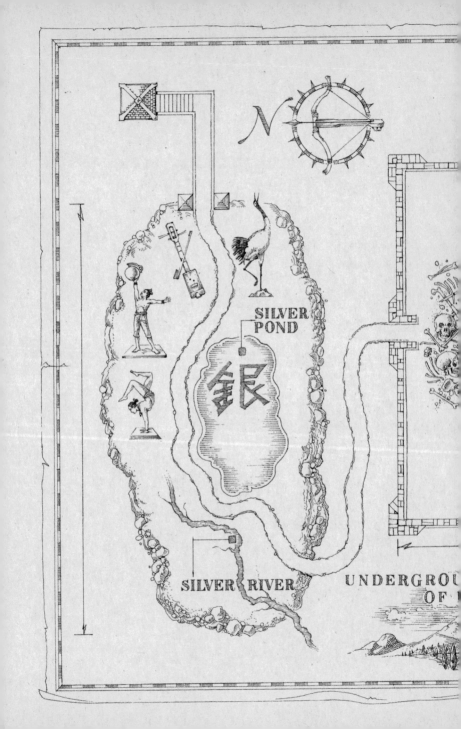

SILVER
POND

銀

SILVER RIVER

UNDERGROU
OF

N

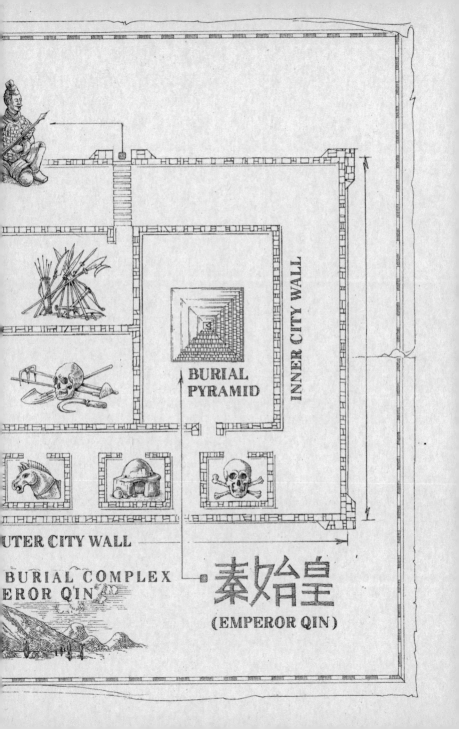

BURIAL
PYRAMID

INNER CITY WALL

UTER CITY WALL

BURIAL COMPLEX
EROR QIN

秦始皇

(EMPEROR QIN)

*To kindness and wisdom we make promises only.
Pain we obey.*

—MARCEL PROUST, *IN SEARCH OF LOST TIME*

A THIEF IN THE
HOUSE OF WISDOM

As he crested the hill, perched on the back of his Arabian horse, what struck him was how the whole city seemed to be made of sand. Tan houses and towers and mosques scooped right out of the surrounding desert and packed into perfect squares and rectangles and half circles. It seemed impossible that the fierce desert winds wouldn't one day reduce the whole thing to dunes.

"Are you regretting not changing your clothes, Lord Winterbottom?"

The Persian gentleman smiled at him as he asked the question. He had tried to get Lord Winterbottom to dress like the locals—blowzy pants and robes, with the traditional Persian headgear—but the Brit had insisted on wearing his official uniform as Royal Surveyor of Britannia. That was, after all, the reason he was here.

"A little," he admitted, wiping his brow. His navy wool jacket, adorned with ribbons and medals of rank, was soaked through with sweat. His thighs, which had been straddling the large horse for half an hour, were on fire with heat rash.

The Persian nodded. "It will be cooler inside," he promised.

They continued along the main road, passing a mina-ret—a narrow tower of baked bricks encircled with arches near the top.

"The Tower of Death," said the Persian, with a sweep of his arm. "We throw prisoners from it."

"Indeed?" said the Brit.

"Our city's name translates to 'The Place of Good For-tune,' " added the Persian, "but you aren't very fortunate if you fall from there."

"I would imagine not," said Lord Winterbottom. But any fears he had of plunging to his death were erased when they came in sight of an imposing brick wall, visible through a promenade of palm trees, and the tall wooden gates set within—the entrance to the House of Wisdom.

Two soldiers met them at the outer wall.

"This is Lord Nigel Winterbottom," said the Persian, handing a scroll to one of the guards, "in the care of Sufi Rouhani, faithful servant of the House." The guard studied the Brit's papers, which were like a small work of art, written in calligraphy with the shah's colorful seal at the bottom. He returned the scroll and the two soldiers withdrew into the recess of the wall to the wooden gates, holding them open for the visitors.

Lord Winterbottom's guide escorted him inside, where he found a courtyard that reminded him of the quad of his beloved Jordan College back in Britannia—except with stone tiles instead of a lush square of grass. Directly in front of them was a two-story building with a grand, barrel-vaulted entrance of ornately carved stone. On either side of this main building were identical buildings stretching off into the distance.

"A city within a city," said Sufi Rouhani. "One built on a foundation of knowledge, growing larger and more resplendent through the ages. Come, let me show you around."

Lord Winterbottom, who had paraded through some of Europe's grandest palaces and cathedrals, was in awe of what he saw that day. The interior of the buildings was a puzzle of geometric wonder and trickery. Every wall, it seemed, was carved with dramatic arches and arabesques, a honeycombed hive of stone and mosaic tile and filigree.

The House of Wisdom was indeed a city within a city. Or perhaps, a university was more accurate—one surpassing Oxford and Cambridge in size and splendor. Within were separate buildings dedicated to the study of mathematics, medicine, science, art, philosophy, and literature. A music room was carved with niches in the shapes of different instruments—not just for decoration, but to enhance the acoustics of the dome-shaped room. There was an observatory with the largest telescope Lord Winterbottom had ever seen, and within the zoology building was an actual zoo filled with exotic animals. The main library, boasted Sufi, was the largest repository of texts in the known world, and as if to prove it, he led his guest through room after room of books, scrolls, and other manuscripts stacked floor to ceiling.

As they walked, the Persian told Lord Winterbottom this story:

"It was early in the thirteenth century that the Mongol horde tried to destroy the House of Wisdom. A young scholar named Tusi, apprentice to the Royal Astronomer, had calculated the rate of expansion of the Mongol Empire, and had determined the precise date the horde was likely to arrive. Sadly, his warnings were ignored. So he began to dig a hole—"

"A hole?"

"Yes. Under the floor in one of the study rooms of the

library. And night after night, he would secret out books under his robe and hide them underground—more than four hundred thousand manuscripts in all—until the invasion came."

"Four hundred thousand?" said Lord Winterbottom. "How large was this hole?"

"Just listen," said Sufi. "I'm sure you know the story of the great siege? The fires, the looting, the massacres. When the Mongols defiled the library, books were torn from their shelves and thrown into the river. The waters ran black with the ink. But Tusi did a very remarkable thing."

"More remarkable than single-handedly hiding four hundred thousand books, one at a time?" said Lord Winterbottom.

"A few at a time," said Sufi. "I never said one at a time."

"Very well. Go on."

"The very remarkable thing," he continued, "was that Tusi diverted the ink-stained river into a vast underground cistern, until he had collected all of the bleeding texts. You see, the volumes he hid were but a fraction of those that were destroyed, and he refused to let the others be lost forever. So he devised a special pen that, when dipped into the cistern, allowed him to transcribe all the works the Mongols had tried to destroy. The diluted words flowed through him, as if by magic, and re-formed through the nib of his pen."

"That is truly remarkable," said Lord Winterbottom.

Sufi nodded. "Through all the years of turmoil that followed . . . the Mongols, Tamerlane, the Ottomans . . . the House of Wisdom persevered."

They walked on in silence for some time, through what seemed like endless passageways and studies, until they came to a deep green leather door.

"And now we come to what you *really* want to see," said Sufi. "The Hall of Maps." He pulled forth a large silver key, inserted it into an ornate keyhole, and slowly pushed open the green door, which swung silently on its hinges. Lord Winterbottom followed him inside.

At first glance, the interior of this room seemed like all the others: arched recesses from floor to ceiling, filled with books; ornate rugs; scholars sitting cross-legged on the floor, reading books propped in X-shaped stands. Every bit of wall not devoted to bookshelves was covered by maps, as might be expected of a Hall of Maps, but when Lord Winterbottom looked more closely, he could see that these were no ordinary maps.

Along with Persian maps of antiquity were scientific maps of the human body—brain, nervous system, circulatory system, even the systems of humors and emotions. There was a map showing the birthplace of every Persian ruler through history, and another highlighting the places where the prophet Zarathustra had overcome major obstacles on his way to composing the seventeen holy hymns. There were maps of the moon and the wind, as well as maps of Heaven and Hell.

When he glanced down to avoid stepping on a scholar, Lord Winterbottom noticed that the lush rugs he was walking on were also maps, arranged so that the floor of the hall as a whole showed a map of the known world. In a corner, a scholar was hunched over a glass case where a beetle was making tracks in a tray of sand, and the scholar was carefully recording the pattern.

"Extraordinary," mumbled Lord Winterbottom as Sufi guided him out of the main hall, down another corridor, through another locked door, and into a small chamber where on a blue-and-gold pedestal a book two arms long and two arms wide lay open.

"The Atlas of Ptolemy," said Lord Winterbottom with reverence.

"The only known copy in the world," said Sufi. "Rescued from the Library at Alexandria."

"Some would say *stolen.*"

"Would those people rather the Atlas had burned with the rest of that long-lost city?"

Lord Winterbottom reached out a hand to touch it, but Sufi stopped him.

"I must insist that you do not," he said apologetically. "Quite delicate, you understand."

The Brit arched a thin, plucked eyebrow at his host. "But then how am I to examine the Atlas? Was this not part of Queen Adeline's arrangement with the shah? In preparation for our survey of India, and the mutual benefits it will bring to our two nations?"

"No need for a lecture," said Sufi. "I will turn the pages for you. All of the rare-book librarians here have had our fingertips cauterized, so that they secrete no oils or sweat."

"Indeed?"

"Quite painful, but necessary," said Sufi. "Now, please, if you will clasp your hands behind your back and remain perfectly still, no matter what. No matter what," he repeated, quite emphatically.

Lord Winterbottom reluctantly obeyed, and promptly felt something cold and dry winding around his wrists.

"What the . . . ?"

"Don't move," said Sufi. "The Persian asp strikes only if provoked. Remain calm and all will be well."

"Easy for you to say," said the man fighting the urge to panic.

"Just be still; breathe normally," said Sufi, carefully opening the large book to the midway point. "The first half is a treatise on cartography and astronomy. Rather tedious. Here now, we come to the maps."

Sufi turned the page to a spread entitled ROME, followed by SARMATIA, NORTHERN BARBARIAN LANDS, AFRICA, and then THE ORIENT.

"Hold on now," said Lord Winterbottom. He was growing agitated yet desperately trying to remain calm. "Where are the maps?"

Sufi smiled. "Ptolemy left no maps. Only detailed instructions for *making* maps."

"I beg your pardon?"

"Shall I go on?" said Sufi, turning to a spread entitled NETHER REGIONS and another called THE HIDDEN SEA.

Lord Winterbottom almost flinched, but caught himself. "There," he said. "Tell me more of this one."

But Sufi Rouhani was now standing behind his guest. Lord Winterbottom was about to protest when he felt the Persian's hands come up and grasp him across the chest.

"What the devil are you doing, Rouhani?"

"Don't move," said Sufi. "Remember—your hands are tied."

"Are you mad?"

"No, just lonely. We servants of the House are required to take . . . *vows*. Also, I've lived in Persia for thirty years now, where men and women dress quite similarly. I've learned to tell the difference."

"Sufi . . ."

"You've got fewer curves than I like, and you're not very pretty, especially with that fake mustache. But I could tell you were a woman the moment I saw you."

"Sufi, I have to sneeze."

"What?"

"Dust," said the Brit, his long nose twitching. "From the pages, I think."

"No dust here."

"In the middle of a desert?" His nostrils were spasming now. His narrow mustache was wriggling like a worm.

"I assure you, this is a highly controlled environment. . . ."

"I can't stop it. . . ."

"You're bluffing," said Sufi. "Remember, the asp . . ."

Achoo!

It all happened in an instant. Lord Winterbottom flung up his hands to cover his nose. In that same moment, the Persian cried out. Sufi Rouhani looked at his guest, who slowly pulled his hands away from his nose to reveal a wicked smile. Sufi held his own hands up to his face, just in time to see the asp pull its venomous mouth from his thumb.

"Sorry, old chap," said Winterbottom as Sufi collapsed to the sandstone floor and the small asp slithered away into the darkness. The Brit turned to the Atlas, ripped out the page open before him, and a moment later the person

—10—

known as Lord Winterbottom was running down the corridor, back into the Hall of Maps, screaming, "There's been an accident!"

In the chaos that followed, Lord Winterbottom fled the hall, the shiny medals on his bright blue coat going *clankety-clank*. He ducked into an empty nook of another reading room, where he stripped off his coat, vest, shirt, boots, and trousers, leaving him in the blowzy pants and kaftan that Sufi had given him the day before. Even in this traditional Persian man's garb, it was obvious that Sufi had been right—the lord was a lady. She kicked her old clothes into the darkest corner, peeled off her mustache, covered her head, and strolled back the way Sufi had led them, stopping briefly in a room of ancient weapons, where she nicked a sword that had caught her eye—a brilliant scarlet sheath with gold ornament, and a gold and scarlet hilt with a gold pommel. Just in case. She hid the sword under her baggy clothes, and then walked out of the House of Wisdom into the bright, broad daylight.

PART ONE

THE
ORACLE
BONE MAP

CHAPTER
1

THE NAMES

Bren had never much remembered his dreams, until this one: a house at the base of a mountain where two rivers meet. And a door made of wide planks of larch wood, hanging on heavy, black iron hinges. The door is inscribed with writing that is foreign to Bren, and yet he understands it. It is a list, read from top to bottom: David Owen; Emily Owen; Brendan Owen.

The next time he comes to the door, though, his mother's name has been crossed out and another has been added. The door now reads: David Owen; ~~Emily Owen~~; Brendan

Owen; Archibald Black. The third time, Mouse's name has been added to the bottom. But the fourth time he comes to the door, everyone's name but his mother's has been struck.

"Mouse, what sort of dreams do you have?"

She was hunched over their makeshift game board. She had taught him how to play Go, an ancient Chinese game of strategy involving black and white stones. She had drawn the board in the firm sand near the water, and had collected light and dark pebbles from one of the island's streams.

"Dreams?"

"Yeah. I don't mean hopes and dreams. I mean the kind you have at night. Do you remember them?"

Mouse shrugged. "Sometimes."

"Do you ever have the same dream over and over?"

"I guess," she said. "Doesn't everyone?"

Bren examined his remaining black stones. The object of Go was to capture more space than your opponent by surrounding her stones with yours. In their three days since being shipwrecked on the island, Bren had not yet won a game, and Mouse currently had him cornered all over the board.

"I don't mean the exact same dream. I mean, almost like one big dream, chopped up. That you have in a particular order, night after night."

She looked up, and even though her face and eyes

rarely showed any expression, he could tell she was confused. "Never mind," he said. Back to the board. "I resign. Again."

Mouse carefully set up the board once more, this time giving Bren white and herself black. "You give up too easy," she said.

"Maybe you should let me win once." Mouse moved her first stone. Bren just sat there, then realized he was fingering the black stone around his neck. "Mouse, what did you do with the jade eye?" If she had used it, or tried to use it, since the night in the cavern, Bren hadn't seen her do so.

She reached into her pocket and pulled out the milky white stone they had found in the cave. The stone had been set into the eye socket of a girl named Sun, who had been exiled to this island from China in the company of Marco Polo when she was only a child, because Kublai Khan had feared she was a sorceress prophesied to overthrow his empire and restore the Ancients.

Admiral Bowman had wanted that stone, and the great power he believed came with it.

Mouse held the stone up in the palm of her hand, and Bren felt his stomach lurch as she struck the same pose she had then, summoning the quicksilver dragon to attack the admiral.

In that moment Bren had been terrified of Mouse. And

then, when it was all over, she had gone back to normal. Marooned together, they had just been two children foraging for food, playing games, praying that part of the *Albatross* crew had survived the storm and would find them. They hadn't talked much about what had happened in the cavern. But now Bren was reminded that Mouse was never just a child. She was the orphan with a fantastical past, a soul-traveler, a friend he knew less about the longer he knew her. And now she had this . . . object.

"Aren't you worried about losing it?" said Bren, thinking about how tattered his own trousers were after their ordeal. They had rips and holes all around. "The old man who was with the skeleton, he said *you* were the stone's guardian now."

"The stone found me," said Mouse. "It doesn't want to lose me."

"Back on the *Albatross*," said Bren, "the admiral told me that reaching this island meant having a chance for 'power of our own.' He thought the jade eye was magical, but he didn't say how exactly. Do you think he knew this girl—this sorceress, if that's what she really was—had transferred her spirit to the stone, like the guardian said? Assuming she really did?"

Making statements like that—*assuming she really did*—was one of the tricks Bren was using to try to get Mouse to tell him more. She had done precious little explaining of what happened back in the cave, either because she didn't want to, or because she couldn't.

"I don't think he knew for sure," said Mouse. "He never told me that, anyway. I think . . . he knew that whatever the stone was, it had to be powerful."

"And is it?" said Bren. "Can it get us off this island?"

Mouse shook her head.

"No, it can't? Or no, you don't know?"

"I really don't know," she said, her voice breaking. "I wish I did. I want to leave here as much as you. I have to find this Dragon's Gate. . . ."

"Then why don't you talk to the birds here?" said Bren, trying not to let his frustration spill over, but failing. "Send a message to someone? Or better yet, do your soul-traveling trick and fly away until you find help?"

"It's not a trick!" said Mouse. "It's not that easy. I've never soul-traveled for more than a few minutes, like what I showed you. What if I fly off and can't come back? What if I forget why I'm a bird? I'm afraid to try. I don't expect you to understand. . . ."

She trailed off, now looking past him, toward the sea. Bren barely turned at first, but when he saw the oars of the longboat flung high over the waves, he jumped up in a blur of sand, charging into the water like a madman, running face-first against the slapping waves, his trousers filling with water until he was half running, half floating through the surf.

"That's him, Mr. Graham!" came a shout. "I see him!"

"We all see him, Cornelius," came the shout back. "Put your spyglass away and hold out your arms—the fool boy is going to spoil our reunion by drowning himself."

Bren could feel the bottom dropping away from him, and the water was sloshing over his head. He thrust both arms into the air, and Sean grabbed him and pulled him into the longboat. Bren's trousers were so sodden that they promptly fell down around his ankles.

"Mouse is right behind me!" said Bren, hugging Sean and then pulling up his pants.

"Demonstrating that she's got more sense than you," said Sean. He pointed to where Mouse was standing and waving, only ankle-deep in the water.

"From the shore I thought you were Mr. Leiden," said Bren, looking at the man holding the spyglass. He glanced around the boat, but Sean put his curiosity to rest.

"Aye, lad, the good surgeon didn't make it. I'll tell you about it later."

They hauled the boat ashore and ten men besides Sean got out—men that Bren recognized from the *Albatross* but didn't know well. He didn't care about them right now. He never thought he'd be so happy to see Sean's sunburned Eirish face and that untamed lick of red hair.

"I'll show you where we've been sleeping," said Bren, leading them to the shelter they'd made out of bamboo and palm fronds. He realized the wobbly lean-to wasn't much to brag on, saying, "It's served its purpose. Nights have been warm enough."

"I keep forgetting it's summer this side of the equator," said Sean. "And summer in these latitudes means rain. Possibly bad storms. I think we should look into better shelter."

"There are caves farther inland," said Mouse.

"Big enough for all of us?" said Sean. Mouse nodded. "Any wild animals?"

Besides magical dragons? thought Bren.

"We haven't seen anything like boars or bears here," said Mouse. "Not even snakes."

Sean let out a mock sigh of relief. "Thank the good Lord. You know how we Eirish hate snakes! Ah well, I guess that makes sense given how remote this place is."

Despite his age, Sean's good spirits and obvious fortitude made him a natural leader for what was left of the crew. There was no talk of how they would rescue themselves from this unknown wilderness without a proper ship, nor talk of the disaster that put them here. Just one step at a time, and always forward. They had some food and freshwater. And they had natural shelter available. That's all they needed for now.

But Bren's spirits didn't remain high for long as they walked inland. There had been no evidence that the admiral was killed—Sean and the men obviously thought he went down with his ship—and Bren, as he had every day, kept scanning the trees for blue-eyed blackbirds. He couldn't forget the image of the admiral, transformed into a crow, looking down from the sky when Bren had been in the water. Of course, based on what Mouse had told him about the admiral's powers, maybe he didn't have to be a blackbird. Maybe he could be *any* of these birds. Or a lizard, or a plant. Constantly distracted and looking around, he stumbled half a dozen times as they climbed into the forest.

"You okay, lad?" said Sean. "Shall I carry you?" When he saw he'd embarrassed Bren, he added, "I'm only kidding, lad. You've endured more than any boy your age should've. And who makes it to shore after the shipwreck? Besides the ones lucky enough to claim the longboat? Grizzled, experienced sailors? Nah. A young boy and girl. I would say it's a miracle, but that wouldn't be giving you and Mouse enough credit."

Bren smiled, and his spirits stayed up the rest of the way. To his relief, Mouse did not lead them to the cavern behind the waterfall, but a different one she must've found while exploring on her own.

It did storm that night, but it was warm enough that they didn't need a fire, and Sean and the crew had saved some provisions from the *Albatross*, so Bren and Mouse got to eat something besides fruit and seeds. Over supper, they swapped stories about what had happened after the ship went down.

"How'd you decide who went in the longboat and who didn't? Did you draw lots?" Bren wondered, remembering an especially terrifying adventure story he'd read once.

"No time for that," said Sean. "The ship broke up so fast, it was chaos. Men were in the water, and it's one of the great mysteries of this business that most sailors can't swim. Mr. Leiden was our hero, helping me make sure the longboat went in right side up and insisting I get in it. He fell into the water right after, and I could never find him."

Mr. Leiden was one of the few Bren had gotten to know well, and his death hurt. He fondly remembered the surgeon's excitement when he was showing a skeptical crew how he could combat brain swelling by drilling holes into a man's head.

Bren looked around at the ten other men, most of them dozing off to the sound of the rain. "Did you see what happened to Admiral Bowman?" he asked.

"I didn't see him go under, but I know he wasn't with us, and he obviously isn't with you."

"He's gone," said Mouse. "I saw him. I couldn't save him."

"No, of course not," said Sean. "You needn't feel bad about that. How'd you even get your own tiny self to the island? The waves were fierce!"

"Luck, mostly," said Bren, answering for both of them. "My mother taught me to swim when I was a boy. A younger boy, I guess I should say. I just started swimming and prayed for the best."

"And you can swim, too, little one?"

"No," she admitted. "The waves carried me."

"Lucky indeed," said Sean. "The tide was coming in, and you were on the right side of the waves. The longboat wasn't. The ocean kept beating us back, and what was left of the *Albatross* nearly rolled onto us. Then night fell, and when day broke again, the island had disappeared!"

"Disappeared?" said Bren.

"I don't mean literally, of course," said Sean. "But we had been carried out of sight. It took us a while to get our bearings and a favorable current to make it here. And the last thing we expected to find was you two."

"So what do we do now?" said Bren.

Sean dug around in his rucksack. "I did manage to salvage some things from the *Albatross*. Tools, medical supplies, rations. Canvas to make a good enough sail, and we could hew a small mast from one of these trees. But it's still a long shot we could make it to any known inhabited land. Cape Colony was in an uprising last we saw, and we're more than two thousand miles from the Dragon Islands, which are the closest islands in the East Netherlands."

"We have to try, don't we?" said Mouse. "We can't stay here."

They all fell silent for several minutes, until Bren remembered something: "Mr. Tybert's map!"

"What about it?"

"He had a map he showed me once, where he had plotted possible locations for the Vanishing Island. This island," said Bren. "Based on the admiral's studies."

"And do you have this map?" said Sean.

"No, but I remember it."

"You said you only saw it once."

"That's enough," said Bren, and he began to scratch out what he remembered in the dirt floor of the cave: the Indian Ocean; the equator and the Tropics of Cancer and Capricorn; the East Netherlands; India and Madagascar. Those were the boundaries, the reference points. He then drew five spots where Mr. Tybert had marked possibly unmapped islands. "He said his theories were based on what the admiral had read, plus trade winds and other things that would make it more likely that an ancient ship had sailed there."

"Amazing," said Sean. "I forgot about your devilish memory."

He reached into his sack one more time, and what he pulled out made Bren's eyes light up: a small leather folio, filled with paper, and a graphite writing stick.

"I know you kept that journal," said Sean. "Didn't have time to look for yours, but I saw this in the chart room when I went to grab some instruments. I thought it might bring good luck in finding you."

Bren smiled and took the folio, reverently running his fingertips over the rough leather cover, thumbing through the edges of the stiff parchment, which Sean had managed to keep safe from the water.

"Let's try it out, yeah?" said Sean. "Make that map you just showed us in the sand. Then we'll get a good night's rest and do our best in the morning to figure out how to make land from here."

CHAPTER 2

A MEMORY
OF FIRE

Bren opened the journal and ran his fingers down the gutter of the folded parchment, pressing it flat. He thought about that time when Mr. Tybert had shown him the map. He recalled all the times he had joined the navigator at the back of the ship, learning his trade and listening to his stories. He could picture the old man's vacant eye socket and remember the sound of his voice the first time he called Bren "jongen." He could see and hear the navigator so vividly that his ear began to buzz, as if Mr. Tybert had just cuffed him for saying something foolish.

And then he remembered the last time he saw him. Not the last time he talked to him; rather, the sight of the navigator's lifeless legs behind his equipment locker, near the mangled birdcages. The blood pooling on the deck. Killed by the madman, Otto.

Even when they had sewed Mr. Tybert up in his hammock for burial, all Bren had seen was a glimpse of the old man's pale hands, folded peacefully at his waist.

He would never see his friend's face again. Not really. No matter how brilliant his memory.

Bren began to draw. He sketched the same framework as he had a moment ago, the Indian Ocean and the coastlines that shaped it. To this he added Mr. Tybert's navigational details, the longitude and latitude lines, and the coordinates of known islands. When he was done, he showed his work to Sean.

Sean pulled out the compass pair he had saved from the ship, placed one arm on their present location, and stretched the other to each of Mr. Tybert's five possible islands. He then made a few calculations in the margins of Bren's map, and when he was done, his bright blue eyes were a bit dimmer.

"Farther than you'd hoped?" said Bren.

Sean nodded. "There's only one spot on here less than a thousand miles from us. Most of the others, between a thousand and fifteen hundred."

"How long will that take?" said Mouse.

"Hard to say. The boat's got ten oars, and like I said, we can rig a sail, but . . ."

"Even small Viking longboats could make five to ten knots," Bren interjected. "They did have sixteen oars, though, the smallest ones." When he saw the look of surprise on Sean's face, he added, "My friend Mr. Black owns a bookstore."

"Six extra oars would make a big difference, assuming we had the crew to man them," said Sean. "And I don't believe the Norsemen were sailing the open ocean. Still, let's be optimistic, and say we can make land in three weeks. I figure we saved a week's worth of rations from the ship. Bare-minimum rations, mind you. But we can forage here while we hew a mainmast, and there's freshwater."

"I think we can do this," said Bren.

"Me too!" said Mouse.

"Little one," said Sean, "if you'll be on board with us, then I have no doubt. I've come to believe you're invincible."

Bren smiled. If they only knew.

They had a rough plan, and they spent the next several days on the island preparing to leave. Mouse and Bren had become expert fruit gatherers, but a few of the other men were practiced at setting traps for birds and fish, and by the time they had crafted a small mainmast, they had a good supply of dried meat. They also carved several containers to carry freshwater from the island. Just a week after Sean had found them, they were ready to leave.

▲▲▲

It had been less than a fortnight since Bren had been on the water, and yet it was like a whole new experience to him. The longboat was a fraction of the size of the *Albatross*, and even small waves pitched and bucked it, despite the best efforts of the oarsmen. He had never rowed before either, except for a small rowboat on one of the lakes in his mother's home county, but this was something else entirely. It was like being in a wrestling match with an opponent ten times your size.

The longboat had ten oars and there were thirteen crew members counting Bren and Mouse, so everyone could get a break from rowing even when they couldn't use the sail. Bren and Mouse were by far the weakest and spent the least amount of time athwart. No one could really be considered off duty in their situation, but when he had the chance, Bren pulled out his new journal and began to re-create the old one from memory.

Imagery flooded his mind as if he were flipping through the pages of the actual book: the sketches of the *Albatross* and all the rigging; the knots he had learned; the odd pieces of equipment with odd names, like Jacob's staff and loggerheads; faces of the men he had worked most closely with; lists of items on the ship and slang the regular crew used (most of it unprintable); typical menus from break-fast, lunch, and dinner; how the bells and watches system worked; diagrams of all the navigation instruments Mr. Tybert had taught him to use, and his notes on all of them; and then, of course, his own daily "logs," as if he had been the captain of his own personal adventure.

These journal entries covered everything from the mundane to the extraordinary to the barely believable. He thought he would scarcely be able to rewrite the details of the insurrection at Cape Colony, or the Hunger that had driven his nemesis, Otto Bruun, to murder. But even more emotional for Bren was remembering how it all started—him, standing at the rail of the *Albatross*, having made his bargain with the admiral, facing his father and deciding to leave Map. Before that moment, he had never had any doubt that he wanted to leave the place of his birth. Not since his mother died. Part of that, he had come to realize, was believing that he could return any time he wanted. That he was in control of his own fate. That he was the one charting his course. Something about the way his father had looked at him from the dock . . . the desperation in his eyes . . . Bren understood for the first time what his father must've felt—that there was a very real chance they might never see each other again.

Now, here he was, however many months and however

many thousands of miles removed from home, wanting nothing more than to reassure his father that they *would* see each other again. To reassure David Owen that he wouldn't have to spend the rest of his life without his wife *and* his son. To plot a course that would take them right back to Map.

There was just one big problem with that: Mouse. The girl who had become his best friend didn't want to go to Map. She wanted to find something called the Dragon's Gate, and she'd made it clear she wanted Bren's help.

"Have you drawn the bone map yet?"

Bren nearly jumped out of the boat. He couldn't fathom how Mouse was able to sneak up on him in a longboat.

"Not yet," he said. He knew how important this was to Mouse; he just wished he could understand why. "I will though, soon. I promise."

She just stood there.

"Okay, I'll do it now," he said, turning to a fresh page and putting himself where he least wanted to be—back in that cavern, among all those things that couldn't have happened. Not unless he had been dreaming.

He caught his hand playing with the black stone necklace around his own neck. The one that had protected him these past few years, according to Mouse. Remembering how she seemed to control the dragon, to attack the admiral, the thought crossed his mind that he might need the stone to protect him one day from *her*.

"Okay," he said again, forcing himself to bring the graphite stick to the paper. He sketched the girl's skeleton as they had found it, the bleached bones etched with black ink. Oracle bone script, the guardian had called it. More like pictograms than the Chinese writing Bren had seen elsewhere. Mouse had read them in vertical columns, starting on the girl's left: from her left shoulder down her upper and lower arm bones; then the left side of her skull and breastbone down to her hips and femur, her lower leg and left foot; then up and down her right side; and then the right shoulder and arm.

And then the sudden, intense fire and the cracking of bone. It had made Bren flinch then, and it made him flinch now, to hear and remember the sound of them breaking. As if this girl, whoever she had been, might feel her body being destroyed. When the smoke had cleared, there were fractures in the bones, and while Mouse didn't tell him what the oracle bone script had said, she did tell him what the fractures were: a map to this place called the Dragon's Gate.

As Bren reproduced the image of the cracked skeleton, though, it didn't look like a hidden map. To Bren it just looked like broken bones, or an ornate piece of pottery dropped on the floor. What was left of the skeleton's left shoulder blade, brittle with cracks . . . her tailbone, barely intact with a web of hairline fractures . . . her right breast-bone, looking as if the girl had taken a musket ball to the chest . . .

"Are you sure you read the bones right?" asked Bren, a touch of sarcasm in his voice. He avoided looking Mouse in the eyes when he said it, and for a while she said nothing.

"No," she admitted. "I didn't even know I could read that language. I had never seen it before. It just . . . came to me."

"Why do you think you need to find this Dragon's Gate?" he said. "Does it have something to do with the girl, Sun?"

"It must," said Mouse, "but I don't know how, yet." She surprised Bren by grabbing his arm. "Bren, I need to find out who I really am. I don't believe the admiral's story any more than you do. And this is the only way to learn the truth, I just know it. But I need help figuring it out. *Your* help, don't you see?"

Bren didn't see, but he couldn't tell her that now.

She was right that he had never believed Admiral Bow-man's story about her. The admiral had found Mouse in an orphanage in a fishing village at the mouth of the Pearl River. He had been drawn there by rumors of a strange girl who could talk to animals. Later the admiral had told Mouse that she came from a lake high in the mountains of China. A flock of cranes had landed on the shores of the lake, and when they touched the earth they transformed into beautiful girls. They undressed and hung their robes on a willow tree by the shore, and then went to bathe in the lake. What they didn't know was that in that very willow tree was a hunter who had come to hunt geese and hidden himself when the cranes landed.

When the girls finished bathing, they dressed and flew away. But the last girl couldn't find her robe—the hunter had stolen it. He jumped down from the tree and forced her to come with him, lest she freeze to death. She agreed, and the hunter took her home, asking her to marry him. She refused, and he in turn refused to return her robe, and this went on for weeks and months until she finally gave in. But she vowed never to name their children, so that they could never grow up.

Years later, the hunter's wife finally tricked him into returning her robe. As she flew away to rejoin her sisters, the hunter begged her to at least name their sons, so they could grow up to be leaders of their tribe. And so the crane wife agreed, calling out the sons' names as she departed, but the daughters were left nameless, and eventually cast away by the hunter.

That was the reason Mouse could talk to animals, the admiral claimed, because her mother was a crane.

Bren could understand Mouse wanting to know the truth of it all—where she really came from and how she came by her uncanny abilities. And he wished he could help her. But deep down, he wanted to go home even more. Sean and the other survivors had nothing on their minds but making it to safety, which meant sailing north across the Indian Ocean until they reached the East Netherlands, that archipelago of Dutch possessions in Southeast Asia. From there they would be able to sign on with a ship to take them back to Western Europe. And Bren had every intention of going with them.

CHAPTER 3

THE
SILK ROAD

The woman formerly known as the man pretending to be Lord Winterbottom wasn't sure how long she had been riding her stolen horse, because the sun never seemed to move in this part of the world. It hung there high above her as she rode over one scorching dune after another, and anything like a breeze was just a slap in the face. What she wouldn't have given for those overcast London skies and afternoon showers she was forever complaining about. To say nothing of the perfect Mediterranean weather, under which she had squandered most of her inheritance.

And then, a sight that made her spirits go up an octave—assuming it was real. She had heard about these phantom oases in the desert. Mirages, they called them. A trick of the mind, all perfectly explainable by science. Or was it mathematics? She wouldn't know, having been expelled from Jordan College in the middle of her first year for impersonating a boy.

But this seemed so real. A house. Perhaps a church? Salvation, indeed.

Jean Barrett rode her horse almost into the side of the building, so unwilling was she to believe her good luck. It was like a small inn, with a courtyard, abandoned in the middle of nowhere. Which it probably was. She was on the old Silk Road, that great artery of trade between East and West until the rise of the Ottoman Empire. Along the road the Chinese had built caravansaries—way stations or rest stops—every so many miles to make the four-thousand-mile journey bearable. She must've stumbled upon one.

She fed and watered her horse, then fed and watered herself. Afterwards she sat down on the floor of the building and removed the large page she had torn from the Atlas of Ptolemy. She unfolded it and read the title again, written in Greek: THE HIDDEN SEA.

Beneath the title were two columns of handwritten Greek text, with a couple of mathematical diagrams sprinkled in. Not a map, but instructions for making a map. So said Sufi, God rest his groping soul.

"Bugger," said Barrett as she set the stolen pages aside and dug in her rucksack for something else—a letter, folded twice and heavily soiled.

She unfolded it and began to read:

My dearest Lady Barrett,

   I wish you safe passage through the Holy Lands and into Persia. I trust my sources have provided the most current intelligence on the least hazardous routes. Arranging your visit to the House of Wisdom was something else altogether, and a thousand highway bandits will seem like nothing if you fail to convince. To that end, take care with the disguise I have provided you. Winterbottom clings to that blue coat as if his life depends on it—and yours will. Don't remove it under any circumstance. He certainly wouldn't. And he always wears it buttoned to the top, to ensure that all his medals are showing. No one there has ever met him, that I know of, but it would be good to be aware of a few of his personal tics and habits. . . .

Barrett skimmed past this, as it was over and done with.

   . . . the papers are what's critical, of course, and I have managed to create a brilliant forgery, if I may

say so myself, through a connection I have at Rand
McNally's Map Emporium . . .

More skimming, past the author's rather tedious description of his cleverness, until she came to the relevant part:

> *I'm afraid I can't tell you with absolute certainty*
> *which map you will need. You'll have to trust your*
> *instincts. What you will be looking for is an Indian or*
> *Eastern Ocean that no longer exists to us—one explored*
> *and mapped by Chinese navigators who had their life's*
> *work erased by emperors bent on convincing their people*
> *that there was no world beyond China, no history but the*
> *present.*
>
> *Ptolemy was in a unique position to capture this*
> *knowledge, and if I'm right, his is the only collection of*
> *maps in existence to plot the locations of islands and way*
> *stations that have since been lost to modern navigators.*
> *And it is here that I believe my friend, Brendan Owen,*
> *was taken and quite possibly abandoned by his captors.*
> *You've never met Bren, but you've heard me speak of*
> *him, so you know how important he is to me. That,*
> *plus the substantial fee we have agreed upon, will I trust*
> *make this worth your while.*
>
> *Yours faithfully,*
> *Archibald Black*

Barrett refolded Black's letter and looked again at the stolen map. Or rather, the alleged map. Her Greek was a bit rusty (yet another subject she'd failed to master before being expelled), but it began, "Beneath the jeweled surface of the sea, where laughing waves play, there lie the phantom lands, sunk from men's view of the world." From there were somewhat flighty phrases about winds and storms, boats tossed, tropical islands spangling the Indian Sea, wild places terrible and remote, and those places talked about but never seen. On the back was a cramped, two-column list of places and their coordinates.

"You must be joking," Barrett muttered.

She studied the list of place names, looking for ones that were unfamiliar to her—the "hidden" ones. But far too many failed to ring a bell. After all, Ptolemy had lived and worked in the second century. Barrett, having trained as an antiquary, knew that names of cities and regions had changed many times through the centuries with the rise and fall of empires. She would have to do her homework. Or, she could plot all the places listed here, and compare the result with a modern map.

But how long would that take?

The edges of the torn-out "map" were wanting to curl up at the ends, so she laid the whole thing on the stone floor of the abandoned building, pinning the corners down with loose stones. A desert breeze almost immediately tossed a handful of sand on the face of the map, and when Barrett brushed it off with her hand, a remarkable thing happened. Where she had brushed the sand away, there was a picture.

A map, or part of one, lay horizontally across the page.

She picked up the parchment and shook out the remainder of the sand, then held it in front of her for a better look. To her disappointment, it looked just as it had before—like a page from a written manuscript.

She tilted it this way and that, trying to catch it at the right angle, or let the light hit it in just the right way, trying to detect more than one surface, or two pieces of parchment stuck together. But she could find no such thing.

Beneath the jeweled surface of the sea . . . those were the first words of the "instructions."

Barrett laid the map down again, pinning the corners, and grabbed a fistful of sand. She casually scattered the grains across the parchment as if she were sowing seeds. Nothing happened.

She lay prone on the ground next to the parchment, and gently swept the sand from one corner. And once again, a picture appeared.

She pulled herself up into a squat, removed the silk scarf covering her head, and ran the delicate fabric from one side of the parchment to the other, until the loose sand was gone. Then Jean Barrett stood there, not believing her eyes.

It was a complete map of the Indian Ocean, framed by the borders of Africa, India, and Southeast Asia. A diagram made of grains of sand, right below the text.

"Well, I'll be damned."

She stretched out on the ground again, extended her index finger, and barely traced the lines of the map. It would seem that it had been etched into the parchment with miraculous precision, and became visible only when the tiny grains of sand settled into the otherwise invisible crevices.

Barrett just shook her head and smiled. "Oh, Archibald. You don't even know the half of it."

She ran her fingers through her short dark hair and then pulled them back with disgust. Her hair was still greasy with the pomade she had used to make herself look more like a man. Greasy and filthy—she hadn't bathed properly in days.

She couldn't spare much water, but now that she at least had shade she disrobed to her undergarments and splashed two handfuls onto her head and body, rubbing herself down with the only scrap of clean fabric she had left.

Outside, her horse neighed.

Barrett hurriedly rolled up the map and stuffed it into her sack, just as she saw the shadow of a stranger fall through the door.

She had time for one move: grab her clothes or her

sword. When she heard a voice—a man's voice—she went for the sword.

The man who walked in was slight of build and appeared to be Chinese. He had short dark hair, a trim mustache, and a fuzzy beard that dangled off his chin. He wore a wide-brimmed, black silk hat and a black robe that reminded Barrett of a priest's, except the robe was cinched with a colorful belt and had a pair of white cranes embroidered on the front. It was obvious from the look on his face that the last thing he expected to find in an abandoned caravansary on the abandoned Silk Road was an armed woman in her underwear.

"I don't speak Chinese, but I'm sure you can understand this," she said, brandishing the sword with the flair of a stage actor.

The man stopped in his tracks, his eyes going from the silver blade to the scarlet sheath. "The Tamer of Beasts," he said breathlessly, and then he fell to his knees in front of her.

SHARK
BAIT

B ren and Mouse sat opposite each other in the middle of the longboat, each gripping an oar. Mouse could barely wrap her small hands around the handle; Bren had started to get the hang of it, and marveled at how much stronger he was now than when he had left Map. Sitting on the bench, he looked down at the muscles visible in his left leg through his tattered trousers. His browned arms, while still long and thin, were now roped with muscles around his forearms, and when he pulled the oar toward him, a small apple appeared in the crook of his arm.

He momentarily took one hand off the oar and touched his face to see if he might have started growing a beard.

Sean, sitting astern, helped the crew keep the rhythm by leading a chant.

"Mouse, like this," said Bren, noticing that his rowing partner was having trouble keeping her oar in the water. He demonstrated, executing the J-shaped stroke that the other men were using to propel the boat. "Watch Pieter in front of you . . . do what he's doing."

"I am watching," said Mouse, a tiny bit of irritation in her voice.

Bren brought the oar around several more times, watching Mouse out of the corner of his eye. "Mouse, you're barely getting the paddle in the water. If we don't do it together, the whole thing is off!"

"Watch your own side," said Mouse.

"It's not my side versus your side," said Bren, "we have to work together."

"Then stop yelling at me."

"I'm not yelling . . ."

But he didn't finish what he was saying, because two of the men who had been on break—Willem and Rem—walked up and grabbed Bren and Mouse by their collars.

"You're both doing it wrong," said the one clutching Bren, and he unceremoniously removed the boy from his seat and took over the oar. His partner did the same to Mouse.

Sean was grinning when the two deposed rowers came to the stern.

"What's so funny?" said Bren. "We're not expert rowers, you know."

"I know," said Sean. "You don't have to be. I told the men beforehand we'd more or less be rowing with eight oars every time you two sat down. You're taking your turns, breaking a sweat—that's what matters."

Bren felt his muscles shrink back to normal.

"Besides," said Sean, holding up the map Bren had made with one hand and handing him the backstaff with the other, "you're both our cartographer and our navigator. Make sure we're still heading in the right direction."

"Aye, Captain," said Bren, sitting next to Mouse at the stern. Sean was being kind, he knew. Any one of them could have used the backstaff to measure the sun's height above the horizon, which told them their latitude, or north-south position. Guided by Bren's map, they were aiming north-northeast, toward the closest possible island— approximately 850 nautical miles, if they were lucky.

And they would need luck. They had a backstaff and a map of possibly nonexistent islands, and little else. No hourglass, which left them guessing at time. No traverse board to dead reckon their longitude, or east-west position. Mr. Tybert had often spoken fondly of the old-timers and their uncanny ability to sail by instinct, to recognize the swell of the waves, the color of the sea, and the patterns of fish. Bren had none of that.

But he did have Mouse. When the *Albatross* had been lost in the doldrums of the Atlantic, she had noticed the migration of birds and helped them decide which way to sail. She had uncanny ability in abundance.

"Mouse, you let me know if you think we're off course, okay? I know you have a sense about these things."

She nodded.

The sea had been calm since they managed to push off from the island, with just enough wind to use their make-shift sail occasionally for power as well as shelter from the sun. Mr. Tybert had told him the Indian Sea was calmer than the Atlantic, but Bren wondered how long that would last. On a voyage this long, good weather was bound to be followed by bad, and the bad in turn followed by good.

If you made it through the bad.

Bren pulled out his journal and held the oracle bone "map" for Mouse to see. "Does anything here look like a gate to you? Or a dragon?"

She studied Bren's drawing, but eventually shook her head. "We'll figure it out," she said.

Bren nodded, without much conviction. He then noticed Mouse's hand resting against the pocket where she was keeping the jade eye. It could have been coincidence, but he wondered if she *was* worried about losing it, despite how unconcerned she had seemed on the island.

"Mouse, I need to ask you something. Did you mean to summon that dragon? Were you trying to kill the admiral?"

"No!" she said, with surprising ferocity. She glanced toward the front of the boat as if to make sure no one was eavesdropping. But the crew couldn't have cared less about their child passengers, and their rhythmic chanting with every oar stroke drowned out most other sounds.

"I was just trying to keep the stone away from him at first," she said. "But I was scared of him, too, in a way I never had been. I knew he could be cruel, but I had never been afraid he would hurt me. Until that moment. But when the quicksilver began to change . . . it was as if I remembered something I had forgotten long ago, and then I knew what I was doing, even if I didn't know how. Does that make any sense?"

"I suppose," said Bren. It didn't really, not to him anyway. But he wanted to trust Mouse. "Just out of curiosity, you told Sean and the others that the admiral was really gone. You are sure about that, right?"

She rubbed her hands together nervously. "No. When the dragon flooded the tunnel and disappeared, I lost all sense of control. Like the stone was suddenly empty."

Bren slumped a little, not wanting to admit how often he'd looked for blue-eyed birds or other creatures on the island, terrified Admiral Bowman might still be out there.

Their first sighting of land came almost a week into their journey. At first someone thought they'd spotted a ship— a large, black triangle of a sail on the horizon. But as they neared they saw it was an island, if you could call it that. Little more than a rock, cleaved in half so that one side was sheer cliff, and the other a jagged stairway to a sharp point. They circled the pyramid, which was scarcely half a mile around total, but they could find no obvious place to land their boat.

"Nothing but a lifeless rock," said one man.

"It's not lifeless," said Mouse. "Look up there, near the top."

Bren could just make out the shrubbery at the peak of the pyramid.

"Aye," said Sean. "But assuming there is any sort of food and water up there, that must be five hundred feet or more."

"How 'bout we send Mouse up," said one of the men. "Never saw a more nimble climber."

"No!" said Bren, suddenly and with unexpected anger. He saw the shock in everyone's faces and immediately looked down in embarrassment. His hands were trembling.

He hadn't meant to yell like that. But that horrible day, just a few weeks ago, had flashed into his mind—the day the *Albatross* foundered. The ship, breaking apart, listing to one side, and Mouse, who had gone above to scout the horizon, being jarred from the crow's nest and clinging to the side, her legs dangling over the raging sea. And then falling.

Bren could never forget the sight of it, and how he had felt. That he had suddenly lost something that he was just beginning to realize was vital to him. It didn't matter that Mouse was okay now . . . he couldn't get that terror out of his mind.

"I'm sorry," he said.

"It's okay," said Sean. "I understand. Besides, we're in no need of food and water right now, and it's not one of the islands Mr. Tybert speculated about. Hardly worth the risk of trying to make land amidst all these rocks."

So they rowed on, and soon discovered they had picked up a companion near the towering rock—a shark. Mouse was the first to notice it, the dread grey fin carving the water. The fin would occasionally vanish, only to resurface, time and again, until it had the full attention of every man in the boat.

"It's an omen," said one man.

"No, it's not," said Sean, eager to stem any talk of superstition that might panic the crew. "It's just a shark doing what a shark does . . . swimming."

"Hunting," said another.

"Then let's not be prey," said Sean. "Bring the oars in

and use the wind for a while."

Everyone was happy to take their oars out of the water. It felt too much like trailing your hand in the waves.

"Maybe we should throw it some food, so it won't be hungry enough to follow us," said Bren as the dorsal fin once more breached the surface.

Sean shook his head. "Will just make him hungrier, and likely attract more."

Another disturbing thought came to Bren. What if it was the admiral? Or the admiral's spirit? He stopped himself—he was being silly. Still, he watched Mouse lean casually against the side of the longboat, as if she were wishing the shark would come nearer.

He had to see the shark's eyes. That would tell him for sure.

He looked around the boat. It was small, too small for anything like real privacy. But all the men were deliberately ignoring the shark, he noticed, refusing even to look starboard. Even Sean.

"Mouse," he whispered. "Are you wondering the same thing . . ."

"Yes," she said, her eyes following the gliding fin.

"Can you *talk* to the shark?"

She shook her head. "I've never tried to talk to a sea-fish. Every animal I've ever talked to I could hold in my hand, or at least touch."

"What about soul-traveling?" said Bren, trying to imagine the soul of his friend in the body of such a beast. "I know you said you're not sure what your limits are. . . ."

"There's no connection," she said. "I don't know if it's because it's a shark, or . . ."

"Or because someone else is already inside it?" said Bren.

He glanced around the boat once more, then silently dipped his hand into their rations bag, fishing for one of the dried pieces of meat. He pulled up a nice stringy bit of some island bird one of the men had trapped. It had tasted like the floor of the vomitorium to Bren, but he would still be in big trouble for wasting a valuable piece of food.

If Admiral Bowman were somehow back with them, though, none of that would matter.

Mouse saw him with the dried meat and grabbed his arm. He pulled away and leaned against the gunwale. "It's okay, I have this, remember?" he said, showing her his black stone. "You told me it was my protector."

"It might not protect you from losing an arm, though," said Mouse.

Bren hadn't thought of that, and he drew his arm back. But he had to know. He inched his right hand toward the water and immediately began to tremble. He recalled some of the stories he had heard in the Gooey Duck back home, the kind that really made his ears perk up—sharks swarming a body buried at sea as soon as it hit the water, or gathering between ships squaring off for battle, as if they could smell blood before it was spilled. And then there was the tale of the sadistic captain who dangled one of his own men overboard until a shark leaped out of the water and bit off the poor soul's foot.

Bren pulled back his right hand and switched the meat to his left. If he were to lose a hand, he'd rather lose his weaker one.

He dipped the meat into the water, as far from the side of the boat as he dared lean, keeping his eye all the while on the grey fin some thirty yards away.

Gradually the fin submerged. A spasm ran through Bren's arm.

He looked to Mouse for reassurance, only for a moment, but in that moment, he saw it all happening in her eyes.

The shark had broken the waves, lunging for Bren's hand. All Bren saw was a giant pink cavity, not so much a mouth as an abyss, ringed with teeth like some primitive gravesite. The strip of meat fell from his hand, disappearing into the dark chasm of the shark's mouth, but Bren's open hand still hung there, his arm paralyzed by fright.

He watched the gaping mouth close around him. He saw the bloody stump where his left arm had been. He felt the cold shock of the wound. He was sure of it.

But then he heard yelling, and saw the filthy faces of

the crew above him, and when he held up his hands, both were still there.

"What the bloody hell were you doing?" said Sean.

Bren realized he was flat on his back in the boat. Sean must have yanked him away at the last second.

"Shark," said Bren.

Sean looked around at the others, not sure whether to laugh or be concerned that the boy was daft. "Aye, it's a shark. I think we figured that out already."

But that's not what Bren meant. In the last second before the shark had plunged back into the sea, its head had turned sideways, just enough for Bren to see the large, glassy black eye, soulless, nothing more than a polished stone set in leather.

Not a blue eye. Not the admiral's eye.

"Get some rest," said Sean. "In the shade."

Bren nodded, but he was fine, now. And the shark, apparently with a distaste for bird meat, disappeared for good.

THE EIGHT IMMORTALS

"I must admit, I'm not accustomed to having men fall at my feet," said Barrett, her sword still raised and the man still on his knees. Not sure what to do, she finally made a standing motion with her left hand and said, "Erm, you may rise?"

The man stood, and his eyes moved from the sword, which Barrett slowly lowered, to Barrett herself.

"My apologies," he said. "That must have alarmed you."

"Which part?" said Barrett.

"Please," he insisted. "Dress yourself."

He turned away as Barrett slipped back into her blowzy pants and kaftan. She left the head scarf off for now, but kept the sword front and center.

"You can turn around now," she said. "And I think it's about time you told me who you are."

"My name is Yaozu," said the man.

"Are you alone?"

"Yes and no," said Yaozu. "I am alone here, now. But I am one of many."

"How many?" said Barrett. "And are they on their way?"

Yaozu smiled. "With all due respect, you seem mistrustful of me, yet you have not introduced yourself. And you are the one holding the sword."

Something about the man's way was disarming, and so Barrett slipped the sword back into its sheath. "I am Lady Jean Barrett of Wolveren Hampton, northern Britannia."

"Pleasure to meet you," said Yaozu, bowing slightly.

"Where did you learn English?" said Barrett. "If you don't mind."

"I was a language scholar in Damascus," Yaozu explained. "And if you don't mind, how did you come to possess that sword?"

Barrett hesitated for a moment, then admitted the truth. "I stole it. From the House of Wisdom in Persia. I was on a mission there, one that put me in danger, and when I was fleeing I nicked this thing you call the Tamer of Beasts. I guess that doesn't make me sound very honorable, does it?"

"Depends," said Yaozu. "Is it stealing to take something back from whom it doesn't belong?"

Ethics. Another one of Barrett's least favorite subjects. As someone who collected artifacts from other countries, she was always tripping on that one.

"Whose sword is it, Yaozu?"

Yaozu looked at the sheathed sword with a glint in his dark eyes. "Spiritually, the sword might be said to belong to Lu Dongbin."

"And who might that be?"

"One of the Eight Immortals," said Yaozu. "There is much to explain, I see. Please, may we sit down and talk?"

Barrett agreed and they sat together on the stone floor, Barrett laying the sword between them crosswise, like a barrier.

"How familiar are you with the history of China?" said Yaozu.

Barrett shrugged. "I'm an antiquary by trade, so I have a healthy interest in foreign cultures. I know the Marco Polo stories, of course, though I don't know how much to believe. And I know the empire has been shut off from the rest of the world since the Ming succeeded the Mongols."

"China has a long history of empire," said Yaozu. "But

our people go back thousands of years before the Imperials. The Ancients, many call them. And before them, the Three Sovereigns and Five Emperors, demigods who ruled Heaven, Hell, and the Middle Kingdom, or Earth.

"As it is told, these demigods allowed the Ancients to use magic to rule the Middle Kingdom so they could concentrate on ruling Heaven and Hell. No sorcery or dark arts, but gifts such as healing and divination, altering weather and domesticating wild animals. But maintaining these gifts, learning them and teaching them, is most difficult. So the Ancients created eight magical objects instead, one for each of the demigods' gifts."

Yaozu began to draw pictures in the layer of sand on the stone floor:

"The lotus flower, given the power of persuasion;

"The jade tablet, for divination;

"The flute, which can call the wind and rain;

"The bottle gourd, offering protection from evil;

"The basket of flowers, which can heal;

"The bamboo drum, for summoning;

"The fan, which can bring the dead to life;

"And the sword," he concluded, nodding at the one between them.

"The Tamer of Beasts," said Barrett. "So it's a person? Like a genie's in here?"

"Not exactly," said Yaozu. "More like the spirit of the

demigod. Which is why the objects themselves came to be known as the Eight Immortals, or the Covert Eight Immortals."

Barrett gently ran her fingers from the gold cross guard, along the scarlet grip, to the ornate gold pommel. "It is striking. But how do you know this is the real thing?"

"There is one way to be sure," said Yaozu. He stood and walked out of the building and was gone for several minutes. He returned holding his black silk hat upside down in his hands.

"You want me to tame your hat?" said Barrett.

Yaozu laughed and turned the hat over. A black scorpion the size of her hand landed in front of Barrett, its fat tail curled over its back, dangling a stinger the size of a fishhook. Barrett sprang to her feet and backwards in one motion, colliding with the wall behind her.

"Bloody hell!"

"The sword," said Yaozu, calmly returning his hat to his head.

Barrett yanked the sword from its sheath and raised it above her head as if she aimed to cleave the scorpion in two, but Yaozu was quick to stop her.

"Lady Barrett, do not kill the scorpion! Subdue it!"

"How?"

"I do not know," Yaozu admitted. "I've never had the good fortune to wield the sword."

Barrett sidled away from the scorpion, which slowly rotated toward her on articulated legs, continuing to threaten with its tail.

"Okay," said Barrett. "Subdue it. Let's see if you can dance, little scorpion." She pointed the sword at the scorpion, half closing her eyes and murmuring. The scorpion seemed to quiver, and then it raised itself on its back two legs, resting on the curve of its tail, and began clicking its pincers together over its head.

"Yaozu, am I doing that? Or is that some scorpion attack ritual?"

"I believe it is you, Lady Barrett," said Yaozu, smiling broadly. "One more test," he added, and to Barrett's horror he rolled up one sleeve of his robe, scooped up the scorpion, and placed it on his bare, outstretched arm. "Prevent it from stinging me."

Barrett stood there, wide-eyed, pointing the sword and mumbling again as the scorpion's tail twitched and twitched, seemingly on the verge of striking. But it didn't.

"Most remarkable!" said Yaozu.

"Drop it!" said Barrett, and when Yaozu turned his arm over, Barrett impaled the scorpion with the point of the sword as soon as it hit the floor.

"Are you mad?" she said, panting. "I had no bloody idea what I was doing!"

"Ah, but the sword did," said Yaozu.

She stood there, trying to regain her composure, but her irritation at the stranger with a death wish wasn't helping. Then it sank in—they *were* strangers.

"Yaozu, why are you telling me all this? Why not just nick the sword and run?"

He reached inside his tunic, and Lady Barrett immediately brandished the sword again.

"Do not be alarmed," he said. "I just want to show you something." And he pulled out a small slab of pearlescent green stone, polished to a mirrorlike reflection on one side.

"Is that . . ."

"The jade tablet," said Yaozu. "I used it to find you."

"You were looking for me?" said Barrett, the hairs on her neck standing.

"You looked different in the mirror," said Yaozu. "You looked—"

"More like a man?" said Barrett.

Yaozu nodded. "I wasn't looking for Lady Barrett, I was looking for the inheritor of the sword. The Immortal who empowered it was considered the true leader of the eight. You plucking that sword from the House of Wisdom . . . it's a bit like the story of King Arthur, isn't it, pulling the sword from the stone? I believe you were meant to possess it, Lady Barrett. You must be a most remarkable woman."

Barrett lowered the sword, breathing normally again.

She wasn't going to argue with Yaozu if he insisted on thinking she was remarkable.

"What exactly would I be leading?" she said. "What are you getting at?"

"How about an expedition to find the rest of the Eight Immortals?" said Yaozu. "You said you were an antiquary."

"That doesn't really answer my question."

"Come with me, back to where I'm from," said Yaozu. "I will explain more."

"No offense intended, Yaozu," said Barrett, "but I'd like you to explain a bit more now. Before I hitch my wagon to your horse. What do *you* plan to do with these artifacts, assuming they can be found?"

He cleared his throat, causing Lady Barrett to fear that a long story was coming.

"The Ancients never should have created the artifacts. They did not consider that those not guided by wisdom could use them too. Or perhaps they did, but did not care."

"You're saying you want to destroy these magical artifacts?" said Barrett. "Or lock them away? Or do you believe that you and these others you've mentioned have the wisdom to use them?"

Yaozu evaded the question. "The first step is to find them, and make sure they do not fall into the hands of the wrong people."

"If you'll pardon me," said Barrett, "I don't quite see

how a flute that makes it rain or a sword that makes scor-pions dance is exactly a threat to world peace."

"You don't think like a conqueror, Lady Barrett. Imagine being able to flood a valley where your enemy is camped. Or possessing that sword when your enemy is on horseback."

She thought about it. If what he said was true, then shouldn't she want to help him find these objects? For the good of humanity, of course. The fact that they might be among the greatest historical finds to date, making her famous and quite possibly rich again, only slightly factored into her decision.

Still, she had made a promise to Archibald Black. . . .

"Yaozu, you say this jade tablet helps you find people?" she said, taking the tablet from him and looking at herself in the surface. The polished jade cast her reflection in pale green, which made her think of some sylvan spirit, alien but oddly enchanting. "If so, I think we can help each other out."

"Who are you looking for?" said Yaozu.

"A boy named Bren Owen," said Barrett. "He went off from Britannia on a Dutch ship, and his family believes he may be lost in the East somewhere."

Yaozu took the tablet back and held it so they both could see, and said, "Show us Bren Owen, of Britannia."

Bubbling up as if from a pool, the image of a thin,

sunburned boy appeared, his hair windblown.

"Amazing," said Barrett. "But where in the world is he? It looks like a boat, but not a full-blown ship."

"At least you know he's alive," said Yaozu. "If he were dead, or if no one had any knowledge of him, I do not believe he would have appeared."

"Okay," said Barrett, "let's try this. You said the tablet had the power of divination? Show me where I will rescue Bren."

The image of Bren in the boat disappeared, replaced by nothing at first, and Barrett feared what that might mean—that the rescue wasn't to be. But then they were looking at a tropical forest, and an elephant marched across the scene.

"That's not good," said Barrett. "Black was convinced Bren was taken to an island."

"These powers are difficult to understand, and to master," said Yaozu. "I am only just learning."

"Wait," said Barrett. "I want to try something else."

She retrieved the atlas page she'd stolen, laid it on the floor, and gently spread the sand so that the hidden map appeared. Yaozu's mouth opened in amazement. "I'll explain later," she said. She then took the jade tablet and said, "Show me where I'll find Bren on the map of the Hidden Sea."

In the mirror appeared the image of the floor of the caravansary, with the map laid on it, as if she were looking through a window instead of at a tablet. She then saw her-self crouch down over the map and extend her hand, her right index finger hovering over the sea and moving slowly from one island to another, until finally the mirror image of Barrett set her finger down on top of a small island in the north Indian Ocean, the northernmost island, in fact, of the ones shown on the map.

"Remarkable," said Barrett. She looked up at Yaozu, who was smiling. "Now the question is, how do we get there?"

CHAPTER
6

DRAWING LOTS

A week after Bren and company lost the shark, a tropical storm blew across their path, battering the long-boat and nearly swamping it. Their makeshift mast was snapped, and though they kept the boat upright, it was filled with water. They counted themselves lucky that it hadn't been a full-fledged typhoon, but when Bren measured their latitude, he discovered that they'd been blown backwards during the two-hour storm, and they'd lost their east-west bearings entirely. Sean had hoped for a journey of no more than three weeks in all, but they'd already been at sea nearly that long with no end in sight. And they had exhausted their food rations.

A seaman can go a fortnight without food, but only days without water, and that was their real concern. They had been able to save some of the rainwater from the storm, but it wouldn't last long spread among thirteen people. Even still, Bren marveled at the way veteran seamen could stick to routine under any circumstances. When it was their turn to sleep they simply tucked themselves against the inside of the boat, between the thwarts, stretched their legs out, and were soon snoring.

Bren had never gotten used to sleeping on the *Albatross*, except when overcome with exhaustion, and the longboat was no different. If there was moonlight, he spent most of the night writing in his journal or looking at Mouse's oracle bone map, trying to remember anything he'd read or seen in Admiral Bowman's secret books that might be a clue to deciphering it.

Days later, they came in sight of another towering pyramid of rock, remarkably similar to the first one. Every man in the crew cursed the rock with parched mouths, as if it were a mirage of salvation, more proof of how lifeless this stretch of sea was. Having stared into the deadly mouth of a shark, Bren couldn't help but see these jagged triangles as giant, prehistoric teeth, as if the ocean were concealing the mouth of some colossal beast lurking just beneath the surface. Compared to starvation at sea, though, being devoured in one gulp by a monster would be considered a lucky break.

Suddenly Mouse grabbed Bren's sleeve with one hand while she pointed to the rock with the other. "Bren, look!"

"Look at what? It's a rock. Same as the last one."

He'd no sooner gotten the words out of his mouth than he realized that's what Mouse meant—it looked almost exactly like the last one. Half the rock was smooth and concave, as if it had been cleaved in half.

"You don't think . . . we haven't been sailing in a circle, have we?" said Bren.

"No," said Mouse. "Different rock, but it looks the same on purpose."

"You're saying they're carved?" said Bren.

Mouse nodded. "Could it be a signpost?" she asked.

"Maybe," said Bren. "We immediately recognized the shape. That would have been valuable to the people first sailing this ocean, before our modern navigation equipment."

"What are you two so animated about?" said Sean, trying to be playful but sounding as weary as he looked.

Speaking only loud enough for Sean to hear, Bren said, "Mouse and I think these rocks we've passed may be wayfinders, left by ancient sailors."

"Do you?"

Bren couldn't tell if he was taking him seriously or not. "If they are, at least we know we're on a course back to land, don't we? If men sailed this way before?"

Sean half smiled and agreed without much enthusiasm, and Bren took note of the limits of positive thinking when your situation was dire. After all, even if they knew for sure they were on a course that would lead them to civilization, they were still out of food and nearly out of water.

They were slowing down, too. The men were rowing with less vigor, from the combined effects of fatigue and hunger. When they passed their third black pyramid, as forbidding and lifeless as the previous two, Sean pulled Bren and Mouse to the back of the boat to talk to them.

"Children," he began, trying to wet his cracked lips. "I hate to call you that, after what you've been through, but the fact is, you are children, and I'm about to have to do something no captain wants to do, and that no one your age should have to witness."

Bren's already parched throat shrank even more in anticipation of what Sean was about to say. He had an inkling, from horror stories overheard at the Gooey Duck, and from his adventure books, but he still wasn't entirely prepared for what Sean told them.

"I'm going to have to call a lottery," said Sean, his voice quaking. "Of course, you two will be exempt. No one would tolerate sacrificing a child."

Bren felt overwhelming relief, followed quickly by shame. It seemed cowardly to allow Sean to exempt him after these men had rescued him and Mouse.

"No," he said. "Include me."

"Me too," said Mouse.

When Sean tried to protest, Bren stopped him. "If you're going to do this, Sean, the men have to know it's fair odds."

Sean clasped Bren on both shoulders and just shook his head. His speech to Bren and Mouse served as his rehearsal, and when he told the men his voice was strong and sure. They took the news in silence, unable to look one another in the eye.

It was a bright blue day with no wind, so that the whole of the Indian Ocean seemed empty but for them. Sean took a length of flexible rope and cut it into thirteen pieces of varying length. He then put all the pieces into a sack and let each man—and boy and girl—draw in turn, taking care not to let anyone fish for a longer piece.

Mouse went first and drew a piece as long as her forearm.

The next four men took their turns, and then the fifth drew out a piece barely the length of his forefinger, and his sun-scorched face went ashen.

Seeing this, the next five crew members confidently dipped their hands into the sack; none were gloating, but the looks on their faces as they compared their pieces to the pale-faced man's were unmistakable. *You've been a fine mate and an able seaman, but better you than me.*

That left Bren and Sean. Bren's mind was distracted by the poor soul holding the short rope, and the look on his face, and the horrible thought of men having to survive by eating one of their own. *How would they kill him? How would they cook him? Would any of them really be able to keep human flesh down?* Those were just some of the unimaginable thoughts troubling Bren when he noticed that the expression on the poor soul's face had changed, as had the faces of the others. Bren looked at his hand: the piece of rope he was holding was no more than a stub, the length of his thumb knuckle if he was lucky.

Sean, looking like he might be sick, drew the obligatory final piece, which was of course much longer than Bren's.

An already somber mood in the longboat took a turn for the worse. A veteran seaman getting the short end, a man who had fully embraced the profession and all its risks, was one thing. A boy like Bren losing out was something else entirely. The only person who didn't seem horrified was the other man with the very short piece.

"Let's lay them out," said Sean, pointing to Bren and the other man. "Measure for measure."

What's the use? thought Bren. He could tell his piece was shorter.

But then something extraordinary happened. Sean stretched the older man's piece across the thwart, and when he stretched Bren's piece next to the other, it proved to be a hair longer.

Bren couldn't believe it. Sean didn't seem to be able to believe it either, and a grin broke across his face.

The other man also didn't believe it, and he certainly didn't appreciate Sean's reaction, lunging for him and pushing him back with great force, so that Sean tripped on the thwart behind him and nearly fell over the side.

"You rigged it!" said the man. "Or switched 'em! You two are friends."

Sean scrambled to his feet. "You know me better than that, Bakker. And you saw for yourself how careful I was to keep it aboveboard. You all did." He spun his head in all directions, to see if he could detect any mistrust among the rest of the crew.

"Mr. Graham is true to his word," said another, and the rest of the crew quickly backed him up. Bren didn't know if it was because they really believed what they saw, or simply because no one relished the idea of sacrificing a child.

"Everyone here could see I had the longer piece!" shouted the man called Bakker, whose desperate anger made Bren think of Otto, shortly before he'd gone mad.

"Optical illusion," said Sean. "The eyes, and the mind, play tricks. You saw me lay them out equally, fair and square."

Bakker tried to lunge at him again, but the others stopped him. "You're friends with him! You're all in cahoots!"

Bren couldn't look at him. He turned to Mouse . . . what had she seen? She said nothing, but touched her hand to her chest, near her throat. Bren did the same, touching the stone necklace.

A chill went through him. Had some sort of magic just saved Bren's life, at the cost of another's?

The rest of the crew had to restrain Bakker, until they decided exactly how to carry out this most unspeakable of options.

Bren sat down at the stern, exhausted by fear and relief, and now regret. If he were truly brave, he would offer to take his rightful place as the sacrificial lamb. But he couldn't bring himself to do it. He *was* a coward.

NEW AMSTERDAM

Two men hauled a bound Bakker to the middle of the boat. As soon as Sean drew his knife, Bren had to look away. He'd witnessed enough bloodshed for a lifetime, and there was no way he could watch Sean do what no captain wants to do.

"Wait!" cried Bren suddenly, jumping up from the stern and clumsily stepping forward over the thwarts.

Everyone froze. One of the men holding Bakker said, "You offering to switch him places, boy?"

"No," he said feebly, overcome again by his lack of

courage. "But I think I can buy him time. Buy *us* time."

"How?" said Sean, eager for any alternative. Even before Bren answered, he was sheathing his knife.

"There may be a way to make saltwater drinkable, by removing the salt."

Sean slumped a little; others grumbled. "Bren, lad, it's not like dirt swirling around. The salt is dissolved in the water."

"I know that," said Bren. "I didn't say it would be easy. But apparently it can be done. Mr. Leiden once told me he'd read about it in a scientific journal."

That was a lie. Bren had actually read this in a cheap adventure book, but he wasn't about to tell them that.

"Here—give me one of those tin drinking cups. Now, something to cover it . . . this!" Bren ripped a blank page from the back of his journal. "Parchment is made from animal skin. Strong yet flexible, and not too porous. When we stretch it over the cup like this, you see, it becomes somewhat translucent."

"Does anybody understand a word he's saying?"

"Listen!" said Sean. "Go on."

Bren removed the parchment and dipped the cup over the side of the boat, filling it with seawater. He then stretched the parchment back over it and set it in the sun.

"He's trying to grow fish," someone said.

"No, trying to create some steam, which will condensate

on the paper, leaving the salt behind," Bren explained. "Don't look at me like that. I know it will hardly produce enough to wet your tongue and lips, but it's better than nothing, isn't it?"

"It's worth a try," said Sean. "If we can buy a day or two, we may get another one of those typhoons. Bren, lad, are you willing to sacrifice your journal?"

"Of course," said Bren.

"What about pieces of cloth from our shirts?" Mouse asked. "Might that work, too?"

"It might," said Bren.

What followed was tedious, and the results hardly quenched any man's thirst. But the most desperate did revive a bit, and it gave them all something to focus on besides the alternative.

Then a miracle happened. They sighted land two days later, and it wasn't a lifeless black pyramid or some other forbidding place. It was a wide, white beach sloping gently toward a verdant jungle, and a lagoon the color of a robin's egg. The air was pleasantly warm and humid, and birds Bren had never seen before were congregating in the tree-tops. It looked like Paradise.

"What is this place?" asked one man.

Sean was shaking his head, looking at the chart Bren had been keeping. "We can't have reached the Eastern Netherlands yet. It's simply not possible, even accounting for errors of measurement on our part."

"So what?" said another man. "If it's not already Dutch, we'll claim it!"

That was met with a roar of approval from the rest of the crew, except for Bakker, the man who was now spared. Bren expected him to be happiest of all, but he just remained slumped near the prow, a vacant look in his eyes.

They rowed the longboat into the lagoon, and Bren and Mouse both leaned over the side to look into the clear blue water, where strange and colorful fish darted about. They took their shoes off to feel the warm sand with their bare feet, and Bren wanted nothing more than to lie down and stare up at the tropical sky until he fell asleep.

But of course, that wasn't possible. He was a member of a crew, and there was work to do. Finding freshwater and food was their first concern. Then they would worry about where they were, and whether anyone else lived here, friend or foe.

"Any volunteers to explore the island?" said Sean. "Besides Mouse?"

Mouse was already running into the jungle before any-one could stop her. Then a crewman named Cornelius led another group, leaving Bren, Sean, and six others to stay by the beach, secure the boat, collect wood for a fire, and keep a watch for any other ships at sea. It was perhaps an hour later that Cornelius emerged from the jungle, carrying fresh fruit and a hat full of freshwater.

"This place *is* Paradise," he said, his lips wet and spread wide in a smile. He shared what he'd brought and then led them all to a freshwater stream and a thicket of fruit trees. After they'd all had their fill, they went back to the beach to finish preparing shelter. They were desperately in need of rest.

They had hardly made it back when Mouse came tearing through the undergrowth and onto the beach: "People are coming."

"How many?" said Sean. "Hostiles?"

Mouse shook her head. "A large number," she said. "I don't know if they are friendly or not."

They all looked at each other. They were outnumbered, that much they knew. They also knew they were exhausted. Getting back in the boat wasn't an option.

Before long, they heard the *swoosh* of people moving—lots of people. The friction and the crunching of leaves and twigs underfoot grew louder. Bren could have sworn he heard music . . . and singing? Was it a war call? And then, he couldn't believe what he saw next. Two great elephants emerged from the jungle, surrounded by a dozen white men on foot. On the backs of the elephants were men dressed in the sober black and white of Netherlanders, seated in embroidered pavilion-like structures. The larger of the two elephants held a larger pavilion, and a larger man—pale and fat, with yellow hair and a beard, and overdressed for a tropical island. Bren could only assume he was the leader.

"Welcome to New Amsterdam!" bellowed the presumed leader. "Castor, down!"

His elephant slowly bent its front legs until it was kneeling, and then did the same with its rear legs. The man riding it was still ten feet above the ground, though, and a small coterie of assistants helped him out of his pavilion and onto the ground. He fussed with his waistcoat and sleeves, rearranged his hat, and then walked over to where Sean and Bren were standing.

"Welcome to . . . I already said that." He cleared his throat. "I am Governor Wycoff, at your service." He removed his hat and bowed. He reminded Bren of a jollier Mr. Richter, the wealthy businessman from the Dutch Bicycle & Tulip Company that Bren had despised. "My lieutenant governor, Gertjan Oomen," he added, waving his hat at the man atop the other elephant.

"Governor Wycoff, my name is Sean Graham, formerly bosun of the *Albatross*."

"The *Albatross*?" said the governor. "Reynard Bowman's ship?"

Sean nodded. The governor craned his neck to see who else was with them.

"Where is he?"

"The thirteen you see before you are all that's left,"

said Sean, and he proceeded to introduce Bren, Mouse, and the other ten surviving crewmen. "I apologize for our appearance, and our unannounced arrival. I'm afraid we've had a . . . bit of an ordeal."

The governor clapped his hands together. "Of course, how rude of me! You will share your story later, over a welcoming feast. But now you men clearly need fresh food and water, and rest. And, I daresay, a bath."

Bren could tell Mouse and he were thinking the same thing: *Please let us ride an elephant to wherever we're going.* Once the governor had remounted his elephant, and it was standing again, Mouse walked over and stood right next to its trunk.

"Careful now, little one," said the governor, but Mouse reached out a hand and gently ran it along the elephant's trunk, which twitched up into a J and danced a little back and forth. The elephant's ears flapped up and back several times, and Bren could have sworn he saw something like delight in the giant's eyes. Even the governor was impressed.

"Extraordinary!" he said. "Would you like to . . ."

Before he could even finish, the elephant wrapped its trunk around Mouse's legs and hoisted her straight up like a torch, setting her on its back right behind its ears. The governor let out a great laugh.

"Would anyone else like to—"

Bren was at the other elephant's side before the governor could complete a sentence. The governor laughed again.

Bren was helped into the pavilion with the lieutenant governor, an owlish Dutchman who smiled and nodded and patted the cushioned seat next to him. Sean and the rest had had enough of riding unpredictable vessels, and were grateful for solid ground beneath their feet.

When the elephants rose, Bren felt as if he were halfway up the mast of the *Albatross* again. And then the beasts began to walk . . . a slow, rhythmic rocking, not unlike a ship in calm waters. Still, Bren felt nervous, afraid he might fall right out of the open pavilion if the elephant suddenly changed its stride or stepped on a limb.

Mouse, of course, took to the elephant like it was old habit, tucking her knees behind its ears, stroking the stiff hairs atop its head.

"You really saved us, Governor Wycoff," said Sean, who was walking between Bren and the governor. "I never would have dreamed a day ago that we'd all have the chance to return home so soon . . . if at all."

The governor laughed. "Well, don't be too hasty, Mr. Graham. After a night or two with us, you may never want to leave!"

Once they arrived at the village, Bren decided the governor might be right. Back in Map, he had always measured his father's shabby wooden house against the stone and slate homes of the wealthy. Here the Netherlanders had built a beautiful village from the resources they had: large wooden houses made of palm wood; streets of crushed shells that glittered like jewels; wooden aqueducts carrying freshwater.

"Is this what all the Eastern Netherlands looks like?" Bren asked Sean.

"Not exactly," he said, taking in the village with as much awe as Bren. "Most look more like fortified trading posts. This reminds me more of Cape Colony, which until now I had thought of as the crown jewel of the colonies."

"Maybe this is the new crown jewel," said Bren. "The governor did call it New Amsterdam."

"Aye," said Sean. "He did say that."

Their welcome feast that night took place outside, since the weather was perfect, and though Bren was starving, he took his seat warily. He had only attended one banquet, back at Cape Colony, and he shuddered at the thought of how that one had ended. After everyone else was seated, the governor appeared, and Bren, Sean, and the others, following the lead of the thirty or so Netherlanders, held their palms together over their heads, bent forward, and said, "Prosperity."

Governor Wycoff bowed and said, "Prosperity," in return.

"Where are we exactly?" said Sean, once the banquet was under way.

"New Amsterdam!" said the governor. "Oh, you mean

geographically, of course. I couldn't tell you in sailor's terms . . . such and such degrees north and west and all that jibber-jabber . . . but I can tell you we're a week or so's journey southwest of the Dragon Islands. I had been stationed at Sunda, doing typical governor's work, when I was asked to lead a group looking for new resources on nearby islands. Turns out this place is filthy with tin."

"Tin?" said Sean.

The governor nodded. "Important in making bronze, you know. Bronze artifacts have been found all through the archipelago. The company figured there must be a wealth of tin around here somewhere."

"How on earth did you get elephants here?" said Bren.

The governor laughed. "With much difficulty!"

There seemed to be so many other questions to ask, but for now the group of weary sailors, having narrowly avoided a terrible fate, seemed more than happy to enjoy the feast and the local wine, and, best of all—real beds. After the feast, the governor took them to a longhouse of sorts, the floor of which was lined with wood-frame beds topped with cozy down mattresses and pillows.

"Do you frequently expect large parties?" said Sean.

"A good host is always prepared," said the governor, and he bid them good night.

Bren took a bed next to Sean, and before everyone collapsed from exhaustion, he said, "Sean, I get the feeling something is wrong. That something's bothering you."

Sean finished undressing and lay down on his back, clasping his hands together behind his head.

"Aye, I suppose you're right, lad. Something feels a bit off to me."

"Like what?"

"Like, I've been sailing Far Easters with the company for several years now, and I've never heard talk of a New Amsterdam, and certainly never ported here. And I've never heard of a Governor Wycoff, either."

WHITEHALL

Winter in London is cold, but even worse, it's wet. The rain puddles in the holes and ruts left by horses and carts, softening up the mud until streets are pocked with minor sinkholes. For David Owen, a slight man whose worn boots already looked like old potato skins, this presented little difficulty. But Rand McNally—powerful British map mogul who also happened to be a man of no less than three hundred pounds—was finding himself calf-deep in the muck in his brand-new, handmade leather riding boots. He had, in fact, planned to ride into London for an audience with the queen properly, on a fine horse, except that none could be found to support him.

"Why don't you just ride on the cart with the equipment?" said Owen as McNally extracted his right leg with a great sucking sound. McNally turned his beady eyes on him.

"I'll not be carted to Whitehall like an invalid," he snapped.

They had come this far by boat, hiring out a small craft from the seaside port town of Map, sailing up into the Channel and then along the Thames. McNally didn't like coaches, and the roads this time of year from Map to London were treacherous. But once off the boat, they had only been able to hire out a rickety cart for their things, along with a couple of swayback horses, from the closest livery stable.

The roads into the palace grounds were little better, furrowed by the daily comings and goings of dignitaries in ornate carriages that must have weighed twice as much as a typical coach, what with the weight of precious jewels and metal on both the carriages and their occupants. David Owen realized that he and McNally must look like a couple of wandering tinkers come to sharpen the queen's knives.

The palace guards must've thought that too, judging by their faces, and McNally's Papers of Invitation did little to impress them. They could've been stolen, after all.

"You'll have to go around to the servants' entrance," said the first guard. "Mind your shoes."

"Happy to," growled McNally. When they were both seated in a mudroom, cleaning their boots under the supervision of a stern butler, he said, "You're here to assist me, Owen, nothing else."

"I am aware."

"Be invisible until it's time for the queen's gifts, and then disappear again when you're done."

"I understand."

"This is good for *your* family, too, you know," said McNally. "Head draftsman for the queen's Royal Surveyor? And you'll get proper credit for your work on the new instruments."

While I'm being invisible, thought Owen, but it was something else McNally said that almost overwhelmed him—*good for your family, too.*

What family was that? His wife, Emily, had been gone for almost three years now. And his only son, Bren, had been gone from home more than six months. David still remembered their exchange on the dock as if it had just happened. The Dutch admiral promising Bren not just treasure, but the most extraordinary treasure he could imagine. The admiral couldn't have known how reckless that promise was, could he have? David Owen knew just how limitless his son's imagination was.

And then his boss, Rand McNally, who could have put an end to it all right there. Who had the power to overrule the admiral. Instead, he gave the final shove—*I can't knock sense into him, maybe you can.*

He glanced at McNally, who looked like a muddy boulder right now, hunched over his filthy new boots. Why hadn't he made Bren stay? He was the one who had been so determined for Bren to apprentice at McNally's Map Emporium, and then at the moment of truth he'd driven him away.

David Owen didn't understand, and he would never forgive him.

Once McNally had made himself presentable, the butler led them from the mudroom, through the larder and kitchen, down a long and winding corridor past the servants' work areas, upstairs, and into a long, high-ceilinged hall that was somewhat less impressive than David Owen had been expecting. No thrones, no tapestries, no gold ceilings . . . just a simple marble floor, tasteful paintings on the wall, and at the far end a raised area with a single wooden chair. Scientific appointments obviously didn't get the lavish treatment of military or royal events.

Their equipment had been brought in and was waiting there, near the platform, covered with a cloak. A guard walked them to the front, where they were instructed to stand until the queen arrived.

The queen obviously had better things to do; David Owen and Rand McNally waited there for no less than twenty minutes, Owen quietly fidgeting while McNally began to boil, judging by his ever-reddening bald head.

Finally, a curtain parted, and Queen Adeline was escorted in, dressed neck to feet in a blue and silver brocaded gown, a funnel of pearls around her neck, and her hair done up like a hornets' nest. She came to the edge of the stage and stood there while her two guests knelt. When David Owen rose he saw that the queen was trying to suppress a smile, and that's when he noticed that Rand McNally was having trouble hauling himself back off the floor.

"A hand, Owen?" he whispered.

David Owen hooked an arm under McNally's, but instead of lifting his boss up they both nearly went down in a heap.

"I'll wait over here," the queen said drily, and she turned away and walked over to her chair, making a big show of arranging her gown while the bumbling mapmakers got themselves upright again.

Queen Adeline looked McNally up and down. They had met, once, during the queen's Ruby Jubilee, when she had toured Britannia to celebrate her twenty-fifth year on the throne. She had thanked McNally for his prominent role in elevating Britannia's global trade profile, which led to her granting him additional legal prestige for his so-called treasure maps. She had toured the Map Emporium and the Explorers' Club (though not the vomitorium, where Bren was once employed), and within weeks of her departure, ladies in Map were sporting fashionable new clothes from London and Cloudesley Swyers had designed a whole new line of royalty-inspired wigs.

So, she knew what McNally looked like, and how large he was, and upon seeing his tight pants and knee-high boots, she asked, astonished, "Did you ride here on a horse?"

There was a faint sound of sniggering from her attendants.

"No, Your Majesty," he said. "I had planned to, but—"

More sniggers.

"Enough," said the queen. "This is a solemn ceremony, is it not?"

She went through a short but formal presentation of naming Rand McNally the Royal Surveyor, explaining the title's duties and privileges therein, and then the previous Royal Surveyor came forward, a somewhat frail older man, holding a royal blue coat that was the size of a horse blanket—McNally's official new uniform.

The queen glared at the man. "And where is *your* jacket, Lord Winterbottom? You were quite proud of it, as I recall. With all those medals pinned to it, one normally heard you coming long before they saw you." More laughter.

Lord Winterbottom cleared the phlegm from his throat. "It was stolen, Your Majesty."

"Stolen?" she said. "Who on earth would want to steal the coat of the Royal Surveyor? And how did they get away unnoticed with all the jangling?"

Lord Winterbottom raised a fist to the heavens: "Your Majesty, I can only speculate at the knavery that led to such a dastardly deed."

The queen turned back to McNally; it looked to David Owen like she was trying not to laugh.

"Mr. McNally, you see what a dangerous world we are living in. We have mercenaries involved in the Mogul War in India, Iberia is growing stronger, my treaty with King Max of the Netherlands has been jeopardized by a rogue admiral of the Dutch Bicycle and Tulip Company, and now Lord Winterbottom has lost his coat. Are you quite prepared to assume the risks of becoming Royal Surveyor?"

"I assure Your Majesty that I am," said McNally, "and that I will see to the repair of the treaty with the Netherlands. The benefit to both our countries is too great to let a traitor and his rogue crew muck it up."

The queen waved McNally to the stage, where Lord Winterbottom helped him into his official new coat. The new Royal Surveyor then asked permission to present the queen with a few gifts.

First, there was the map.

McNally was very proud of this, and David Owen had spent many long nights at the Emporium in order to finish it in time for the London trip. It was a map of the future— one that showed how large Queen Adeline's realm would be after the signing of two vital treaties, one with the Netherlands and one with the Mogul emperor Akbar. The Netherlands would receive Britannia's military help against the growing Iberian kingdom of Spain and Portugal. They would also get access to Rand McNally's valuable maps of the New World. In return, Britannia would get a share of the Netherlands' coveted foothold in the East.

This is where the Mogul alliance came in. Akbar had already expanded Babur's empire from the Himalayas to the Deccan Plateau, in the middle of India. But the growing empire was proving unwieldy, so Britannia would help Akbar strengthen his current territory in return for Britannia's license to colonize south of the Deccan, including the islands of Ceylon and the Maldives. Britannia would then share control of the Indian Ocean with the Netherlands.

The queen's green eyes out-sparkled the many jewels she was wearing when she saw the map, with all the new territory swathed in Britannia blue. McNally smiled; he was back on firm footing now, in every way.

"As for the other gifts," he said. "Mr. Owen, if you please."

David Owen went to the covered table and removed the cloak, revealing a number of strange mechanical devices.

"Dear me," said the queen, "I hope you aren't planning to torture me."

McNally laughed politely, waving his assistant forward with the first device: a long staff attached to a single circular object the size of a wagon wheel. It made a clicking noise as David Owen approached the stage.

The queen frowned. "Is it broken?"

"Not at all, Your Majesty," said McNally. "This device will revolutionize surveying. Owen, make the room."

David Owen walked parallel to the stage to the wall, made a right turn, walked the length of the hall, along the back wall, down the other side, and then back to the front of the stage.

"That clicking noise!" said the queen, whose face was a mask of irritation.

"It's a counter, Your Majesty," said Owen, who looked down at a small box where the wheel met the handle. "Two hundred fifty feet!"

"The size of this room, Your Majesty," McNally explained. "You see, with this device a single man can more accurately measure distance in far less time than a team with the Gunter's chain. Enough men with enough instruments, and we can survey southern India in a fraction of the time it would otherwise take."

"Have the borders of India changed?" said Lord Winterbottom. "There it is, on a map."

McNally glared at the deposed Royal Surveyor, but quickly recovered. "Her Majesty knows full well the importance of an accurate accounting of her realm, not just for revenue but for military intelligence."

"It's called a surveyor's wheel," said David Owen, who thought he could defuse the tension.

"We haven't decided on a name yet," said McNally.

"Or the perambulator," said Owen.

"It's definitely not going to be that," said McNally. "Perhaps something in Her Majesty's honor—"

"The Royal Walker!" suggested Owen, who immediately regretted it.

"I beg Your Majesty's pardon," said McNally.

Queen Adeline let out a deep sigh. "I have other engagements, you know. Let's see what else you've brought."

They rushed through the rest of their presentation—an instrument called a theodolite, which measured angles more accurately than the transit, and a special McNally compass with the queen's royal seal on it. And that was that. They were ushered out of the hall and granted the privilege of leaving Whitehall through the front gates, where their rickety wagon and crooked horses were waiting.

McNally stripped off the blue coat and tossed it in the back.

"Let's hire a coach," he said. "I'm not walking back to the river."

All the way back, David Owen kept thinking about what the queen had said, about the rogue admiral who had possibly scuttled their treaty with the Netherlands. He had heard the same story from two sources: McNally, of course, and Archibald Black, Bren's bookseller friend whom David Owen had never liked.

There had been the big announcement of the treaty, and then a few months later the truth came out—that this Admiral Bowman was to have been arrested at Cape Colony and the businessman, Mr. Richter, installed as the new governor—but something had gone wrong, and now the Netherlands was focused on repairing the damage.

Owen had swallowed his pride to ask Archibald Black to find out more. In fact, the bookseller had already begun an investigation of his own, since he thought of Bren like a son. Black explained to Owen that he had never trusted the admiral, and there was something about a secret order called the Black Tulip, and a mysterious medallion called a paiza, which took on greater weight when Owen told Black that the admiral and Bren had spoken of a map and a lost treasure.

Black had concluded that this admiral was in search

of an island that had been erased from modern maps. All David Owen knew was that his son had gone off with a madman.

"Should be easy enough to repair things with King Max," said McNally. "We'll need to draw up some new maps for the Netherlanders, of course. Perhaps spread the New World a bit wider than we have previously, show him how good it will look in orange. And of course, if there really is a war at Cape Colony, Britannia could help resecure the colony. Yes, this will all work out."

Despite his boss's bravado, David Owen thought he sounded more hopeful than certain.

▲▲▲

When they got back to Map, David Owen first went home, but the small house was empty and cold, and he didn't feel like starting a fire. So he walked into the Merchant Quarter until he was standing in front of Black's Books. It was after hours, but he knew that Archibald Black spent most of his evenings at his store. He knocked.

"Ah, David, I thought you might be a customer," said Black, who somehow seemed to have grown thinner in the months since Bren left, even though he was barely more than bones to begin with.

"People besides Bren come in here?"

"Occasionally," Black said stiffly. "Come in."

He made tea for them, but Owen just held his cup without ever drinking it.

"How did Whitehall go?"

"Fine. McNally is officially Royal Surveyor, but he's fretting about things with the Netherlands and how that will affect his India plans."

"I'll bet," said Black.

"I want to go after Bren," said Owen, surprising both Black and himself.

"And how do you propose to do that?"

"The Indian Royal Survey," said Owen. "I can get assigned to that, and I could take you with me. You've always wanted to travel."

"You're not talking about a holiday," said Black. "You're talking about finding Bren. How exactly will going to India help?"

"The mercenary you hired . . ."

"Barrett," said Black. "And she's an antiquary, not a mercenary."

"Yes, well, you hired her not to dig up artifacts but to steal a map."

"Indeed," said Black. "We've been through this, David. The paiza . . . what you overheard the admiral say to Bren . . . a certain rogue admiral's obsession with vanished islands . . ."

"And you still haven't heard from her?"

Black took a sip of tea. "No. But that could be for any number of reasons."

"If you still believe there could be a map in that Persian library that could help one locate this treasure island Bren may be stranded on, then I want that map," said Owen. "And I have to assume at this point that Barrett failed to steal it. But the Royal Survey gets us close enough that we could go after the map ourselves. Passage secured and paid for by Her Majesty, the queen."

"We're not explorers," said Black.

"You love Bren, don't you?" said Owen. "Almost as much as I do?"

Black said nothing.

"Well, then," said David Owen, standing up. "Thank you for the tea."

"Wait," said Black. "Give it more time. Barrett's message could've gotten lost."

David Owen nodded, his eyes full of sadness. "Think about what I said, Archibald." And he left the store.

CHAPTER 9

ROGUES

The first few days on the island of New Amsterdam were like heaven to Bren. The weather was perfect, warm without being too humid. The food, despite being mostly fruit, fish, and vegetables, was delicious, as fresh as anything he had tasted. And his bed—his bed! Softer and more comfortable than any place he had ever lain down to sleep.

And yet, there was the occasional sign that something was off.

One night Bren was awakened from a deep sleep by the

far-off sound of music, and possibly chanting, in the middle of the night.

At lunch the next afternoon he could have sworn one of the men called Governor Wycoff "Lord Ananda," or something odd like that.

And after a few days it dawned on Bren that no one seemed to be native to this tropical island—just a few dozen Netherlanders, most of them men.

Sean was clearly bothered as well, and one day he asked the governor to show them the tin mines that the Dutch Bicycle & Tulip Company had sent him in search of. If the governor was ill at ease with this request, he didn't show it. He agreed to throw together a little tour of the far side of the island, where hills ringed the northern coast.

"Now we'll see just how legitimate this settlement is," Sean told Bren.

When they arrived, Bren was horrified by what he saw—a huge pit where trees had been cleared and rock torn away. When he used to go with his mother to lake country, she would always take him on walks through the unspoiled countryside and talk about how the earth was a living thing. But looking at this, Bren didn't see how any living thing could tolerate such a gaping wound.

"Horrific, isn't it?" said the governor. "I don't care how valuable the metal, it can't be worth the cost of this much destruction, can it?"

"How would you suggest we dig for gold, silver, and the like?" said Sean.

The governor threw up his arms. "Why dig it out at all? What value is gold, really, except that kings want to fill their castles with it? You've been here a week already. Has this place not provided everything you could want? Fresh air, water, food, shelter? The pleasure of my company?"

"So you shut the mine down?" said Sean, looking around. There appeared to be just one mine entrance, and it was sealed shut. "And the company approved of this?"

The governor shrugged. "The company wants for nothing."

Sean wasn't satisfied. "That's beside the point, isn't it? If they sent you here to mine tin, how are you not delivering tin?"

"We convinced them there were other resources here," the governor said. "If they just gave it time. And speaking of time, we should get going if we want to make it back by evening feast."

And that was all the history of the island they got out of him on that day. But the feast that night was a bit less festive than usual. The governor hardly talked to anyone. Bren went to bed restless, worried about Sean, and had barely dozed off when Mouse shook him awake.

"I need to show you something," she whispered.

Their guesthouse was down a road from the governor's house, separated by jungle, perhaps a hundred yards away. But as soon as they stepped outside, Bren heard the rhythmic and foreboding beat of a drum, and this time, for sure, chanting—a language Bren didn't understand.

All he could think about was that horrible rebellion at Cape Colony . . . the screams and the panic and the butchery. Of course, the admiral had been the cause then, and the only inhabitants of this island, as far as he could tell, were Netherlanders. But then who was drumming and chanting?

They crept closer. Bren tried following Mouse step for step, as she had the uncanny ability to move through the undergrowth without so much as bumping a leaf or crunching a single twig. By comparison, Bren felt like one of the governor's elephants.

The drum beat louder, and the chants rose higher, and before they reached the clearing they heard the crackle of fire. When they were close enough, they saw the Netherlanders circling an enormous bonfire. To Bren's great surprise, they were all stripped to the waist, and some barely wore trousers, either.

"Mouse, what's going on?"

"I don't know. The chanting woke me up, so I snuck over here and saw this. Then I came back for you."

"We should go get the others—"

"Wait," said Mouse, and before Bren could stop her she had moved off to her left, circling the bonfire by perhaps a quarter turn. After a moment she motioned for Bren to join her.

What he saw shocked him. The governor was there too—he was the one beating the drum and leading the chant, dressed in nothing but an animal-skin loincloth, his otherwise naked body glistening with sweat from the heat of the fire. Another man was doing an odd dance next to the fire—it was Bakker, the man who'd lost the lottery.

"What in heaven's name . . . ," said Bren.

"I daresay those chants are rising up to heaven."

The whispered voice behind them nearly made Bren jump out of hiding. Even Mouse spun around, frightened. Bren had never seen anyone successfully sneak up on her, ever. It was a young man, perhaps Sean's age, slight of build but neatly dressed in cropped grey pants and a linen shirt, sporting a thin mustache that looked like it might've been penciled in with a graphite stick.

"Who are you?" whispered Bren.

"Your only chance of getting off this island," said the man.

"We have a boat," said Mouse.

"Take a closer look at that fire."

Bren and Mouse turned back to the bonfire. What had looked like ordinary pieces of stripped wood stacked around the edge were in fact oars. And at the heart of it Bren could make out the thwarts and curved parts of the keep and hull, along with their makeshift mast and sail.

Their longboat would soon be a pile of ashes.

▲▲▲

"Sean, wake up. Wake up!"

Bren was trying to whisper and shout at the same time; it wasn't very effective, but finally Sean lifted his groggy head from the pillow.

"What is it, lad?"

"We need to go."

He sat up all the way. "Who is this?" he said, looking at the stranger next to Bren and Mouse.

Bren opened his mouth to explain, then hesitated. "I don't actually know, but—"

"We have to get off this island," said Mouse. "Trust us."

"Okay, okay," said Sean, getting up and fumbling for his shoes. "Wake the others. Do you know if the governor left our boat at the beach, or brought it inland?"

"Inland," said Mouse.

"And then he burned it," said Bren.

Sean stopped mid-lace. He turned to the stranger.

"That's where he comes in," said Bren.

Sean just shook his head and helped Bren and Mouse wake the others, which was no small task. Proper beds and soft pillows had had the effect of a strong drug on all of them, and it seemed as if they would never draw them all back from the land of dreams. The fact that Bren and Mouse were children didn't stop anyone from cursing them for waking them up.

"We're going to the far side of the island," said the stranger. "Opposite of where you came in."

"Who exactly are you?" said Sean.

The stranger stood at attention, then bowed slightly. "Lady Jean Barrett, of the Staffordshire Barretts. My father is the Earl of Wolveren Hampton."

"Lady?" said Bren and Sean at the same time.

"Naturally."

When they said nothing, she added: "Do you need proof?"

They both blushed and fumbled over their next handful of words, before Sean managed to ask, "Are we really in danger?"

As if to answer his question, the drumbeat grew louder, as did the chanting. Barrett led them out of the house, around the back, and into the jungle without so much as a lantern or torch.

"You have a boat on this side of the island?" said Bren.

"Not yet," she said.

That didn't sound promising, but Bren and the others could do little more than follow the stranger, who passed through the jungle as if she had night vision.

"I memorized the way this morning," she said, reading Bren's mind.

"Are you alone?" said Mouse.

"For now," said Barrett, "but give me a minute."

The drumbeats had stopped, but now they heard shouting and running. The vacant longhouse had been discovered.

"On a positive note, they don't know which direction we've gone," said Barrett. The end of her sentence was trampled by the sound of an elephant trumpeting, followed by a crashing through the jungle, like some elemental force was destroying every palm tree in its path.

"I suppose they guessed right," said Sean, and the whole escape party began to move faster, no longer worried about making too much noise.

Barrett whipped out a striking scarlet sword and began whacking at the thick undergrowth, clearing a path as they went. Her use of the sword wasn't wild, Bren noticed; she sliced vines and pared back ferns with the skill of a surgeon, her aim even more remarkable considering they were on the run.

"Watch your step!" Barrett called out, just before Bren felt the ground begin to slope downward, and then fall off entirely. Bren and Mouse went down the hill first, rolling like barrels, and the others were right behind them. When they broke the last ticklish barrier of ferns, they were scattered about the beach, except for Barrett, who was already poised with her sword drawn and one fist braced defiantly at her hip.

There was just enough light from a half-full moon and a sky full of stars to see that everyone was there, so Barrett turned toward the sea and, raising her fist, opened her hand all at once, as if she were scattering pixie dust. A bright flare of light shot upward, arcing toward the night sky, hanging there for an instant before exploding like Chinese fireworks.

"Probably should have done that sooner," said Barrett. "Didn't want to set the trees on fire."

"How—" Bren started to say, but just then the half-naked governor, riding his elephant, and the other bare-chested Netherlanders came marching down toward the beach.

"Lady Barrett, I'd say we need that boat you promised," said Sean.

"Should be here shortly," she said.

Bren clasped the black stone around his neck, wondering if it could protect them all, the way everyone aboard the *Albatross* had been saved from the Iberian warships. He felt like a fool as soon as the thought crossed his mind; after all, he had never been sure what had happened then. Instead he looked at Mouse, wondering if she could do something. She nodded and opened the palm of her hand, showing Bren the white jade.

"Why on earth are you running from us?" said the governor, who seemed genuinely hurt that they were trying to escape.

"You burned our boat," said Sean.

"Don't take it personally. It's just that, in my experience, people sometimes need convincing of the ideas we hold dear on this island."

"And what ideas are those?" Sean asked.

"Look around! This is Paradise! Netherlanders are so intent on imposing their ways on the East: the ridiculous European clothing, completely unsuitable for island life; the outdated ethics of international trade; the fear of anyone not born with blond or red hair."

"Right now, it's you we fear, Governor."

"Please, call me Bung Ananda."

"I beg your pardon?"

"Bung Ananda," repeated the governor. "I'm not a Dutch governor here. This is not a Dutch colony. This is Utopia."

Bren looked at this overweight, sunburned Netherlander standing there in his altogether and thought he could have made a better advertisement for his so-called Utopia.

"If this is Utopia, then you won't mind if we leave you to it," said Barrett.

"Ah, well, you see, it's trickier than that," said the governor. "Utopias are delicate. They require full investment, if you'll pardon my using the crass business language of my former employer, and a certain amount of privacy. You are all welcome to stay, but I can't let you leave."

No one said anything for a moment as Sean and Barrett took the measure of the man who now called himself Bung Ananda. Standing near the back of the group was Bakker, still mostly naked. Apparently the fact that his fellow crewmen were willing to kill him made Utopia sound appealing.

"These aren't all the Netherlanders who came here to mine tin, are they?" said Sean. "The longhouse we were sleeping in . . . all those beds . . ."

Bung Ananda smiled, but it was an expression of pure sadness. "They couldn't see the forest for the trees, if you'll pardon the cliché. We found Paradise on this island, and they wanted to destroy it. They wanted their precious tin so badly, so I left them to it. Simple enough after that to convince the company that our entire tin-seeking expedition had come to naught."

Bren thought of the sealed mineshaft and a chill went through him. *This man buried his countrymen alive.*

"Now what?" said Sean, half turning to Barrett as he asked the question. Just where was that rescue boat?

And then Bren noticed two things happening at once. First, he saw Barrett raise her sword again—the only weapon any of them had, save for perhaps a small knife here or there. Did she mean to take on this crazy man's entire army single-handedly?

He then saw Mouse put her white stone away and close her eyes, standing there motionless in the sand.

Barrett began to move sidelong across the beach toward the jungle, her sword still raised high. The elephant followed her, despite Bung Ananda's best efforts to stop it. "Castor, stay!" he bellowed, but the elephant seemed hypnotized by the sword.

Which is when a third thing caught Bren's eye: a ship coming into view around the island. A small ship, with two fin-shaped sails, listing badly in the wind.

"Castor, give your master a hug," said Barrett, at which point the elephant lifted its trunk and plucked Bung Ananda from his back, the end of his trunk cinched around the stunned man's chest, pinning his arms.

"Castor, release!" he pleaded, but the elephant just held him aloft. And then, quite suddenly, Castor slammed his master to the ground, cratering the sand.

"Wait—don't do that," said Barrett, holding the sword with two hands now, pointing it directly at the elephant. Castor lifted the former governor up—he was still alive, groaning—and then slammed him down again.

Bren and Barrett flinched.

"Castor, no!" said Barrett, but suddenly there was a

violent trumpeting sound from the jungle, followed by the thunder of footsteps. The other elephant charged onto the beach, the lieutenant governor barely clinging to its back.

"Rogue!" cried one of the other Netherlanders, who all began to scatter. Sean and his crew did the same, but when Bren saw Mouse still standing there, eyes closed, he knew what was happening.

"It's okay!" he called to Sean. "Head for the water!"

The ship was now almost to shore. The rogue elephant charged Castor, trampling what was left of Bung Ananda in the process, and a moment later the two elephants were locked in combat, their ivory tusks clashing, while the Utopians continued to panic and flee.

Barrett was just as confused as the others, but when Bren grabbed her by the hand she put her sword away and started running toward the water.

The ship wasn't all the way to shore, so they waded out as far as they could until they could grab the rope ladder a deckhand had lowered. The small ship started turning out to sea even as the last few men were reaching for the ladder, but they all made it, and before long they were sailing away from the island, all the survivors of the *Albatross* but Bakker on board and accounted for.

CHAPTER 10

THE MAGICIAN
REVEALS
HER TRICKS

Not much was said that night. All Bren remembered before being ushered below was a strange man dressed nothing like a sailor helping him over the side of the ship while someone else navigated them away from shore. But the next morning, Bren could tell Sean was sizing up their new captain. What was left of the *Albatross* crew sat on the deck of the small ship, drinking terrible coffee and eating cold porridge, while this Jean Barrett—*Lady* Jean Barrett!—stood before them. She still sported the thin mustache, which in daylight definitely looked drawn on.

Barrett couldn't have been much older than Sean, maybe twenty-five or so. But there was an element of refinement to her—the neat clothes; the close-cropped hair; the expensive-looking sword; the title "Lady." She must have been some privileged young woman playing at being an adventurer, thought Bren, and that's what Sean seemed to be thinking as well.

But she had rescued them, with a considerable amount of skill and calmness under pressure. And she could clearly wield that sword. Maybe she hadn't learned everything the hard way, but she had learned, somewhere.

Barrett walked up to Mouse.

"I didn't know the Dutch crimped young girls."

"You can tell she's a girl?" said Bren.

"I've had some practice telling the sexes apart," said Barrett.

"Mouse wasn't crimped," said Sean. "Bowman, our former admiral, rescued her from an orphanage in China."

Barrett arched a thin eyebrow that also looked penciled on. "Really? And your name is Mouse?"

"That's what I'm called," she answered, her voice barely more than a whisper.

"I'm Bren," said Bren, holding out his hand to Lady Barrett. He'd never met anyone like her. She was like some character sprung from his adventure books. Barrett took his hand firmly and pumped his arm.

"I know," she said. "Bren Owen, of Map. I was sent to rescue you."

Bren's jaw went slack.

Barrett reached inside her tunic and pulled out a letter, handing it to Bren. As soon as he unfolded it, he thought his legs would go out from under him. It was as if he was standing on a ship for the very first time, conscious of every roll of the deck, feeling unsure and sick. He took the letter and skimmed it, recognizing the handwriting immediately but rushing through to find the scrawled signature, and then he read through it again, more carefully. Still, he was barely able to understand anything.

"Don't keep us in suspense, lad," said Sean.

Bren didn't know what to say. He looked to Barrett for an explanation.

"Archibald Black and I are old friends," she began. "Or I should say, his family and mine are. I'm an antiquary, and when I would go out on assignments I would bring Archibald books and collectibles from all over the world. The prices he would pay for them helped fund my trips, so it was a mutually beneficial arrangement."

Bren couldn't help but smile. Here was someone who had helped make Black's Books the place he had been drawn to since he was a child, and the place that had become his sanctuary after his mother died.

"I spent every day I could at Black's," he said. "I

sometimes met the men—er, people—who brought him books. But I don't recognize you."

"Ah, I was probably in disguise," said Barrett, pointing to her upper lip. "Antiquarianism isn't some dusty old professor's line of work. There's danger aplenty," she added, grabbing the hilt of her sword, "and many places where it's too risky to be seen as a woman."

Barrett held a small mirror up to her face, using her own spit to erase the fake mustache.

"Word got back to Map that this Bowman had gone rogue," said Barrett. "As you know, Rand McNally is the first to learn anything in our part of the world. The way Archibald explained it to me, you had found some secret map and had left him a drawing of it. He concluded, based on what your father told him—"

"My father?"

"Yes, your father is desperate to bring you home too," said Barrett. "Anyway, all I know is that the smartest man I've ever met concluded you might have been taken to and perhaps abandoned on a vanished island, and as you can tell from that letter, he sent me to steal the only map he thought might narrow down your whereabouts."

"Who is Archibald?" said Sean.

"He owns a bookstore in Map," said Bren. "He's like a father to me." Even though his real father was nowhere in earshot, Bren still felt a stab of guilt as he said it.

"What map?" said Mouse.

"This map," said Barrett, reaching again into her tunic and producing the large map she'd stolen. "It was in something called Ptolemy's Atlas, in Persia."

"In the House of Wisdom?" Bren asked, agog.

"You know it?" said Barrett.

"Know it? It's the greatest library known to man, at least since the Library of Alexandria burned to the ground. Mr. Black would talk about it constantly. But how on earth did you manage to steal anything from there?"

Barrett smiled. "Oh, well, that's rather a good story," she said. "Gather 'round."

▲▲▲

Barrett stood before them, her hands behind her back, her eyes wide.

"I knew if I made the slightest wrong move, I was a dead woman," she said. "The Persian asp is one hundred times as venomous as the king cobra."

Bren and Mouse gasped.

"A hundred times?" Sean protested. "Pull the other one."

"It is the deadliest snake on earth," Bren assured him, though to be honest, he wasn't certain about that.

"So here I am, afraid to breathe, trying to think of something before this librarian takes advantage of me."

"What did you do?" said Mouse.

"I sneezed."

"You what?" said Bren.

"I sneezed," she repeated. "Mouse, come up here, I want to show you something."

Barrett was standing on the third step leading to the quarterdeck, with her audience gathered in the ship's waist. Mouse bounded up the steps to her.

"Now, wrap this piece of rope around my wrists." Mouse did so, and Barrett instructed Mouse to stand behind her. When she was in place, Barrett made a big production of needing to sneeze, throwing her head back, scrunching up every muscle in her face, forming a giant *achoo* with her mouth. And then she fake sneezed like a clap of thunder.

Mouse couldn't help it—she flinched, closed her eyes, and turned her head away for a second. When she looked again, the rope was tied around her own wrists, as Barrett stood there triumphantly. The whole crew oohed and aahed, except for Sean.

"Just a trick, lads."

"Of course it's a trick," said Barrett. "Sleight of hand . . . misdirection . . . I sneezed like a banshee, and in that split second slipped the asp onto the wrist of my captor, who was bitten immediately. He felt no pain, I assure you, and died almost instantly. I quickly but carefully tore the map I needed from the Atlas, shed my disguise, beneath which was *another* disguise, and walked scot-free from the compound."

Bren realized he was staring at Lady Barrett with his jaw open. "You're a magician antiquarian?"

"I suppose that would be an accurate assessment, yes," said Barrett. "Although I prefer the word *antiquary*. *Antiquarian* just makes me sound old."

"So what's so special about this map you stole?" Sean asked. "How was it supposed to help you find Bren?"

"Good question," said Barrett. "I couldn't even figure out how it was a map at all. Look . . ."

She unfolded the large map and showed them how it was all text. "I couldn't make heads or tails of it at first. But take a look at this." She laid the map down on the deck and asked Bren and Mouse to hold it. She then pulled a handful of salt from her pocket and sprinkled it across the surface, gently brushing away the excess, to reveal the hidden map.

"Wow!" said Bren and Mouse in unison. Sean tried to act unimpressed, but he wasn't very convincing.

"The Hidden Sea. As you saw in the letter, Bren, Black was convinced the Chinese had covered up all sorts of discoveries. My new friend Yaozu explained . . . this is Yaozu, by the way," said Barrett, waving to the man in the black clothes who had just come up from below. Bren recognized him as the man who had helped them aboard last night, but in the confusion and darkness he hadn't noticed that he was Chinese. "Yaozu explained that ancient rulers were forever in search of a mythical island where the Immortals lived, where they believed they could find the elixir of life. No luck, one assumes, but they did end up charting land that would have served as handy way stations as they explored the Indian Sea."

"And for exile," said Bren, under his breath. But when he took a closer look at the map of the "Hidden Sea," he didn't see the Vanishing Island. It made him feel queasy to realize that if they hadn't gotten off the island, Barrett never would have found them.

"That's incredible," said Sean, looking more closely at the map. "Look at the locations of these islands. They would have been sailing the open ocean with nothing resembling modern navigation equipment."

"So did you just happen to look for us on New Amster-dam first?" said Bren.

"It was the first place we looked," she said, smiling at Yaozu. "Never hurts to be lucky."

"How did you escape Persia?" asked Sean.

"On the horse I rode in on," said Barrett. "Except of course I was dressed like a Persian, so no one took any notice, what with all the chaos back at the library. They were looking for Lord Winterbottom and his jangly blue coat. I rode west until I was on the old Silk Road, where I found shelter in an abandoned rest stop of sorts. It's where

I met Yaozu. He's trying to get back to his home in the South China Sea and knew a spur off the Silk Road that took us south to the Arabian Sea, where we acquired this modest but seaworthy vessel."

Mouse turned to Yaozu. "How did you get so far away from home?"

"I might ask you the same question. . . ."

"Mouse," she said.

"Mouse," Yaozu repeated.

Bren wondered if the Chinese man's story of leaving China was anywhere near as fantastical as the Chinese girl's, but that would have to wait.

"You know, I fought on the back of an elephant once," said Barrett.

Bren's mood immediately improved. "You did?" he said, thinking of the stories of Hannibal's mighty Carthaginian army, crossing the Alps on elephants during the Punic Wars with Rome.

"This was India," said Barrett. "The expansion of the Mogul Empire. I was a freelancer, along with a handful of Iberians and Italians and Britons, lending a hand and expertise to the great Akbar as he enlarged his empire to the south and east."

"Why?" said Bren.

"Because as long as the Indian subcontinent was fractured," said Barrett, "it was vulnerable to the Netherlanders.

They already have their stronghold in Southeast Asia, and it was feared they would soon control everything east of the Ottoman Empire save China. But a unified India made that less likely—and gave Akbar's benefactors a chance to perhaps open trade with the Moguls."

That was enough politics for Bren. "What about the elephants?"

"Would you like to hear about the Battle of the Malabar Caves?" said Barrett.

"Yes!" Bren almost shouted.

"The Malabar Caves were carved centuries ago into the mountains that separate India from Nepal in the north. They were the work of religious zealots looking to live a cloistered life of suffering and prayer. At the beginning of the war, they were considered off-limits, out of respect for the believers."

"That never works out," said Sean.

"Indeed," said Barrett, "and it didn't there, either. The rebels either evicted the believers or forced them to share their caves . . . either way, the Malabar Caves became a rebel hive. That's where the war elephants come in. We used them to flush the rebels out of hiding. We rode them up to the caves, each of the great beasts carrying a huge wooden tub filled with water. Have you ever seen an elephant bathe itself?"

"No," said Bren, at which point Barrett mimed plunging

a trunk into water and then spraying it everywhere.

"Blasted them right out of there," she said. "You can't believe how powerful an elephant's trunk is. Every town should have one to put out fires."

"You rode elephants up the side of a mountain," said Sean, his voice dripping with doubt.

"Hannibal did it," Bren blurted out, a bit more harshly than he intended.

Barrett touched his shoulder affectionately. "You did make good use of Black's Books, didn't you? Yes, Hannibal did it, and so did we. I captured the rebel leader and brought him to the emperor. Akbar always wore this long strand of pearls, and he stood there before the leader, twisting the strand with his finger. Then he passed sentence."

"And?"

"Death by elephant. They made the poor chap kneel and put his head on a stump, and one of the war elephants was brought over to step on his head."

Bren flinched. He immediately thought of Map's custom of dropping stones onto prisoners' heads. "Lady Barrett, if you're from Britannia, you must've been to the Explorers' Club at Rand McNally's."

She scoffed. "I haven't, nor do I desire to. He's an important map peddler, to be sure, but real explorers are out in the wilds, not sitting in posh chairs sipping brandy."

Bren smiled. He liked her even more. "I can't wait to

see the look on Mr. Black's face when you walk into the store with me."

"Archibald will be over the moon to see you," said Barrett. "Your father, too, I'm sure."

The broad smile on Bren's face disappeared when he noticed Mouse scowling at him.

"Lady Barrett, if I may make a suggestion," said Sean, "I think we'd all have much better chances of getting home safely on a Dutch ship. Let us help you navigate to one of the East Netherlands ports, and I'll make sure we get signed on with a Far Easter going back to Amsterdam. *Old* Amsterdam," he added.

"I think that's a splendid idea," said Barrett. "Now, since we spent most of the night on the run, why don't we all try to get some rest."

CHAPTER 11

SECRETS AND STONES

"Mouse, I know you're mad at me."

Silence. They were lying side by side in hammocks belowdecks—the only deck of the small ship. Sean and half the other men were snoring across the way; the other half had agreed to work above, helping the one man Barrett and Yaozu had hired out to work the sails.

"I know you want to find this Dragon's Gate," Bren continued, "whatever it is, but you don't know how much I miss home right now. My father, and Mr. Black . . . besides, Sean and the others want to return home too. He's going to want you to come with us. Mouse?"

"I don't like the name Mouse," she said. "It makes me sound like a pet."

"Oh," Bren stammered. "I—"

"I told you why the matron called me that. She thought I was evil."

"I'm sorry," said Bren. "What would you like me to call you?"

She said nothing at first, and then Bren heard her sigh. "That's just it, don't you see? I don't know who I really am. And you keep talking about home, but your home isn't my home."

"It could be," said Bren. "You could live with us. My father would love having you around. And you'd like Mr. Black and Beatrice—ooh, and especially Mr. Grey, this big grey cat that hangs around. 'Course you met Duke Swyers and his gang. I'd forgotten about that. They're rotten, but I'm not scared of them anymore."

"Stop," she said.

She went silent again, and Bren, in the darkness, thought he heard her crying. But it might just have been the unfamiliar noises of the ship.

▲▲▲

Barrett invited Sean, Bren, and Mouse to join her and Yaozu for lunch in her cabin. They assumed she was just being hospitable, but it turned out she had a proposition for them.

"How'd you like to earn a little extra money for the return trip, Mr. Graham?"

"I'm listening," he said.

"We're still on board with the plan to sail to the East Netherlands, but Yaozu and I want to go farther. Into the South China Sea, specifically. And to do that we need to sail through the Rotterdam Straits. It would help immensely to have a Dutch crew, for obvious reasons."

"To go where exactly?" said Bren, trying to hide his disappointment that Barrett wouldn't be staying with them.

"To China," said Yaozu. "My home."

"And he's invited me to go with him," said Barrett. "As I've told you, I'm an antiquary—I go digging for lost civilizations, or at least their artifacts. And there's no civilization more lost to outsiders than ancient China. Yaozu can get me in. But our initial destination will be an island called the Pearl Cliffs, which is our reason for wanting to avail ourselves of your seamanship. According to Yaozu, we'd be approaching during the spring gap, that delicate time when winter hasn't yet let go, but spring hasn't arrived. A heavy fog descends upon the island. Tricky for amateurs like us."

"When you say you can pay us, how much?" said Sean. "Negotiating our way through the straits is one thing—and I'm talking politics as well as seamanship. But the South China Sea's a different animal . . . tricky this time of year, as you say. . . ."

"Okay, Mr. Graham, you don't have to lay it on so

thick," said Barrett. She set out an iron chest, unlocked it, and flipped the lid to reveal rows of gold and silver coins. Sean tried to remain stoic, but his blue eyes were counting the coins.

"I think we can work something out, Lady Barrett," he said.

"I want to go with you," said Mouse, and everyone turned toward her. "To China. I don't want to go back to Europe with them."

"You can't just decide where you want to go," said Bren, who felt an unexpected frustration taking hold of him. "You're a child."

Mouse refused to look at him, and he suddenly regretted his tone. She had just told him how lost she was feeling, but he didn't understand how she could just abandon him now, after all they'd been through together.

Sean tried to defuse the tension. "Little one, I know you came from there," he said kindly, "but you told us you were an orphan. There's nothing there for you now."

Mouse glanced up at Bren, as if giving him the chance to step in and stick up for her, but he refused.

"Look, I'm not asking anyone to go to China with me," Barrett assured them. "I just need your political connections and your sailing experience. Then you have my word, you can take the boat and head back to the East Netherlands, and home from there."

"How will you get home?" said Bren.

"By land, I hope."

Sean and Barrett shook on it, and they continued to sail for the Dragon Islands, toward a port called Bantam. Bren had been so excited about returning home, but now he felt conflicted because Barrett wasn't going to be with them. He was drawn to her . . . traveling the world, fighting on elephants, digging up ancient artifacts. But there was something else, something he couldn't quite put his finger on.

Later that day, after he'd helped clean the deck, Bren went below to fetch his journal—what was left of it, after his freshwater-making experiment—taking it to the saloon to write. Barrett was already sitting in there, alone.

"Oh," said Bren. "I'm sorry, I was just . . ."

"Come in, Bren. Please, sit down."

Bren obeyed, but didn't know what to say. He just sat there dumbly, waiting for Barrett to say something first.

"I see you're a journal keeper," she said.

Bren nodded, too anxious to speak.

"Perhaps it's not my place to interfere, but I can't help but notice that you and your little friend haven't been on the best of terms lately. I may talk a good game," she persisted, "but I'm an awfully good listener as well."

Bren had learned a hard lesson in trust from Admiral Bowman. But Lady Jean Barrett was a friend of Mr. Black's. This was different.

"We haven't been friends all that long, really," said Bren.

"Still, I gather you've been through a lot together in that short time," said Barrett. "You really must've had to depend on each other on that island."

"I guess," said Bren. "It's just . . . she's good at keeping secrets."

Barrett nodded. "That's not always a bad thing, you know. When you first met me, you thought I was a man. That wasn't an accident, of course. I've gotten good at it, pretending. Makes things easier sometimes, navigating this world as a man. But keeping secrets like that can be hard on the keeper, too." She leaned back in her chair and let Bren consider this.

"I guess you know Mouse used to pretend to be a boy?"

"I assumed as much," said Barrett, "given that you seemed surprised when I was able to tell she was a girl right away. You can hardly blame her under the circumstances, living on a ship. My double life was forced on me as well. My father desperately wanted a boy, for all the usual reasons. To take his name, to inherit his estates . . . four daughters in and he'd had enough. He sent me, Lady Jean Barrett, off to boarding school as *Jean*—the French pronunciation. It wasn't hard to pass in grammar school, but when I got older, things got a bit more . . . *complicated*."

"Because you started to . . . ?" began Bren, who

blushed a painful shade of red before he could even get the words out.

Barrett laughed. "Actually, my physical appearance was the easy part." She looked at Bren, hesitating. "Oh never mind. My point is, Mouse probably doesn't think about keeping secrets the same way you do."

She had a point, Bren realized, but of course he wasn't telling Barrett the whole story. It was all that had happened on the island that was causing the friction between Mouse and him, but there was only so much he could reveal without seeming crazy.

"What do you have there?" said Barrett.

She was talking about his necklace. Out of habit, he had nervously grasped the black stone, turning its smooth shape between his thumb and finger, as if hoping it might ward off doubt as well as danger.

"Oh. Just a necklace my mother gave me before she died. Sort of a lucky charm, I guess."

"May I?" Barrett held out her hand, and Bren noticed how long and slender her fingers were. He slipped the leather lanyard over his head and handed it to her.

"Where did this come from?"

"According to my father, she bought it from a curiosity shop in the lake country in Britannia, where she was born. She used to take me back there when there were threats of plague in Map."

Barrett turned the stone over and over in her hand. "Curious indeed."

"Why?" said Bren. "It's just a black stone. I'm not sure why she even thought to buy this one in particular." Of course, Mouse had told him something very different about it—that it was the stone, not the paiza, that had been protecting him all along. Could his mother have even known?

"Do you know what sort of stone this is?" said Barrett.

"I just assumed it was something quarried in the lake country," said Bren.

"I don't think so. The glassy appearance, the hardness . . . I think this may be jade."

Bren almost fell off the saloon bench. "Jade? Like from China?"

"Well, jade has been found in places apart from China," said Barrett. "But not black jade, as far as I know." She looked Bren directly in the eye. "Are you quite sure you didn't know this was jade?"

Bren realized he was holding his breath. He exhaled now—at least he could tell her the truth. "No, I had no idea. I didn't even know jade could be black. How can you tell it's jade anyway?"

"My field requires a working understanding of rocks and minerals," said Barrett, still turning the black stone over in her hands, and then perching it at the tips of her fingers, as if it were a ring and her hand were the setting.

"You know, they say jade has certain . . . powers. Easterners have long thought jade blesses anything it touches. The Chinese in particular thought it had powers to heal, and to protect."

"Protect?" said Bren. "Do you believe all that?"

Barrett laughed. "I don't know, but it's a nice thought, isn't it?" She handed the necklace back to Bren, who held the black stone between his fingers once more, feeling how smooth and yet imperfect it was, with its warped surfaces and indentations.

"Did you know jade could also be white?" said Bren.

Barrett seemed surprised. "I've heard rumors, but I've never had the pleasure of seeing white jade myself. Why?"

Bren didn't answer at first. Wasn't it for Mouse to tell Barrett about the jade eye if she wanted her to know? Maybe, he thought, but he had been through the ordeal on the island just like her. This was his story, too.

"Mouse has a piece. We recovered it on the island. It's what the admiral was looking for," he said, measuring his words. He was still afraid of sounding crazy. "It was a stone Marco Polo supposedly left there. We found it in a grave of sorts."

He hesitated again. Should he go on? Then he remembered that his best friend had sent Barrett to find him. If Mr. Black could trust her, so could he. "And then, there was a fire. This skeleton . . . it sounds crazy, I know, but all the bones were tattooed with Chinese writing. Not regular Chinese writing—oracle bone language, according to Mouse." The words were tumbling out now. "Mouse read this ancient language—it was a question, she said, and then a fire cracked the bones, which gave the answer."

"Pyromancy!" said Barrett, with a snap of her fingers. "Fortune-telling by fire."

"I suppose," said Bren. "Except she said the answer was a map, to someplace called the Dragon's Gate. I know that's why she wants to go to China with you—her white stone came from there—and she wanted me to go with her."

"Hmm," said Barrett, who appeared to drift off in thought before returning. "Bren, it may be true that you and Mouse haven't known each other very long, but you two *are* friends. That much is obvious. And if a friend says she needs you—if *she* really believes she does—well, you may not agree, but you should be there for her. Imagine how it must feel to be her age, an orphan from China, passing as a boy . . . she may just need to believe that she's not in this alone."

Bren suddenly felt very selfish.

"But I don't understand what she wants, and she won't tell me. Not exactly, anyway."

"Maybe she doesn't quite know," said Barrett. "Or she doesn't know how to explain it. It doesn't mean she's lying to you, or manipulating you."

"Are you saying you want me to go with you, Lady Barrett? Both of us?"

She didn't answer him right away. "I was charged with getting you home safely, and I take that responsibility very seriously. But I was wondering if you could show me this map? I assume you've recorded it in your journal?"

Bren opened the journal to the pages where he had drawn the aftermath of the cavern fire. Barrett stared at it first one way, then another, rotating the journal until she came back around to where she'd started.

"Remarkable."

"What is?" said Bren.

"I think . . . no, I'll have to show you, and the others," said Barrett. "Wait here."

CHAPTER 12

THE ORACLE BONE MAP

Bren held open his journal to the place where he had redrawn the fractured oracle bones from memory. Yaozu and Sean leaned in for a look. Mouse was there, too.

"What are we looking at?" said Sean.

"The oracle bones Bren and Mouse found," said Barrett. When she saw how confused Sean was, she added, "Oh, the children didn't tell you?"

The look on Sean's face made Bren feel sick. He knew exactly how he must feel, learning that Bren had trusted Lady Barrett, a woman he'd just met, with things he hadn't told Sean.

"One of you has to explain what she's talking about," said Sean. "Might as well be you, lad."

"I'm sorry," said Barrett. "Of course I assumed you and Mouse would have told your friends about the map."

"What map?" said Sean, growing more confused by the second.

Bren, flustered, looked to Mouse for help. There was no worming out of it now. So they took turns telling Sean about the cavern and the skeleton and the oracle bones that were supposedly a map to something called the Dragon's Gate. They explained about the Marco Polo letter and Mouse showed all of them the white stone the admiral had been after. They still left parts out—the quicksilver dragon, the soul-traveling, the admiral becoming a bird, the centuries-old man guarding the centuries-old skeleton. As if they silently agreed that Sean could only take so much.

"Did you say this is a map to the Dragon's Gate?" said Yaozu. "And that you read oracle bones to reveal it?"

Mouse nodded.

"Doesn't look like any map I've ever seen," said Sean. "And I've seen all manner of them."

"Two reasons for that," said Barrett. "First, Bren has drawn the broken bones, and that's all you see. But look at this."

She was unfolding the page from Ptolemy's Atlas again when Bren suddenly stopped her.

"Wait! I see what you mean." And he flipped to a clean

page in his journal and began to draw the Hidden Sea map from memory.

"How did you do that?" said Barrett.

"My own magic trick, I guess," said Bren. He tore the page from the journal and gave it to Barrett, then turned back to the oracle bones.

"Now look," she said, folding the Hidden Sea map so that what was primarily visible was the northern border of the Indian Ocean—including mainland Southeast Asia and Indochina. "Compare the curves of the coastline with the shape of the bones here. And don't these bone fractures align with the rivers that empty here?"

"The oracle bone map is a map of China!" said Bren.

"These other fractures could be more rivers, or roads," said Barrett. "Pieces of bone are mountains or deserts, the holes could be lakes. At least, that's my working theory. What do you think, Yaozu? You would know better than any of us."

"I believe you are right, Lady Barrett."

"And that's the second reason it didn't look like a map to you, Mr. Graham," Barrett continued. "You've never seen a detailed map of China, have you?"

"I don't reckon I have," said Sean. "But does someone want to explain to me what a Dragon's Gate is?"

Bren's excitement dimmed. "We haven't figured that part out. At least, I haven't. Mouse?" He couldn't help himself. There was still a part of him worried that she was hiding something from him. But she just shook her head.

"I may be able to elucidate that," said Yaozu.

They all turned to him at once. Bren wondered what "elucidate" meant.

"There is a story they tell in China of how Paradise was lost to the Angry Mountain," Yaozu began. "The most fertile of valleys in all the land was the one fed by a river that came from the Roof of the World, as the great mountains are known. To the east the river ran all the way to the sea. To the west, it ran through Paradise. But one mountain grew envious of this valley, and in his festering anger he began a quarrel.

"*Look at my River,* said the Mountain, *which flows from on high and brings you fish to eat.*

"*See how I lay low,* replied the Valley. *Would you seem so tall and proud without me?*

"*The snow from my peaks melts to water your soil,* argued the Mountain.

"*You would drown if I did not take the burden of your waters,* said the Valley.

"*I stand tall against the wind, which would trample your grains.*

"*I lay naked under the sun, which would scorch you.*

"*I give you life,* said the Mountain.

"*I keep death from your feet,* said the Valley.

"And on it went, almost from the beginning of time. It

was for the River to settle things, so that there could be peace again. *I belong to no one,* it said, *but flow through time.*

"The River searched his waters for two stones, one of black jade and the other of white, and devised a game of pure skill for the Mountain and Valley to play. The game went on for months, but in the end, the Mountain lost, because brute force cannot win a game of skill and cunning."

Bren felt as if he'd been struck by lightning. It was obvious Mouse was having the same reaction.

"The Mountain began to tremble with rage. The Valley shook and the River flowed backwards. As the Mountain's anger grew, the earth was rent and flooded, and fires spread through the land, and finally, the Mountain threw down stones to keep the River from flowing into Paradise.

"*None shall pass through here except in death,* it said. The Valley, refusing to lie at the foot of the mountain, withered and died. The River, unable to flow across the Angry Mountain, divided itself in two, passing by on both sides, and to symbolize the rending of harmony, one side took the black jade and the other the white."

Yaozu touched his finger to the oracle bone map, in what would be the northwest part of China, if their theory were correct. "This I believe to be the Takla Makan Desert, which some call the Sea of Death. And these two hairline cracks, converging . . . the Black Jade and White Jade Rivers."

"And there's a mountain between them?" said Bren.

"I believe so," said Yaozu.

"What will I find there?" said Mouse. "What is the Dragon's Gate?"

"That I do not know for sure," said Yaozu. "Only that many consider it a key to the search for immortality."

Sean could only shake his head. "What does all this mean?"

"Well—when I told you I wanted to go to China," said Barrett, "I left a little something out."

"Aye. There's a surprise."

"I don't believe it was any of your business, Mr. Graham, seeing as how I only asked you to take me to the borders. You certainly didn't turn your nose up at my gold and silver."

Sean's mouth opened but only hot air came out. Finally he laughed and threw up his hands. "You know, I'm just a hired hand taking you to the coast of China. What difference does it make if I think you're crazy, or what fool errand you're on?"

"Because I want Bren and Mouse to go with me," said Barrett.

Sean stopped laughing. He stood up from the table and then leaned forward on his fists, his face stopping just inches from Barrett's. "You must be mad."

She kept her seat and didn't flinch.

"You were charged with finding Bren and bringing him

back home. By someone you claim to be a friend, no less. And I presume you were paid to do it, am I right?"

"You are."

"Then how on earth can you justify putting Bren at risk instead? And Mouse too? How can two children help you?"

The question seemed to catch Barrett up short. Bren realized everyone, including him, was waiting for a good answer. Perhaps it was all those adventure books he'd read at Black's, or what he'd been through already, but he'd grown accustomed to thinking it was normal for a twelve- or thirteen-year-old boy and an even younger girl to risk their lives side by side with adults, for the adults' benefit, no less.

Barrett, normally so quick with her words, thought about her answer and responded carefully. "Okay, Mr. Graham, fair question. Back your face up and I'll tell you."

"I can hear you better up close," he said.

Barrett stood suddenly and drew her sword so swiftly that Sean stumbled trying to retreat, tripping over the saloon bench. From his backside he drew his own short dagger, realizing immediately he was at a severe disadvantage.

"Remember how the governor's elephant attacked him? That was me," said Barrett. "Or rather, *this*," she said, brandishing the sword.

"A magic sword," said Sean, slowly getting back on his feet and sheathing his dagger.

"Before the first imperial dynasty," said Yaozu, "thousands of years ago, China was governed by people we now call the Ancients. And before them, the universe was ruled by—"

"Three Sovereigns and Five Emperors," Bren interjected.

Barrett smiled. "You really did spend time in Archibald's bookstore."

"Actually, Admiral Bowman explained all that to me. Are you saying that sword is one of the Eight Immortals?"

"Yaozu calls it the Tamer of Beasts," said Barrett, resheathing it and handing Bren the scarlet-and-gold scabbard. It was obvious Sean was lost again. "Eight magical objects, Mr. Graham, empowered by the gifts of the eight demigods who once ruled Heaven and Earth."

She turned to Bren. "And it wasn't just luck that we found you so quickly."

Yaozu showed them the jade tablet.

"Another one of these Eight Immortals?" said Sean. "And let me guess, you're after the rest of them?"

"You catch on quick for an Eirish," said Barrett.

Bren returned the sword to her. "You think you know where the others are?"

"Yes and no," said Yaozu. "At one time I didn't think

the artifacts existed. Now I fear they may all be waiting to be found, and that is a problem."

"How so?" said Sean.

"Because anyone could use them," said Barrett. "We wouldn't want them to fall into the wrong hands."

Her choice of words made Bren cringe. Admiral Bowman had said almost the same thing in justifying his pursuit of Far Eastern magic.

"The fact is, I believe someone already has used them for ill," said Yaozu.

"Oh, you mean Lady Barrett," said Sean. "Using the 'Tamer of Beasts' to ruin that poor man's Utopia."

Bren was sure he could hear Lady Barrett grinding her teeth.

"I mean the Emperor Qin Shi Huang," said Yaozu. "The founder of China's first imperial dynasty. The one who ended the time of the Ancients."

"By using their magical objects against them?" said Mouse.

"Most forget—Qin was just a boy of thirteen at the time of his conquest," said Yaozu. "There are many who believe he could not have succeeded without the Eight Immortals, or some of them, anyway."

"Thirteen!" said Bren. "That's how old I am . . . I think."

"Natural disasters, in particular, played a key role in

his victory," Yaozu explained, "weakening his enemies and giving his army strategic advantages."

"And the Eight Immortals can have power over weather and the environment, right?" said Bren. "The admiral explained that to me, about how the magic of the Ancients was more tied to the natural world."

Yaozu nodded.

"But you're literally talking about ancient history," said Sean. "This emperor has been dead . . ."

"Almost two thousand years."

"Almost two thousand years!" said Sean. "He probably had his toys and weapons buried with him!"

"Precisely!" said Yaozu, smiling broadly. "But that is what we must find out."

Sean ran his fingers through his hair, tugging at his cowlicks. "You need Bren and Mouse to help you dig up an old emperor?"

"Not at all," said Yaozu. "If I or anyone else knew where Qin was buried, his tomb would have been pillaged ages ago. No, I need them—specifically Mouse—to help us find it."

Sean cursed him loudly. Yaozu calmly ignored this and went to Mouse.

"The ability to read oracle bones—truly read them— was thought to have been lost with the Ancients," he said. "Few can even read the language, much less divine anything from them. You have an extraordinary gift, young one."

He sat her down at the table and held her hand in his. "There is a relic in a small holy place on an island called the Pearl Cliffs, near where I was born. It is believed to be the collarbone of Di Xin, the last Shang king. No one knows for sure where it came from, or if the story is even true. But if it is true, I believe you could use the bone to divine the location of Qin's tomb. If you let me take you there, I will lead you to the Dragon's Gate."

"This is crazy," said Sean. "You can't believe any of this, Barrett. Even if you do, what do you need Bren for?"

Barrett stood between Bren and Mouse. "Your stone has powers, does it not?" she said to Mouse.

"I think so."

"And yours too?" she asked Bren.

"According to Mouse, it protects me," he said. "I know it sounds crazy, Sean, but I've been wearing the stone every time I've narrowly avoided being killed. Back in Map, when the Iberians attacked . . ."

"Bren! You can't believe all this nonsense!"

"It's true," said Mouse, holding up the white jade again. "When the admiral found Bren and me, he tried to take the stone. He was going to kill us. But I killed him instead, using the stone."

"Killed him how?" said Sean.

"I summoned a dragon from the silver river," she said.

—146—

"I'm not sure how. I didn't mean to kill the admiral . . . at least, I don't think I did."

"Mouse—"

"And back on New Amsterdam, my spirit entered the second elephant, the one that attacked the Dutch governor."

"Soul-traveling?" said Yaozu.

She nodded again. "I tried to use the stone at first, to control the elephant. I don't like to leave myself, become other things, but I couldn't do anything with it. I don't know why; it was just like I was holding an ordinary stone."

Bren remembered how she had showed him the stone in her hand, there on the beach, and then put it away.

"I believe Mouse was destined to find that stone," said Barrett, looking Sean in the eye, "and that I was destined to find her. I can't explain or prove anything to your satisfaction, I'm sure, Mr. Graham, but I think the Eight Immortals are meant to be together, and that our being together only increases the chances of finding more. As for Bren, I'm not sure what role he will ultimately play, and I don't think Mouse does either, but this means something." She reached out and gently lifted the black stone from around Bren's neck. "Two jade stones, one black, one white, just like in the fable of the Angry Mountain. Like the Chinese philosophy of yin and yang . . . opposites coming together to make a balanced whole . . . the one unable to exist without the other."

Sean turned to Bren, his eyes as bloodshot as if he'd been drinking all night. "I wasn't the one sent to rescue you, lad. I can't make you do anything. But I thought you wanted to go home?"

Bren said nothing at first. He did still want to go home. But he didn't want Lady Barrett to leave him. And despite their quarrels, he didn't want to lose Mouse, either. He didn't understand why she felt this need to go to China. But the catfish man had given Mouse the jade eye, told her she was the guardian, asked her to read the oracle bones. Maybe she *didn't* know exactly what she was doing. It was more like she was acting on orders, and if Bren really was her friend, maybe he had a duty to help her.

"I think I want to go with them," he said finally. He could tell that wasn't what Sean wanted to hear, but he didn't seem surprised by Bren's answer either.

"Me too," said Mouse. "I'll help you find the tomb."

Yaozu smiled, squeezing her hand.

"Aye, I guess we're all going to China then," said Sean. "I've grown very fond of Bren and Mouse, and I don't trust you one lick, Lady Jean Barrett. I'm going to see to it they make it home safely."

CHAPTER
13

CHANGE OF PLANS

The two men who got off the boat at Bombay Island couldn't have been more conspicuous. The first was overburdened with large brass-and-leather cases, one under each arm and another one in each hand. You would have thought he was the servant of the second man, tall and rigidly thin, wearing tan pants and a white shirt with a broad-brimmed hat, so that he looked somewhat like a palm tree.

The man with all the luggage was suddenly swarmed by children, offering to carry his bags.

"Don't do it, Owen," said the thin man. "This place is notorious for thieves."

"If you'd like to lend a hand," said David Owen, "I might not be tempted."

The thin man turned and looked at him, children pressing up against them. "Shoo, shoo, urchins," he said. "The British government was supposed to arrange for transport. Just hang tight, David."

David Owen dropped all four cases and stacked them two by two, sitting on one pair. "I'm only guarding this pair, Archibald," he said. "If you're so worried about theft, I suggest you guard the other two with your narrow behind."

Archibald Black arched a long eyebrow at his companion, but proceeded to sit down on the other pair.

"How will this transporter know who to look for?" said Owen.

"We're the only Europeans here," said Black.

David Owen looked around the port, which was teeming with Indians. Map, even on its busiest day, was nothing compared to this. He pulled out a filthy rag to mop his brow. "Must be near a hundred degrees here. And humid to boot!"

"Compared to Map it feels like Hell," said Black. "But at least it's not raining for now."

"What do you mean, *for now*?"

"Didn't you know?" said Black. "Monsoon season

starts in a month or so. This place will be flooded with rain. Hundreds of inches."

Owen seemed dumbfounded. Black laughed.

"Did Rand McNally not bother with those minor details when he agreed to let you lead up a scout team for the survey?"

David Owen mopped his brow some more. "It doesn't matter. We're here for one reason, and one reason only. And it doesn't have anything to do with that damned survey."

Black felt sorry for the man squatting on the two cases, slumped over from the burden of grief and frustration. As much as he, too, wanted Bren to return safely, he didn't have much faith in David Owen's plan. If Lady Jean Barrett hadn't succeeded, why would they? But he understood why Owen wanted to do it. He had nothing left in Map. Not his wife, nor his son. At least being in India, working on the survey, would take him away from his empty house and his old routine. And Black got a chance to go to Persia, and perhaps see inside the legendary House of Wisdom.

A man wearing a turban and a knee-length red-and-gold frock coat came running toward them.

"Sahib!" he said, although it was unclear whether he was addressing Black or Owen. "Your carriage has arrived!" The man, who couldn't have been more than twenty, practically yanked the large cases out from under Black. "Allow me."

David Owen hopped up before he, too, was dethroned.

"Where are you taking us?" said Black. "And be careful with those! They contain expensive instruments."

The boy was half dragging, half pulling all four cases along the dock, until they reached a carriage that was little more than a flat cart with a piece of canvas propped above it on four sticks to shield them from the sun. He loaded the cases onto the back and then leaped onto a warped bench, taking up the reins of a single horse that looked like it had seen better days.

"Hop in! The back, please."

David Owen didn't seem to mind, but Black was scowling as they loaded themselves into the cart next to their luggage.

"Where can I get a boat to Persia?" Black called as the boy slowly steered their carriage through smothering crowds of people.

"Persia?"

"Yes, I'm going north. Not south like my friend here."

The boy laughed. "Oh, but your friend is going north. You both are!"

"What?" said Owen. "I'm part of the Royal Survey!"

"And I'm not!" Black sputtered.

"Yes, yes, Royal Survey!" said the boy. "Change of plans. Emperor Akbar wants you to survey *his* territory first."

David Owen avoided eye contact with Black. "Well, you said you wanted an adventure."

"I most certainly did not," Black replied.

PART TWO

THE DRAGON'S GATE

CHAPTER 14

THE ROTTERDAM STRAITS

"Does your ship have a name?" asked Sean.

They were standing on the quarterdeck, just as the two main Dragon Islands of the East Netherlands—Sunda and Java—came into view.

"A name?" said Barrett, staring off toward the gap between the two islands, the Rotterdam Straits. "Oh yes, you mean, what was she christened?"

"If we're going through on business, this all has to look official," said Sean. "That man you hired out, I assume this is his boat?"

Barrett squirmed a bit before answering. "Well, we may have borrowed it in the Gulf of Arabia."

"Borrowed?" gasped Sean. "From whom?"

"I'm not sure," said Barrett. "The owner wasn't around when we borrowed it."

She half smiled, and Bren couldn't tell if she was proud or embarrassed. Either way, Sean was in neither a humorous nor a forgiving mood.

"We're sailing into Java with a stolen ship?"

"Would Sunda be better?"

Sean almost hit her this time. He stormed to the other side of the ship and then back again, bending the boards with every stomping step.

"You're going to get us all arrested, Barrett. This needs to be a legitimate ship with a legitimate purpose."

"How about the *Sally Turner*?"

"The *Sally Turner*?"

"She was a girl I knew in school. I fancied her quite a bit."

Sean closed his eyes and took a deep breath. "You need a better name than that—and you need papers for the clerk at Bantam. I don't suppose you thought to *borrow* those as well?"

There was an awkward pause that quickly turned into an awkward moment and then a full-fledged awkward silence.

"I can do it," said Bren. "I can forge papers for us. I saw official documents back in Map, in Rand McNally's office. . . . I can duplicate the seal of the Netherlands and Britannia, and I saw King Maximilian's signature in Admiral Bowman's cabin once. Sean, you've been sailing long enough to tell me what transit papers should say, right?"

Sean's face returned to its more normal, calmer shade of pale. "Aye, I suppose. If you're sure about the rest."

Bren nodded. He'd put his memory to far greater tests than this for Admiral Bowman.

"Smashing!" said Barrett. "To my cabin then."

"We need to buy time," said Sean. "Clew the sails to slow us down."

"Yes, I'll relay that to the men," said Barrett. "Meet you below."

While they waited for her, Bren turned to Sean and asked, "Why don't you trust her?"

"Why would I?" said Sean. "You have to admit, she's a bit of a character."

Bren considered that more or less a compliment. "I know you don't know my friend Mr. Black, but he wouldn't have sent Lady Barrett if he thought I couldn't trust her."

"Except he sent her to find you and return you to Map," said Sean. "He didn't mean by way of China."

The cabin door flew open and Barrett bounced in. "Marvelous, you're all here. What do we need?" When no one replied, she asked, "Did I interrupt something?"

"Not at all," said Sean. "We need parchment, pen, and ink."

"I can do that," said Barrett, fumbling around in a drawer that they all realized now wasn't hers, until she found a blank sheet. After a bit more rummaging around, she produced pen and ink.

"Most papers of transit I've seen start this way," Sean began, and he went on to describe the formal language and the general length, spinning an official-sounding tale of scouting the South China Sea, per the new alliance in the works between Britannia and the Netherlands. They would explain in person, if it came up, how the ship rescued the survivors of the *Albatross*, but without mentioning the rogue governor. Bren added the seals of Britannia and the Netherlands and forged the two royals' signatures. The last thing was the ship's name. Sean and Barrett spent fifteen minutes arguing about it, neither willing to approve of the other's suggestion, until Bren finally blurted out, "How about the *Fortune*?"

The two combatants agreed to that and Bren wrote it down.

"My God, lad, you have a career as a master forger if you want it," said Sean.

Bren smiled, until he heard the stern voice of Archibald Black in his head telling him that it wasn't a compliment.

"And you're in luck, having a proper British captain on board."

"You mean me, of course," said Barrett.

"You?"

"You did know I'm British, didn't you? Or did the accent slip past you?"

Sean had to keep from laughing. "You're a lady!"

Barrett marched over to where Sean was standing. He stood his ground, and she punched him in the face.

"Come on, you big red dope," she said as Sean rubbed his chin and tried to blink the water out of his eyes. "Hit me back, if you're man enough."

Sean made a fist over and over again with his right hand, but he couldn't bring himself to hit her. Instead he gave her a good shove, sending her tumbling backwards into the chair and desk. She didn't hit the floor, though.

"Stop it!" screamed Mouse, jumping between them and pushing Sean against the wall. He held up his hands to let her know he was done.

"I just meant, you hired me to take you to China," said Sean. "I assumed you meant me to captain the ship."

"Then you should've said what you meant," said Barrett.

They all kept out of each other's way after that, and in a couple of hours they were pulling into the harbor at Bantam, the port at the narrowest point of the Rotterdam

Straits. It was nothing as impressive as Cape Colony had been. In fact, from a distance it looked to Bren more like the part of Map he'd grown up in—a clutter of shabby wooden houses. Here, though, the ones near the water were on stilts, like a lady hiking up her skirts to traipse through a puddle.

Barrett had no trouble convincing the clerks at the Bantam factory that she was in charge of the ship. Bren had thought she might take the opportunity to pretend to be a man, but she didn't bother. Chief Clerk Boerhaven raised an eyebrow when he met Lady Barrett, but that was it. After all, Britannia was ruled by a queen; who's to say her ship captains wouldn't be women as well?

The bigger challenge was that the chief clerk had received word of Admiral Bowman's treason and the uprising at Cape Colony, and he was on high alert.

"We've also had a trader go missing looking for tin deposits on nearby islands," said Boerhaven. "Fellow by the name of Wycoff. Don't know why I wouldn't have heard that a British scout was passing through to the China Sea."

Sean started to explain, but Barrett jumped in.

"You're quite right, Mr. Boerhaven. These are uncharted waters, if you'll forgive the pun. Top-secret stuff, in fact, and the governor will be getting his own briefing. For now this is for your eyes only, do you understand? This is all part of the new Britannia-Netherlands alliance. Exploring new trade options, if you will."

Whether Boerhaven was dazzled or just outright confused by Barrett, it didn't matter, because he eventually stamped the letters of transit "approved" and returned them to Barrett.

"How about a tour of the factory then, for those of you new to Bantam?"

Bantam itself was small, but Java island was large. Beyond the rickety-looking houses were acres of cultivated farmland: flooded rice fields in one direction; rows of cotton as far as the eye could see in another. The chief clerk walked them through a sea of green stalks twice as tall as any of them, and when he explained that it was sugarcane, Bren's eyes went wide. The last British ship he had tried to stow away on was one bound for Jamaica, where they supposedly had grass made of sugar. Was this the same thing?

The chief clerk laughed at Bren's expression. "Would you like to try some?"

Bren nodded eagerly and the chief clerk pulled out a large knife and cut away a hunk from one of the massive stalks. "Just chew it," he said, and when Bren put it in his mouth, it was like sucking on a piece of soft wood, pulpy and fibrous. But then he tasted the sweetness. . . .

"Maybe Mouse would like a sample?" said Barrett, and the chief clerk cut away a piece for her too.

When they came back to the heart of town, Boerhaven

showed them bushels of spices called nutmeg and clove, which he explained came from tropical trees all through the islands, and burlap sacks of coffee beans. The smell was overwhelming. There were also large flat carts stacked with ivory—elephant tusks longer than a man, and rhinoceros horns. But the chief clerk seemed most proud of an enormous tent, where table after table was covered with small, milky white cakes. It was rubber, he explained, collected and dried and ready to be turned into tires for the bicycles that gave the Dutch Bicycle & Tulip Company part of its name.

"This is primarily a trading post, of course," said Boerhaven. "We do our share of farming here on Java, but the bulk of everything we export comes from all over the Dragon Islands and Southeast Asia. To ensure steady profits, the company negotiated with local farmers to convert to commercial crops like the ones you've seen."

"Negotiated?" said Barrett with a laugh. "What did the farmers get in return?"

Boerhaven was taken aback. "Our protection, of course," he said, waving an arm in the direction of military barracks Bren had missed before.

When the chief clerk walked on ahead, Bren whispered, "Protection from whom?" Barrett whispered back, "Protection from another country wanting to 'negotiate' with local farmers."

"Quiet, you two," said Sean, trying to whisper but not entirely succeeding. "We're guests, remember?"

"Come, children," called the chief clerk. "There's something else here you might find entertaining."

He led them to a part of Bantam occupied solely by local Javanese people, and down a twisting alley they came to a sort of wooden stage, covered with a brightly colored curtain. There was a small crowd gathering—golden-skinned men, women, and children with black hair, some dressed very plainly in loose-fitting clothes, others in draped clothing so multi-colorful it looked as if it had been painted. A few Netherlanders and their children were there as well. Before long the curtain was drawn to reveal a pair of figures against a white backdrop.

"Puppets!" said Bren and Mouse.

The chief clerk smiled approvingly at their excitement.

The puppets were unlike any Bren had seen—elongated two-dimensional figures made of leather, finely cut and decorated, held up on slender pieces of bone. The first show began, performed in Dutch, about a girl named Timun Mas, who outwits a green giant determined to eat her.

The second featured a hideous creature known as the Wewe Gombel, the ghost of a wronged wife who kidnaps children from bad families and cares for them in her nest. This was followed by several episodes from the Panji cycle, about a famous prince of Java, and one of the tales of

Kancil, a cunning little mouse deer who uses intelligence to triumph over larger animals.

The last show they watched was the story of Malin Kundang, a boy from a poor family who sneaks away from home on a trading ship and eventually becomes rich and marries a princess. But he becomes so proud of his accomplishments that he refuses to acknowledge his mother and his humble origins the next time he comes home, and in retribution, his mother turns her son and his ship to stone.

Bren was ready to leave after that.

▲▲▲

"Yaozu, I was wondering something," said Bren. "You said that at one time, you didn't think these artifacts existed. What changed your mind?"

They were all in a common room of a guesthouse the chief clerk had put them in. The remaining crew of the *Albatross* was asleep, while Barrett, Sean, Yaozu, Bren, and Mouse sat up enjoying some sort of homemade spicy ale.

"I told you China was my home, but that wasn't completely true," said Yaozu. "One cannot feel at home in a country that does not welcome you. I was born on one of the many small islands off China's mainland that have become home to outcasts. My parents were scholars, as were their parents and grandparents before them, and scholars were among the first to be shunned under the new dynasty. Research was forbidden.

"My family taught me about the Ancients and the Eight Immortals, which I considered mere folklore, and when I was old enough, they sent me away from a world they considered lost. I've only returned once since then, for my parents' funeral. They were killed in an accident. Then I returned to the Near East, which is when I learned that the Immortals might be real and could be found. I read about a king named Prester John, supposedly a descendent of the Three Magi and the last Christian king of the East. I say *supposedly* because Marco Polo had written of him, and no one knows better than the Chinese that Marco Polo had a flair for exaggeration."

Bren stole a glance at Mouse. He'd always heard the same thing, but the letter of Admiral Bowman's had proved real enough.

"Anyway," said Yaozu, "it was written that Prester John had among his possessions a mirror with which he could survey his realm. I investigated, and found a group of what one might generously call zealots living in poverty in Ectabana, where I met you, Lady Barrett. They had made a shrine around what they believed to be Prester John's magic mirror, though of course they had no idea how it worked."

"So you just took it?" said Sean.

"As soon as I saw it, I suspected it might be the jade tablet. I had to know. It was nothing but a useless relic to those people, and it would have been reckless to leave it there. You know most of the rest of the story."

"I don't get it," said Sean. "You want to find this tomb of Qin; why not use the magic tablet?"

"It was the first thing I tried," Yaozu admitted. "Knowing of these objects and even possessing them is a far cry from understanding and controlling them. Another reason they are dangerous. The only thing I can assume is that no one anywhere possesses the knowledge of Qin's tomb, and therefore the mirror cannot show it to me."

"He's right," said Barrett. "The first thing I tried to do was find you, Bren. It showed me your face, but not where you were. Then it showed me the place you might be, but with no context for me to locate it. Fortunately I had the Ptolemy map and was able to use the two together."

"But wait, neither of you knew about Mouse until you rescued Bren," said Sean. "What was your master plan before that?"

He seemed determined to poke holes in their story, but Yaozu was unflappable.

"To avail myself of Lady Barrett's expertise . . . take her home with me, research the history of the Eight Immortals, make educated guesses about where they may have ended up . . ."

"He's just being polite," said Barrett. "I was going to steal this relic he told Mouse about and take it back to

London. See if we could decipher it there."

"Speaking of maps," said Bren, "maybe I should start working on a more detailed map we can use? Yaozu, would you be able to help fill in more detail?"

"I can try," he said.

"That's a splendid idea," said Barrett. "You really do have mapmaking in your blood."

"Don't say that," said Bren, as if he were afraid his father and Rand McNally might overhear her.

"Oh no, I can tell you have adventure in your blood too," she said, grabbing his hand. "A full share."

CHAPTER 15

THE TEMPLE OF THE FIVE LORDS

Bren got up before dawn to watch the sun rise over Bantam. He had read that the Far East was called the Land of the Rising Sun by old sailors, and he wanted to see what they meant. What was so special? He could see the sun rise just fine from his hovel in Map, couldn't he?

He walked north from the factory, from the barracks where they'd been quartered, past the rice fields and the stilted houses of the fishermen, until he reached the eastern end of the harbor, where he waited. He chewed on a handful of coffee beans that the clerk of Bantam had given him.

They were painfully bitter, but Bren had never felt more alert this early. Despite being exhausted he had tossed and turned in bed, unable to stop thinking about the adventure that awaited them.

And then the first glow of light appeared on the horizon, like a lamp from someone unseen coming up a darkened hill. The light grew in area and intensity until Bren was convinced some great fire was about to consume the earth, a fire that reminded him of that night in the cavern, when he had to shield his eyes from the heat. . . .

He blinked. Just for a moment, but when he opened his eyes again, the sun was right there, not so much rising as poised at the edge of the ocean, as if it were about to roll across the waves. It wasn't beautiful; it was terrifying, and Bren shut his eyes again, as hard as he could.

"I know what you're thinking," came a voice, and Bren spun toward it, still sitting, his eyes still closed. When he opened them he saw Lady Jean Barrett, bathed in light, her arm cocked to shield her eyes.

"What am I thinking?" said Bren.

"That it all seems so close, that the world can't possibly go on and on beyond the horizon. Like the sun is popping up out of a slot between the sea and the sky."

She sat down next to him.

"The emperors saw the same sun, the same close horizon," she said. "Remember Yaozu's theory about the map of the Hidden Sea? That it came from a fruitless search for an island of immortality? Well, Emperor Qin was convinced that the island must lie this way. He sent a naval captain named Xu Fu sailing toward the rising sun. Qin had also once employed a magician named Anqi Sheng, who was already a thousand years old when Qin reigned, and some think it was Anqi Sheng that Xu Fu went in search of, after the magician disappeared."

Bren perked up. "Did the magician look like a catfish?"

"Sorry?"

"Nothing. Did Yaozu tell you all this?"

"Some," said Barrett. "Some I may have read on my own. I stole a glance now and then at those rare books I used to fetch for Mr. Black."

She smiled at Bren, and any doubts about his decision to go with her evaporated.

"Come on," she said, standing and offering a hand to Bren. "Let's help Sean and Mouse load some supplies."

▲▲▲

They estimated a week's journey through the South China Sea and provisioned themselves accordingly. This meant two things: food and water for themselves, obviously; and items they might use to barter—or bribe—their way through the mainland. The first was provided by Chief Clerk Boerhaven, who was happy to give but also drew up a complicated contract that ensured he would be absolved of blame should disaster strike. The second was provided by Mouse, who without the chief clerk's knowledge sneaked into one of the factory's storehouses to pinch nutmeg, cloves, coffee beans, and a handful of other goods that would be desirable to mainlanders. She also nipped two bottles of jenever from the chief clerk's office, since he had not seen fit to provide the crew with any spirits.

None of the Netherlanders had sailed into the South China Sea, nor Sean, but they had acquired a reliable map from the chief clerk that showed them how to navigate north from Bantam, across the equator, through the gap between the Dutch Siamese peninsula to the west and Borneo to the east, until they were hugging the coastline of Indochina, going north-northeast. The Pearl Cliffs, their target, was a sizable island in the northern part of the sea. Most of their week under sail was blissfully calm, and Bren had never been so glad to be bored. He spent the time adding more detail to their map of China, with Yaozu's help.

Then they hit the fog. Barrett hadn't been kidding about that. It was nothing like the vapor that had concealed the Vanishing Island. That had seemed somehow not real . . . *enchanted* even. This was just fog, but it was thick as cotton, and it was everywhere.

"The Pearl Cliffs should be in sight," said Sean, standing on the quarterdeck with Barrett, comparing his charts to their map.

"Are those mountaintops?" said Bren, pointing to what looked like a pair of green peaks above the white shroud.

"I believe you're right, Bren," said Barrett.

"How shallow are the waters?" said Sean. "Do you know, Yaozu?"

"Where most boats land is here, on this side," he said, pointing to the southeast corner of the island. "There was a port established there on an inlet, so smugglers could bring supplies to exiles here."

Sean piloted the ship through the edge of the fog, where they trimmed their two sails until they could see land, and then dropped anchor to hold their position perhaps a hundred yards away. The ship had a six-oar rowboat, and three of the crew lowered it to go scout for a landing. The report was that there wasn't enough depth for even a ship of the *Fortune*'s size to land, so Sean, Barrett, Mouse, Bren, and Yaozu squeezed in with another Netherlander, who dropped them on the island and then rowed back to the ship. The Netherlanders had already agreed to take the *Fortune* back straightaway; they had enough supplies for the weeklong journey back to Bantam.

"It's not too late to change your mind, Mr. Graham," said Barrett, while the rowboat was still within view. "You're a natural leader. You'd make a fine captain for that ship."

"Why, Lady Barrett, one might think you don't want

me to come with you! I'm still young. I'll captain some other ship." He looked at Bren and Mouse. "After we discover the lost tomb of Qin and find the Eight Immortals, they'll probably give me a good one, don't you think?"

He winked at them, and Mouse smiled. Bren did too, but it was forced. He knew Sean didn't want to do this, that he was coming along because he felt some duty to protect these two willful children who had intruded upon his life.

"Is this the island where you were born?" Mouse asked Yaozu.

"No," he said. "A much smaller island, not too far away. This is the island with the Temple of the Five Lords. Our first very important destination."

"Which way to this temple?" said Sean.

"Straight up, I'm afraid."

And so they began their march inland, along a river whose source was the peak of one of the Pearl Cliffs' two mountains, and it didn't take long for them to work up a sweat as the sun rose over the tropical island. Bren took note of all the different animals—ratlike things, rabbits, something that looked like a miniature leopard, and in the trees, small apes, as well as a catlike creature that reminded him of his old friend, Mr. Grey: the same color and size, but with a much longer tail and a stripe down his face like a badger. There were swarming insects, which Bren could only imagine would multiply in peskiness come summer, and everywhere, birds. Hundreds of them. Thousands. The noise of them made the whole island sound like a nervous wreck. Along the river were egrets and herons and pheasants and partridges (at least, that's what they looked like to Bren), cormorants and hens. When they reached the forest, though, it was a pandemonium of perching birds, from parrots to cuckoos to songbirds of all kinds.

Bren was furiously taking notes in his journal, which he would flesh out from memory later.

"Are you secretly a botanist? Or a veterinarian?" Sean teased, noting Bren's enthusiasm.

"Mr. Leiden taught me the importance of studying new flora and fauna," said Bren, somewhat defensively. "That leaf may hold the secret to a new medicine. Or that bird over there may one day teach humans to fly."

Just then the bird in question released a blob of white excrement from its backside.

"Well, for now at least I know how to crap from a tree branch," said Sean, causing everyone to laugh.

It was some much-needed levity. They had all made tough choices about what to do and who to trust. Tension among them had never been less than a low thrum since they came together. For once, it was as if they were all old friends enjoying a day of shore leave.

And as young as Bren was, he wasn't innocent enough to believe it would last.

▲▲▲

Halfway up the mountain they made camp for the night in a shallow cave and used what little daylight was left to find food. They had left most of their provisions with the Netherlanders taking the ship back to Bantam. "We'll have to get used to foraging anyway," said Barrett.

Sean tried his hand at trapping birds with little success, and Bren, who usually left the foraging to Mouse, went off on his own and found a shrub heavy with bright yellow fruit that reminded him of a miniature pumpkin. When he bit into a piece, though, it was as if he had released a sorcerer's curse—his mouth filled with fire, and his eyes turned to puddles, and his lips began to peel away from his face. . . .

They were still near the river, so Bren ran to the edge and plunged his face beneath the surface, but the rushing water just seemed to spread the fire rather than extinguish it.

He collapsed in tears next to the river, which is when he heard someone laughing at him. It was Yaozu, holding what was left of the demonic fruit Bren had bitten into.

"Did you eat this pepper?" he said, more bemused than concerned.

Bren nodded. He tried to defend himself, but his mouth didn't work: "I 'ought it 'as 'uit."

"It is a fruit," said Yaozu. "Notice the seeds. They're what makes it hot. I've never tried this one, but judging by your face I assume it is extraordinarily hot."

"Am I 'oing to die?" said Bren.

Yaozu laughed again. "You will live. Perhaps try eating a piece of sweet fruit. That may help."

Mouse had managed to pry open one of the giant seeds of a palm tree, and the waxy, sweet-sour meat inside was like a salve to Bren's inflamed tongue and lips. He was still in pain for some time, but eventually more embarrassed than anything, as every other person in the party seemed to find humor in his misadventure.

"Should we build a fire, or just gather 'round Bren's face?" said Sean, to much laughter. "Or maybe the lad can start one with his breath!"

"Bren the Dragon!" shouted Barrett, raising her sword in the air, and everyone joined in. "Bren the Dragon! Bren the Dragon!"

▲▲▲

They spent half the next day completing their trek to the top of the mountain, and when they reached the top, there stood an unimpressive red building in a clearing. It was small, two stories, the roof a pyramid of painted tile in need of repair. A stone courtyard was landscaped with palm trees and other species unfamiliar to Bren.

"The Temple of the Five Lords," said Yaozu.

He led them to the front door, a latticed wood frame that slid to the side.

"After you," he said, with a gallant half bow to the others.

The five lords were there waiting for them—life-size statues standing before a red curtain like a theater troupe. They appeared to be carved from wood, each wearing a full-length red silk gown embroidered with green dragons, but with their hands in slightly different positions. All had a black garment on their heads, although there was one different from the rest, and all had black beards and mustaches that grew to the sash around their gowns. Before them was set a copper kettle, a clay plate, and a porcelain sake cup, for offerings.

Bren noticed that each of the statues stood on a short pedestal of painted wood with a brass plate engraved with Chinese symbols.

"Those are the names of the lords," said Yaozu. "In reality, exiled officials who lost power struggles with their imperial government, now martyrs to those of us who long for the ancient ways."

"What now?" said Sean. "Do we make an offering?"

"Of a sort," said Yaozu, and he pulled a necklace from inside his tunic. It was a medallion, similar in size to the paiza that had launched Bren's adventure. But this one had no inscriptions or engravings whatsoever. Just a blank bronze disk.

"Is that a magic mirror?" said Bren.

"You are a curious boy," said Yaozu, with a wry smile. He nodded to Barrett, who went to a small window and folded back the red shutters, letting sunlight stream into the room. Yaozu caught the light with the face of his medallion, directing the reflection toward the face of the one lord who had the different head garment. Bren could barely see the image of a circle reflected on the face of the statue—half light and half dark, each side appearing to overlap the other.

To everyone's astonishment, the statue began to move.

With a jarring scrape of wood against stone, the pedestal upon which the statue stood started to slide backwards. It took perhaps thirty seconds in all, but when it finally stopped, Yaozu led them all to the mouth of a hidden staircase.

Down they went. The stone stairs went straight to a landing, then bent to the left at a ninety-degree angle. The staircase switched back, and as they made the turn, they heard the statue of the lord sliding back into place. They were soon in complete darkness.

"This way," said Yaozu. "Everyone hold the garment of the person in front of you, until we reach the bottom."

Bren blindly felt for Lady Barrett's shirt, terrified he would touch something he wasn't supposed to. He felt Mouse tugging at his trouser waist from behind.

They soon saw a light in the distance, lit torches hanging from the walls of a stone room, hewn right out of the rock.

"Is someone expecting us?" said Sean.

"This temple is maintained by others who study the Ancients," said Yaozu somewhat cryptically as he led them into a large room that reminded Bren of the catacombs his father had shown him under Britannia. Except the recesses carved into these walls were filled with books and artifacts, not bones.

"It's like a secret library!" said Bren, almost unable to control himself. He and Mouse both darted from one nook to another, not daring to touch anything, but looking with all their might. There were tables and storage chests, too, and two other archways leading off into other darkened tunnels. Suddenly Bren stopped cold in front of an arched recess in the middle of the far wall. He'd thought there were no bones here, but he was wrong—he was staring at one now, shaped like the head of an axe.

"The collarbone of Di Xin," said Yaozu. "Technically, his scapula. Mouse, would you like to take a look?"

She came over and peered into the nook. "May I touch it?"

"Of course," said Yaozu, gently taking the scapula and handing it to her.

"What's so special about this bone?" said Barrett.

"The Shang were the last dynasty to read oracle bones," said Yaozu. "Qin officially vanquished the Ancients by destroying all evidence he could find of those who came before him. But the country was already in disarray—the Warring States period, they called it—which set the stage for his conquest."

He led Mouse to a small wooden table and sat her down there with the bone, then fetched a pot of dark red ink and a fine brush.

"I believe the connection between the bone of an Ancient and the gifts of an heir will be strong," said Yaozu. "Oracle bones were once etched with a sharp tool. Later, ink made from cinnabar and brushes were used."

"What question do I ask?" said Mouse. "Where was Qin buried?"

Yaozu considered this. "Perhaps, 'Where is Qin's tomb?'"

Mouse nodded and dipped the brush in the ink. "I've never done this before," she said. "I don't even know how I read the girl's bones."

"It's okay," Yaozu assured her. "Close your eyes and picture yourself writing the question on the bone. Then, do."

She obeyed him, and after a few minutes she began to paint. It was like a spirit was working through her, and Bren quickly recognized the script, more pictogram-like than modern Chinese writing. It was a short question, but it took her a while, and when she was done, most of the scapula was covered.

"Now, for our answer," said Yaozu, taking one of the torches from the wall. "Set the bone on the floor," he said, and when Mouse had done so, he brought the flame to it.

The fire quickly dried the paint, then charred it.

"Grab another torch," said Yaozu, and Barrett held a second one to the bone, until finally one crack appeared, then another. It didn't fracture all at once like the skeleton of Sun had, but the surface soon spiderwebbed, and after several more minutes, Mouse said, "That's enough."

"You can read?" said Yaozu.

"Yes," said Mouse. "I can show you where the tomb is."

CHAPTER 16

INTO THE VAST LAND

Bren opened his journal to a blank page, prepared to draw the pattern on the bone, but Mouse stopped him.

"It's not a map this time. It's a word." She looked to Yaozu. "Does the name Fenghou mean anything to you?"

His eyes widened. "Fenghou! That was the name of Xi'an, before the time of Qin! Bren, show us our map again."

Bren opened his journal and Yaozu pointed to an area in the central part of the country.

"Xi'an was the eastern terminus of the old Silk Road," he said. "In the middle of the Guanzhong Plain. Cradled by mountains south and east, nurtured by the Wei River to the north."

"I'll add it to our map!" said Bren.

"What about getting there?" said Barrett.

Yaozu pulled at his straggly beard. "For that I will need help. First, though, we must get to the mainland. Gather your things."

He left the bone and two extinguished torches on the floor, along with a note that Bren assumed explained to the librarians why their sacred bone was broken. Then they all exited through one of the other tunnels, going down farther into the mountain, until they came to another lit room. This one was bare except for a wooden door on one wall. Yaozu slid the door to the side to reveal a large open carriage, almost exactly like the one in Rand McNally's Map Emporium.

"It's a lift!" said Bren.

Yaozu smiled. "In this case, it is a drop."

When they were all inside, Yaozu operated a pulley that sent them suddenly jerking downward. Everyone jumped, afraid they were about to plunge into the darkness. But the carriage stabilized, and they were soon gliding slowly downward.

"Apologies," said Yaozu. "The mechanism must adjust

to the added weight. Smooth sailing now."

It was a long, dark, slow descent, but when the carriage finally stopped, Yaozu let them off in a room similar to the one above, bare but for one door that opened onto a pitch-black tunnel.

"No torches this time?" said Bren, already feeling short of breath.

"Afraid not," said Yaozu. "But trust me."

The tunnel was so dark Bren couldn't see his own hands. And it was narrow, so that they had to walk single file, and everyone except Mouse had to stoop.

"Yaozu, how long is this walk?" Bren managed to say.

"Quite long," he replied. "Here, come up front with me. Hold my arm and breathe slowly. All will be fine."

Bren did as he suggested, even closing his eyes for periods of time, letting Yaozu guide him. It worked. He lost track of time and let go of the fear that the tunnel walls were closing in. By the end he wasn't sure if they had walked for one hour or ten, but he was relieved when they came out of the tunnel into a room made of mud, and walked up a flight of earthen stairs to a sort of pier along a flooded delta. The pier led to a house in the distance.

"Where are we?" said Sean, looking around, bewildered.

Barrett was smiling ear to ear. "We're in China, Mr.

Graham. What do you think of that?"

Bren spun around in all directions, as if he hoped to take in the entire country at once. They all did, staring at their surroundings with awe. Judging by the sun, it was midmorning, which meant they had walked all night through the tunnel.

"That tunnel went from the island to mainland China?" said Sean.

"Yes," said Yaozu. "An island turned into a place of exile can also become a place of refuge. The Pearl Cliffs had once been mined for jade. Over many decades abandoned shafts were connected to a tunnel dug under the narrow band of sea there." He pointed to the strait of water between them and the fog-shrouded island in the distance.

"You just walked underwater, Mr. Graham," said Barrett.

Sean smiled, despite himself. "So where to now?"

"There," said Yaozu, pointing toward the house. "If it is the same man I remember, we can get more information for our journey, and a few supplies."

They walked along the pier to the house, where they waited for its owner to return. It was the same man Yaozu remembered, and they spoke for a while in Chinese, Yaozu showing him their oracle bone map and occasionally pointing in the direction of Mouse.

"What are they saying?" Bren whispered.

"What you would expect," said Mouse. "Talking about the map, mostly."

It was the "mostly" part that worried Bren. Was Mouse not telling him something?

When the two men finished talking, Yaozu sat down with them at the owner's table and spread out their map. He put his finger to the mouth of a river that emptied into the South China Sea.

"We are at the southern reaches of the delta, here, where this finger of land dips into the sea," he began. "The Pearl Cliffs would be here. We will pick up one of the smaller rivers going north toward the Yangtze, through what is known as the Vast Land. A great distance to cover, over the Nan Mountains, across Big Rattan Gorge. This is Lake Dongting," he said, circling a small area near the center of the map. "South of the lake, we must pass through the jagged peaks of the Forest Above the Clouds. We will have to cross two natural bridges—the Bridge of the Immortals and the Bridge Across the Sky."

Bren felt his stomach clench as he imagined just how high a bridge must be to be called the Bridge Across the Sky.

"We should try to reach the lake before the rainy season begins," Yaozu added. "When the rains come, the lake grows in size almost tenfold."

Moving his finger farther north, he said, "If the tomb

—186—

is indeed here, the most difficult passage from the lake to the tomb will be the Three Gorges. After that, a sandy plain where wind quickly erodes the landscape. There are stories of how Silk Road merchants once carved shelters there against weather and bandits. How extraordinary to think they might have uncovered the tomb of Qin if they'd perhaps dug a few feet more, or in a slightly different location."

"Assuming the tomb is there," said Sean.

"And if it's not, we cross one location off our list and look elsewhere," said Barrett.

"After you've fulfilled your duty to return Bren to his father, of course," said Sean, his voice heavy with rebuke.

Barrett, for once, seemed chastened. "Oh, of course," she said. "I didn't mean to suggest otherwise."

"So how far is it, altogether, from here to there?" said Bren.

Yaozu stroked his scraggly beard for a moment before answering. "A thousand miles. Give or take."

Sean sighed so hard he almost cleared the table.

"They have an old saying around here," said Yaozu. "A journey of a thousand miles begins with a single step."

"Confucius, I assume?" said Barrett.

"No—Laozi," said Yaozu. "Everyone makes that mistake."

▲▲▲

"Marco Polo traveled twenty-five miles a day on foot," said Bren, who had read the legendary travelogue dozens of times. "So if we have a thousand miles to go, it should only take us forty days."

"Forty days and nights, wandering in the wilderness," said Sean, with the flourish of a preacher.

"Feet come later," said Yaozu. "First, dragon boat."

"Dragon boat?" said Bren.

Yaozu smiled. "I think it would help if you looked more Chinese," he said. "I mean new clothes, of course."

Barrett looked disappointed. Bren imagined that she must've fancied the idea of a full disguise.

The owner of the house pulled a heavy wooden trunk from under a bench and handed trousers and tunics to each of them, along with jackets that wrapped around them like robes. Bren marveled at how soft they were compared to his woolen uniform.

"Silk!" said Barrett.

They all stared at one another when they were dressed, giggling at how different they looked. Even Mouse, who was Chinese, looked strange to Bren out of her grey sailor's clothes.

When it was time to leave, Bren rushed ahead of Yaozu toward a small covered boathouse. He was picturing a large, leathery hull, armored with iridescent scales, the prow a massive reptilian head, teeth bared. Instead the dragon boat was barely a boat, as far as he was concerned. It was a long, narrow, teakwood craft, with a draft so shallow it was almost a sled. The bow and stern curved upwards, suggesting a head and tail, he supposed.

"Why the glum look?" said Barrett. "You didn't think it was going to be made from a real dragon, did you?"

Bren turned as red as her magic sword.

"The Chinese do dress up the boats for special occasions," Yaozu assured him. "Very impressive looking then. Now, are we ready?"

"I'm ready for anything in these clothes," said Barrett.

"I have a feeling we'll need to be," said Sean.

▲▲▲

The dragon boat, while unimpressive to look at, was quite agile in the water. Even with only four of them rowing, the boat knifed along the shallow stream through the flooded delta, past rice farms and fishing villages. Yaozu explained to them how this part of the south had become a haven for all sorts of Chinese minorities, through constant turmoil caused by warring dynasties across centuries. Smugglers also called it home. They had little fear for now of being targeted as outsiders.

Yaozu had purchased a few other items from the owner of the house to ensure they were welcomed when they needed food or shelter: tools, supplies, and extra clothes they could barter.

Their plan was to eat any fresh food they had brought from the Pearl Cliffs—fruit, for instance—and save dried meats and other durable rations as long as possible, for when they might need them most. As it turned out, there were plenty of locals along the river willing to share meals and offer sleeping mats without compensation, and Bren quickly learned that the food was far better than he had expected.

When he first looked into a bowl of fish-head stew or rice, some of the glamour of the Far East wore off immediately. It was just like Map! Fish and grain! But this was infinitely more flavorful. Bren was convinced it was some sort of magic, but Sean, noticing the happy look on Bren's face when they were eating, offered a more logical explanation:

"And now you see why the spice trade has made men rich and built empires," he said with a laugh.

Bren again thought of the Jamaica-bound ship that he had attempted to board last year. It seemed that flavorful food had indeed launched a thousand ships.

In the coming days, they paddled upcountry, twisting and turning through several stream offshoots and tributaries, and they passed large groups of men and women out harvesting a tall flowering plant with dark green, leathery leaves.

"Star anise!" said Barrett, and she had them pull the

boat to shore so she could run out and grab one of the fruits from the plant. When she returned, she showed Bren and Mouse an odd-looking eight-legged piece of fruit. It reminded Bren of the starfish he caught in the tide pools of Map's harbor.

"Can I try it?" said Bren.

"It's not that kind of fruit," said Barrett. "You dry it out and then grind it into spice. I tried it in India."

"It's one of the so-called five spices of China," said Yaozu. "Baijao, dingxiang, rougui, huajiao, xiaohuixiang."

"Do you know what those are called in English?" said Bren.

"I don't," he said regretfully.

Bren didn't care. He wanted more. Spices had come to Europe, of course, thanks to traders like the Dutch Bicycle & Tulip Company. But only the wealthy could afford them. Bren had tasted salt and sugar . . . pepper a few times. He wanted more, and he'd had nothing very tasty in Bantam. He guessed the Dutch refrained from eating spices in the colonies so they'd have more to sell.

As they continued traveling north, Yaozu told them some of the history of the region, most of which was tragic.

"The Three Kingdoms period," he began, "was the worst of all. After the fall of the Han. Constant warfare, and the South did not want to give up its independence. By the time the Jin reunited the country, almost forty million people had been killed."

Bren couldn't believe it. "Forty million?"

"So many deaths, it was said that all the rivers turned red carrying away the blood."

Sean was shaking his head. "My God, that's worse than the plague." He seemed to remember a moment too late that the plague had killed Bren's mother.

"I'm sorry, Bren."

Bren shook his head. He realized his hand was clutching the black stone around his neck, and he let go, embarrassed.

"It's okay," said Mouse, grabbing his hand, the one that had been touching the stone.

"I know," said Bren irritably, pulling his hand away brusquely as he said it.

Finally they went as far as the dragon boat would take them, and they traded the teak craft to another farmer for some dried fish and fruit.

"Now what?" said Barrett.

"Now we cross the mountains," said Yaozu.

CHAPTER 17

BIG
RATTAN GORGE

O ver the next several days, they climbed into a land
that seemed impossibly unspoiled to Bren. He had
never seen greener trees or lusher vegetation, drunk cleaner
water, or breathed purer air. It was like a glimpse of the
world at creation, in its most perfect state. The steep hills
and wondrous rocks and abysmal gorges existed to inspire
awe, not guide travelers from one point to the next, nor
provide them shelter or succor. If any mortals had trod this
path, they had been swallowed up without a trace.

And yet the group made its way, slowly but steadily,

and all the while Bren felt he was trespassing on something sacred. In the mornings, a snow-white fog pooled around the mountaintops that Yaozu called "the breath of the dragon waking." At dusk-fall, when the setting sun turned the horizon to flame, Yaozu said that "the dragon was forging his scales in the mountain's furnace."

It was obvious that this landscape had inspired awe and worship since the dawn of time. Yaozu could point to any rock formation or river and recall a story of the gods at play. On the banks of a river there was a cliff face that looked as if it had been carved into a mural of nine horses. They were the stray herd of the Monkey King, turned to stone by his wrath after they tried to escape back into the wild.

Another stream appeared to be a ribbon of yellow cloth, because of the golden flagstone that lined its bed. Seven jagged peaks towered over both sides of the river, and Yaozu explained that they were seven faery maidens who came to the river to bathe and were so struck by its beauty that they refused to leave, turning themselves to stone to avoid being summoned back to heaven by the Jade King.

Bren turned to Mouse as Yaozu told these tales, trying to catch her eye. She had such an extraordinary tale about her own past, where she came from and how she came to be. Admiral Bowman had told her. She had told Bren she didn't believe it, and he wondered if perhaps the admiral had heard one of these local folktales when he was trading on the black market in the Pearl River Delta.

"What sort of wild animals live here?" Sean wondered aloud.

"Are you worried?" said Barrett, a sly grin on her face.

"Just curious. I mean, we have nothing to fear, do we? With you and your magic sword?"

"Still not grateful that I rescued you from a rogue elephant?" said Barrett. "Not to mention a rogue Dutch clerk? With help from Mouse, of course."

"Quibbling won't help us cross the Bridge Across the Sky," said Yaozu, and everyone became quiet, either from embarrassment or because their hearts were stuck in their throats picturing the highest bridge they could possibly imagine.

Bren thought there weren't enough magic swords in the world to tame all the wild creatures here. On the river they had been able to hear the howls of the forest animals . . . warnings, greetings, mating calls, sounds of happiness and irritation . . . he wondered if Mouse could understand any of it. Once they had entered the forest the sounds of the animals had just become a part of the environment, yet taking on a different tone and color from day to night.

Yaozu held out his hand to ask for Bren's journal. He turned it over, and Yaozu slowly flipped through the pages, admiring the precise drawings of the small monkeys they'd seen, the leaf and stem detail of many trees and shrubs, birds of extraordinary variety . . . their deliberate pace had allowed him to do many of these even as they were moving.

"A true appreciation for the natural world," said Yaozu approvingly, and they walked on a while longer until the sound of running water gradually took over the forest.

"A waterfall?" said Bren.

"This way," said Yaozu.

They walked in a semicircular path through the trees, until the roar of the water became almost deafening.

"It sounds like the entire Indian Sea is pouring over a cliff," said Sean.

When they broke from the trees, Bren almost lost his breath—and his footing. They had emerged onto a ridge above a gorge . . . no, a gorge is deep, but finite. This was a black chasm with no bottom, a mouth that reached to the very bowels of the earth.

The stone walls were perfectly vertical, and sheer but for thick clumps of trees that somehow managed to cling to the surface in spots like moss. The waterfall was a raging torrent hundreds of feet wide, plunging into the chasm like a wild animal.

"We don't have to cross that, do we?" said Bren.

"No, we walk around," said Yaozu. "But beautiful, yes?"

"Even more beautiful less close to the edge," said Sean,

who had already backed away toward the trees, ready to take a less precipitous path.

Yaozu smiled again. "I'm afraid you're not going to like what's coming next."

▲▲▲

No one said much after that. What exactly was coming next? Bridges. Natural bridges, high above . . . what? The ground? A bottomless pit?

What came next did not come soon, however. "The Vast Land" proved to be an apt description, and Bren felt like he had walked a thousand miles already. As one day passed into another, he became convinced that the old mapmakers, knowing so little of China, or Cathay, or the Middle Kingdom—whatever name was used by whatever outsider—had made a colossal underestimation of the empire's size. Which would make sense. Bren's father, who had been a mapmaker for Rand McNally for more than twenty years, had told Bren stories about how those advocating for Crusades in the Middle Ages were rumored to have shown the pope maps that made the path to victory look far easier than it was, minimizing the breadth of Moslem territory, shrinking the distance troops would have to travel, even erasing a bothersome mountain range. "We are all at the mercy of the mapmaker," Rand McNally had once said, summing up the powerful position he had secured by trading in information.

They still had dry rations they had saved from the ship, and the forest offered plenty of fruit and seeds and freshwater. But the climate was cooler and damper than it had been, and Bren was worried that his loose silk clothing might not be enough if they continued to head north, and into higher regions, this early in the year. He had never counted on China being so large that they might walk through several different climates in the span of a few weeks.

Finally they began to descend out of the mountains, and Bren secretly hoped they had somehow found another way to pass this way without crossing perilous bridges. When they emerged from the forest, they were on the side of a hill that sloped toward a fast-moving river. The river was walled in by mountains on both sides, bending from sight to the east and west, with another quick turn directly below them.

"Big Rattan Gorge," said Yaozu. "And that is the Xi River."

"Do we swim it?" said Sean.

Yaozu laughed. "Oh no. You would never make it. You would be swept away by the river, likely dashed on rocks. Also, there are alligators."

"So what then?" said Sean.

Yaozu looked up and down the gorge. "There is supposed to be a bridge. Made of rattan. Thus, *Big Rattan*

Gorge. That is the only way."

Barrett walked upriver a bit. "You sure it might not be elsewhere? The Xi looks like a long one."

"It should be here," Yaozu insisted. "We came the only way I know through the forest, and see how the river nearly oxbows here." He showed them the place he was talking about on their map.

Sean sat down. "I suppose we sit here until the bridge appears then? By magic?"

Yaozu said nothing, and Bren thought Sean had hurt his feelings. But then he snapped his fingers. "Magic! I do remember a story from my childhood, about a bridge that rose only at night and sank in the daytime. A means of protection from invasion, if I recall."

He walked over to Mouse. "Perhaps you could try something? See if the bridge is there?"

"No!" said Bren, a little more forcefully than he'd meant to. "She can't just become a fish or anything like that."

"I apologize," said Yaozu.

"It's okay," said Mouse. "I could try, perhaps. I don't really understand how I do it."

"She could become a fish and swim off to spawn and we'd never see her again," said Bren.

"No one's becoming a fish!" Sean bellowed, now lying on his back.

Mouse walked down to the edge of the river and just

—199—

stood there for a while, saying nothing. After a bit she put one hand inside her jacket—where she'd hidden the white stone, Bren assumed—but still just stood there, even as afternoon turned to dusk.

She was still standing there as the others sat together for a small meal at sunset, and when night had officially fallen, she held the white stone aloft in her palm, just like she had in the cavern when she summoned the mercury dragon. The memory of that made Bren's heart start beating rapidly, and his chest grew tight as he wondered what was about to happen. He could see Sean and Yaozu and Barrett wondering, too. The white jade glowed in the dark like a small moon, and then, almost imperceptibly, something began to rise from the river.

Bren jumped to his feet and the others followed, except for Sean, who just sat staring as a pair of long ropes broke the river's surface, stretching from one shore to the other. Not rope—they were stiffer than rope. It was rattan, two long poles as thick as a person's forearm, parallel to each other, with a third pole of rattan connected to the pair above by tendrils of thin cord.

"I'll be damned," said Sean. "It's a bridge!"

"Indeed," said Yaozu. "Shall we cross? Or do you prefer to sit longer?"

CHAPTER 18

THREE BRIDGES

"Just put one foot in front of the other," said Barrett.

"I know how to walk," snapped Sean.

Bren would have laughed, except he was too busy concentrating on doing just that—walking. The V-shaped bridge was simple enough to understand: you walked across a single rattan pole while using the two handrails for support. But even though the bridge had seemingly risen by magic from the depths of the river, it had not magically dried itself off. The smooth, hard stems of rattan were slick, which made footing tricky.

"Stop swinging the bridge," said Bren. "I'm getting queasy."

"Not the bridge," said Yaozu. "The water. Look forward, not down."

Bren immediately did the opposite and saw what he meant. They were only a couple of feet above the river, and it was now completely dark, but there was a near-full moon, and the moving water gave the illusion that the bridge was swaying.

"Rattan is one of the strongest materials on earth," said Barrett. "You could knock a building over with it. Look . . ."

To everyone's horror, Barrett began to jump up and down to demonstrate the sturdiness of the bridge.

"Point made!" said Sean.

"You heard what Yaozu said about the natural bridges to come," said Barrett. "If you chaps can't handle this . . ."

"We're handling it just fine," said Sean.

"Can we just get this over with?" said Bren. They were only halfway across and it felt like they'd been at it for an hour.

Bren was bringing up the rear, and even though he knew how to put one foot in front of the other, he kept looking down to measure his steps, and in doing so, he noticed a dark shape pass under the bridge.

"Yaozu? How big are Chinese alligators?"

"Alligator-sized," Yaozu responded. "I don't know any other kind."

Bren looked down again. "Are they active at night?"

"Especially at night."

"Do you see one?" said Sean, who had paused and was looking down. Everyone was looking down now.

"I don't see anything," said Mouse.

"We're two feet above the water," said Barrett.

"Alligators jump," said Yaozu, who seemed wholly unconcerned that Bren may have spotted one.

"How high?" said Sean.

"Not sure."

"Well, that's helpful."

Bren kept scanning the water, and when he looked up again he saw that he had fallen behind. *Move your feet,* he told himself, but when he looked down to tell his feet this directly, he saw it again—the dark shape, which passed through a ribbon of moonlight, revealing a dark, scaly back just breaking the surface of the water.

"Wait for me!" he said, looking up and trusting his feet to move steadily across the rattan pole. Unlike the time the shark followed their longboat in the Indian Ocean, Bren wasn't worried that Admiral Bowman had somehow turned himself into an alligator—he was worried about being eaten by an actual alligator. It took all his willpower not to look down, and his mind began to unspool one crazy thought after another, but before he knew it his foot stepped off the hard rattan pole and onto land, and he almost collapsed from relief. They all did, except for Yaozu.

"Alligators have legs, you know."

They were all on their feet immediately, running up the hill until they reached the forest on the other side.

"For the love of God, do we need to sleep in the trees?" said Sean. "How far will an alligator chase you?"

They looked back down the hill. No alligator had emerged from the river.

"Not far," said Yaozu. "The Chinese alligator is actually quite docile."

"Docile?" Sean sputtered. "Then why the bloody hell did you make it sound like the thing might leap out of the water and snatch us to our deaths?"

"You were moving so slow," said Yaozu. "Like sloths. Enough time on the bridge already."

They all stood there, dumbstruck. Bren was afraid Sean might actually strike the Chinese man. But then suddenly, unexpectedly, Mouse burst out laughing. She could barely control herself, and her pure emotion was so unexpected that soon everyone else was laughing as well. Bren felt light as air, like he could float to the moon.

"So will the bridge sink now or not until sunrise?" he said.

"That I do not know," said Yaozu. "Nor do I know

how people got the bridge to appear in past times. But Mouse—or perhaps the stone itself—must have been our connection to the ancient magic."

"I told you," said Barrett, not looking directly at Sean but obviously speaking to him. "We need her. And Bren."

The group gathered their meager things and walked a little way into the forest until they found a suitable place to camp for the night. Over the next several days, they descended out of the mountains into the plains, past more rice fields, but also cotton farms and orange groves. Sean seemed especially grateful when Barrett bargained with one of the farmers for some oranges, the sight and taste of which seemed to make him feel a bit less homesick. There was also a keeper of bees, who offered the travelers some honey, which Bren had never tasted before. He wondered if he would ever taste anything so delicious again.

Almost against their will, their pace slowed, even though the going was far easier. The mountainous paths had been hard on their legs, and despite the beauty of the lush forest they had passed through, Bren had felt increasingly closed in by the encircling trunks and the canopy of leaves blocking the sky for days on end. Barrett's single-minded determination to advance went wobbly, and even Yaozu seemed to want nothing more than to lie down among the orange groves and sleep.

"I never understood the allure of a *land of milk and*

honey, from the Good Book," said Sean. "I never cared for cow's milk, and I'd never tasted honey. But after trying that man's honey and milk from whatever that creature was . . ."

"Water buffalo," said Yaozu.

"Water buffalo," Sean repeated. "I believe I could live on water buffalo's milk and honey."

"Not rice?" said Yaozu.

"A bit bland," said Sean. "Like those potatoes they recently started foisting on us back home."

Bren had to agree. British and Dutch food wasn't any better. Why did Europeans like everything to be bland, mushy, or fatty?

"We should get going," said Mouse, who was the only one standing up.

"She's right," said Barrett, who remained lying down on her back with one leg bent at the knee and the other lazily thrown over it.

"Look at those clouds!" gasped Sean, who was lying on his back as well.

"I think you're drunk on honey," said Bren. "They look like ordinary clouds."

Bren, who had struggled to his feet, held his hands out to Sean. "Now come on, Mouse is right. We can't stay here forever."

They eventually got moving again, although still at a sluggish pace, which didn't improve when the plain gave way to mountains again. Up they went, past more trees and caves, streams and waterfalls. This time, though, when they reached a plateau, what Bren saw made his heart stop. The entire forest seemed to fall away into a vast chasm, its mouth as big as a small sea, and rising up from the abyss were thousands of towering stone pillars, some bare rock, some covered with small forests themselves. Below the rim, thick clouds gathered, as if they were standing above the sky itself.

"How . . . how did such a place come into being?" said Bren. "It looks like an earthquake cratered the entire forest, except for a few columns of land."

"Reminds me of a cave," said Barrett. "Those teethlike things that grow up from the ground and down from the ceiling. Except there is no ceiling."

"And no ground, either," said Sean, staring down at the clouds.

"This is the Forest Above the Clouds," said Yaozu.

"How do we get across?" said Barrett.

Bren knew what the answer was already, and so did Barrett—the bridges Yaozu had warned them about.

"We can't just walk around?" said Sean. "It might take a bit longer. . . ."

"Far too long," said Yaozu. "Also, there are dangerous regions east and west."

"There must be a way to reach the bottom," said Barrett.

"There is," said Yaozu. "And I will show you. But from the bottom there is only one way up, and one way out." He pointed off to the northeast, across hundreds of the stone pillars, and at the limit of his sight Bren could just make out what could only barely be called a bridge— a thread of stone connecting the tops of two of the pillars. He knew it would look bigger up close. He dearly hoped that it would look much, much bigger, as well as shorter and wider.

Yaozu showed them a steep path cut in the side of the chasm that zigzagged toward the bottom. It was a dizzying descent, and Bren was thankful for the carpet of clouds that kept him from seeing very far below. They went down and down for hours, until the path leveled out and they were walking across the floor of what had seemed like a bottomless drop from above. They rested and ate, and then kept going.

"How long will it take to cross?" said Barrett.

"Approximately twelve miles across," said Yaozu, "but slow going. Will take two days."

Bren wanted to ask how high the pillars actually were, but decided against it. However, there was something else he was dying to know: "Yaozu, there must be folktales about these rock formations . . . what they look like, how they got here."

Yaozu smiled. "Why don't you tell *me* one? What do

you think? What do you see?"

Bren hadn't been expecting that. He paused and looked around the strange valley, at the petrified fingers grasping for the sky. And he thought of the Chinese books the admiral had shared with him, and the types of stories they told, and the way they were told.

"Before the Ancients," Bren began, "before the Eight Immortals, there were two brothers, Sky and Earth. And Earth raised these great pillars to hold the Sky up, and in return, Sky had a daughter, the Cloud Empress, to give Earth rain. Later Earth had a son, whose job was to dig holes and trenches so the rain could become rivers and lakes and seas."

Yaozu nodded approvingly. "Go on."

"The son of Earth and the daughter of Sky fell in love, against their parents' wishes, and when they sneaked off to be together, there was drought. This angered Earth, who in a fit of spite ripped the tops of these pillars from the Sky, leaving them only as tall as we see them today. His anger nearly caused his ruin, because the Sky would have come crashing down, except for a bargain struck at the last minute. The Cloud Empress would knit together enough clouds to support the Sky, but in return, Earth had to give his son to the Sky, and he became the Moon. Which is why the moon is a symbol of love."

Mouse applauded when Bren finished, and the others

laughed. "You may be an Ancient, too," said Yaozu, clasping Bren warmly on the arm.

"So what's the real story?" said Bren.

Yaozu shrugged. "I don't know one. Except yours now."

Bren smiled, pleased with himself. But the rest of the day's walk would wear the smile off his face. Their path was rarely flat, and being so far below the rim made him feel trapped.

"How the devil will we get to the bridges from here?" Barrett asked, her voice weary and full of frustration. "And why didn't the people who carved out the path that took us down here just carve one back up?"

"The other chasm walls are too sheer," said Yaozu. "As to how we reach the bridges, we come to the way up now."

They broke into a clearing, where one of the stone pillars stood like a religious monument. From a distance they had seemed impossibly tall, but slender. Up close they were massive, as big around as some of the biggest buildings Bren had seen. And on this one in particular, there was a staircase, of a sort: iron rods that had been inserted into the stone, spiraling up and around the pillar.

"You must be joking," said Sean. "And it was the bridges you were worried about?"

"Didn't want to scare you all at once," said Yaozu.

"How high are these things?" said Barrett.

"This one, perhaps six hundred feet," said Yaozu. "But

we only climb partway along the outside. You'll see."

"What do we hold on to?" said Bren, his voice shaking.

Yaozu stepped up onto the first stair and then took several more steps, demonstrating how to use the iron rods like the rungs of a ladder. An extremely high, curving ladder.

"You've done this before," said Sean.

"As a very young boy. My cousin and I used the tunnel to sneak to the mainland and explore."

"And you came this far north once?" said Bren, suddenly admiring Yaozu more.

"We were away from home without our parents' permission for a month," said Yaozu. When he noticed Bren smiling, he added, "The punishment kept me from ever doing it again."

"Keep talking," said Sean. "I find your voice soothing."

And so Yaozu did keep talking, telling them all about how so many people in this part of China had been killed when the Ming invaded the Vast Land, much of which had tried to become independent again after the fall of the Mongols. "All throughout history, trouble in these parts," said Yaozu. "Fertile land, important rivers and ports . . . rulers always want."

Bren was thankful for the time he had spent aloft on the mainmast of the *Albatross*, which had helped him conquer some fear of being so high and exposed at the same time. Although there was always the rigging that might save you if you fell. The ship's mast was around a hundred feet tall, and Bren estimated they had climbed at least that high, and half again, when they came to a doorway carved into the pillar. Or perhaps it was a cave, he couldn't tell for sure.

"Oh thank God," said Sean, practically throwing himself inside.

"We still have far to go," said Yaozu, "but for tonight we stay here."

After dinner, Bren wrote in his journal while Yaozu spoke to Mouse in Chinese. She clearly enjoyed using her native language, and Bren could tell from their body language that she was trying to explain to Yaozu how she read the oracle bones. Yaozu was fascinated by this long-lost ability of the Ancients surfacing in an eight-year-old orphan.

At daybreak they climbed another hundred feet or so through a staircase carved into the pillar, until they saw daylight and then blue sky framed by a stone archway. They had come to the first of the two natural bridges, the Bridge of the Immortals.

It wasn't what any of them had been expecting. The bridge seemed to be nothing more than a handful of boulders that had collapsed between the two pillars, landing in such a way as to wedge themselves several hundred feet above the ground. And they hadn't fallen in a perfectly straight line, either. The first "step" was several feet down from the edge, there was a V-shaped gap midway along, and the final stone was situated highest of all, so that they would have to climb it. The distance was short, but all Bren could think about was the rocks slipping, and plummeting to his death.

"*This* is the Bridge of the Immortals?" said Sean. "As in, you think it looks like something Immortals would fancy as a bridge?"

"No," said Yaozu. "As in, so difficult to cross, only an Immortal would risk it. But we will be fine. Watch me."

Yaozu went first to show them how it could be done. He sat down on the edge of the cliff, adjusting his long tunic and trouser legs, and then half slid, half jumped to the stone below, landing in a crouch. He then took a two-step run up the sloping boulder, toward the V-shaped gap, and leaped across with the grace of a cat. The face of the second boulder sloped the opposite way, and so Yaozu had to stop his momentum by bracing himself against the tall face of the third boulder.

Yaozu turned back to them. "Better idea. You come," he said, pointing to Barrett.

She nodded and plopped down on the edge of the cliff, imitating Yaozu's methods. She jumped to the first step, paused, and leaped to the second, with Yaozu there to keep her from running into rock. Yaozu then bent over, joining his hands together like a stirrup.

"Ah, yes, good idea indeed," said Barrett, and she stepped into Yaozu's hands and let herself be hoisted to the top of the step. From there she was able to reach the next step—a natural wart on the face of the cliff—on her own, and then she was on top of the pillar.

"Not so bad," she called back. "Just don't look down."

Easier said than done, thought Bren, since you had to look down to jump to the first step. But to his relief, the boulder was so wide that when he sat at the cliff's edge, almost all he could see was stone. In a matter of minutes, he was standing next to Barrett, as was Mouse. Yaozu helped Sean up to the top step, and then Sean pulled Yaozu up. They were all intact, at the top of one of the shorter stone pillars, but still dizzyingly high above the chasm.

"One more bridge," said Yaozu. "Much easier."

They walked for perhaps an hour through the forest at the top of the pillar until they came to the final bridge, the Bridge Across the Sky, which connected the pillar they were on to the other side of the chasm. This was the bridge they had spotted from so far away, the day they started out. And if anything, it looked to Bren even wispier and less substantial than it had from miles away. It was probably two hundred feet long, and maybe three feet wide, if the feet measuring it were the feet of children. They all just stood there as if thinking the same thing.

"Easy?" said Sean.

"Easier," Yaozu corrected. "No jumping or climbing."

"It's like a bloody circus tightrope!" said Barrett.

Bren had only seen such a thing once. Never at the circus, which had only come to London, but a daredevil had once strung a high rope from the roof of McNally's Map Emporium to the Church of the Faithful in a misguided attempt to protest the close relationship between commerce and religion. He had fallen halfway and broken both his legs and his back. If you could make that big a mess of yourself from the height of Map's tallest building, then what would you look like after falling from the Bridge Across the Sky?

Bren immediately regretted having that thought.

"Nature made this incredible bridge," said Yaozu. "It likely did not anticipate your needs."

This time it was Mouse who took the lead, scuttling out to the middle of the bridge like a lizard. She stopped, turned around to face the stunned group, then ran the rest of the way.

"See?" said Yaozu. "Even a child can do it."

"Yes," said Barrett. "A mystical child with supernatural abilities."

But Yaozu wasn't listening to any more complaints. He calmly walked out onto the bridge, never stopping or turning like Mouse, but keeping his eyes firmly fixed on his destination until he was standing on the other side. He turned and bowed, inviting the others to cross.

"Fine," said Barrett. "I'll go next." Her bravado was transparent, but it still made Sean bristle.

"No, I'll go next," he said.

"You follow me," said Barrett. "Like always." And before Sean could pick his flattened ego off the ground she had stepped confidently out onto the bridge, and with but a couple of hesitations was safely across in a matter of ten or fifteen minutes.

Sean had no choice but to be brave after that. He marched across with the attitude of a man who thought he needed to cross the bridge faster than Lady Barrett. His pace made Bren nervous, but he made it, bowing sarcastically to Barrett and then turning to Bren. "Come on, Bren. Nothing to it."

Bren looked across the bridge, where the others were waiting.

"Okay," he said, and then again, "Okay."

He took a deep breath and fingered the stone around his neck for good luck as he walked to the edge of the bridge, looking down only long enough to orient his feet, and then he stared directly at Mouse, into her famously opaque eyes, as she stared back at him from across the distance. He felt a certain reassurance come over him. He needed her; she needed him. His black jade and her white jade, two parts of some whole that they would discover together. One couldn't exist without the other.

He stepped out onto the bridge, keeping his eyes on Mouse, and for a while everything was fine.

The wind picked up. A sudden gust hit him like those ocean squalls Bren had come to dread. He looked down again, just to reassure himself that his feet hadn't gotten off track, and when he did, panic set in—the gusting wind had cleared the clouds, giving him a glimpse of the bottomless chasm.

"Steady, lad. You're halfway home!" cried Sean.

Bren knew that was a lie, but he made himself look up, to find Mouse, but he couldn't make his feet move again. Out of the corner of his eye he could see dark clouds blowing in.

"Come on!" Barrett called, barely audible over the howling wind.

"Get down on all fours," said Sean.

Yaozu motioned for him to do as Sean asked.

"Bren, son, Sean and I don't agree on a lot," called Barrett. "But listen to him."

Bren began to bend his quivering legs, hoping to find the bridge with his hands while keeping his eyes on Mouse. But his fear disoriented him. He couldn't be sure he wouldn't lean his hands onto thin air. So he looked down again, and immediately he had to shut his eyes. He grabbed the black stone and clutched it as hard as he could, but nothing worked. He had been a fool to think a magic stone could keep him from falling.

He heard Barrett call out, "Mouse, no!"

He opened his eyes and looked up. Mouse was running across the bridge toward him, and as soon as she reached him, she grabbed his hands and lifted him to his feet, and then she turned around and guided him, pulled him almost against his will, to the middle of the bridge. He wanted to stop, he wanted to resist her, but he just grabbed her hand tighter and kept his eyes on her the rest of the way, and then he collapsed on top of her when they reached the other side.

CHAPTER 19

THE ROAD
TO AGRA

The rain came down so hard the elephants were having trouble keeping their feet. They were trying to climb a short ridge, but water was pouring through the branches and broad leaves of the jungle, hitting the ground with the force of a waterfall and melting the side of the ridge.

"Aziz, Aziz! Get up there and tie the chain!"

The young man who had come to fetch David Owen and Archibald Black from Bombay scrambled up the mud-slide, clutching spindly branches for leverage, dragging a large, heavy chain behind him. When he made it to the top, he secured one end of the chain to the biggest tree he could find and threw the other end back to the mahout—the man giving orders.

The mahout took the other end of the chain and held it out to the lead elephant: "Pull, gajah, pull!"

The elephant took the chain in her trunk, pulling it taut as she attempted to use it as a winch.

Adding only slightly to the elephant's burden was Archibald Black, lying facedown on the elephant's back, his bony knees wedged against her hide, his arms clutching her neck like a giant crab. David Owen was on the elephant directly behind him, sitting upright, but only because he had thrown up twice over the side.

"Pull, gajah, pull!"

The elephant took one cautious step up the ridge, then another, her massive weight supported by feet the size of platters that flattened out the muddy ground, but the tree she was attached to was starting to give.

"Hasan, the tree!" said Aziz.

"Almost there," replied the mahout.

The chain sighed, its heavy iron links stretching at the joints. The trunk of the stout neem tree creaked.

"Hurry!" cried Black, but no one heard him because his face was pressed into elephant hide.

The tree creaked again, longer and louder this time, and the elephant looked at her mahout out of the corner of her eye, as if to ask, *Is this a good idea?*

"Pull, gajah, pull!" came the answer, and so the elephant tugged on the chain again, and with a massive, splintering groan, the roots of the neem tree tore from the ground. The elephant slid back down the ridge, releasing the chain and trumpeting an alarm that drowned out Archibald Black's cries for help.

"You're okay, sahib, you're okay." It was Aziz, at Black's side, helping him down from the elephant, who had knelt in the mud at the bottom of the ridge and refused to move. When he was on his feet, Black immediately teetered backwards against the elephant, resting there upright. Aziz then helped David Owen down from his elephant, walking the pale and nauseated mapmaker over to a stump to sit down.

"Maybe this isn't such a good idea," said Aziz, speaking to the mahout named Hasan. He turned to look at the small army behind them, mostly Indian men on foot, with half a dozen more elephants carrying all their cargo, including the four trunks of surveying equipment.

"You tell Akbar this isn't such a good idea," said Hasan. "I'll just slit my own throat."

"He had to know the rainy season was coming, didn't he?" said Black, catching his breath while resting against the seated elephant.

"Of course he knew the rainy season was coming," said Aziz. "He's the emperor! Perfect time to survey, when the weather is so poor that the armies won't come out."

Black had never seen it rain so hard for so long. "There won't be anything to survey before long," he said. "India will just be one flat mud field."

"Nonsense," said Hasan. "A minor setback. We try again when the rain lets up."

They made camp instead, hundreds of soldiers scurrying about putting up makeshift rain shelters.

"We could be surveying along the way," said Owen, when he had recovered from his first elephant ride.

"The great Akbar is eager to meet you," said Hasan. "Besides, you need more equipment, no? So that many people can help?"

"Yes, but . . ."

"It's politics, David," said Black. "McNally would do exactly the same thing. An official kickoff from his capital. Putting people to work, literally putting India on the map as a global power . . . it's quite obvious."

"No idle hands!" said Hasan, repeating what sounded like a campaign slogan.

Owen nodded. "How far is Uttar Pradesh?"

Hasan screwed up his face, doing the math in his head. "Eight hundred miles, give or take?"

Black and Owen looked at each other, seemingly thinking the same thing—they had gotten in over their heads.

"I'm sorry," said Owen. "Sorry I dragged you into this."

"You did nothing of the sort," said Black. "I care about finding Bren as much as you do."

"I don't doubt that, Archibald, but this was a foolish idea. How were we supposed to find him, even assuming we hadn't been more or less kidnapped by Akbar's army?"

"Theories, investigation, inference," said Black. "Of course we don't know anything for sure. But we have solid leads."

"That admiral never said anything about an island," said Owen, who was twisting a filthy piece of his shirt in his hands. "What makes you so sure?"

"Certainty has nothing to do with it, David. But I trusted a very good book scout from Amsterdam who told me this Bowman had been obsessed with the idea that Marco Polo stashed a treasure on his sea voyage home from China. It makes sense. It may not be perfect, it may not be certainty, but it's the best I could do."

They sat silently for a minute or two, listening to the steady rain and at least one loud argument coming from among the soldiers.

"You're right. I'm sorry," said Owen.

"Stop being sorry," said Black, standing up and brushing off his dirty pants, to little effect. "You need a distraction. Let's check the equipment again."

"We already double- and triple-checked—"

"It will do us good," Black said firmly.

"Okay."

They opened their four trunks in turn, each of which was padded like a violin case, with the surveying instruments fitted into velvet-covered cradles shaped to the particular tool. Owen methodically lifted and examined each instrument, while Black went down an inventory list.

"Four theodolites."

"Check."

"Six quadrants."

"Check."

"Six compass pairs."

"Check."

On and on they went: barometers, thermometers, telescopes, and plotting scales; a heliostat, an aethroscope, a delineator, and something called a four-eyed glass perspective. There were also a half dozen pea-light lanterns and vials of lime to go in them.

The final trunk contained only the large wheel with the handle and counter that David Owen had demonstrated for Queen Adeline. Owen lifted it out and set it aside, then lifted up the velvet cradle, revealing a large, thick black book, covered in leather and bound with a pair of leather straps.

"Just wanted to make sure it's still there," said Owen. "Your admittance to that library."

"The House of Wisdom," said Black. "No ordinary library, I assure you."

"And a Christian Bible's going to get you into a Persian library?"

"It's a Gutenberg Bible, David. One of the originals. My family were early backers of his movable-type machine. This is a family heirloom, and I assure you, their scholars will covet it."

"I can't thank you enough for being willing to—"

"Enough!" said Black. "Have you thought of a name for that yet?" he said, nodding at the large wheeled counting instrument.

"Not officially," said Owen, replacing the velvet cradle over the Bible. "McNally wants to call it the Rand-About."

"Clever."

"I think surveyor's wheel is nice and accurate," said Owen.

"And dull," said Black. "What about the Waywiser?"

Owen swatted away a mosquito. "A bit abstract, don't you think?"

"Not really."

"Bren would have fun coming up with names," said Owen. "That boy's imagination . . ."

"And here's the thing, David. You needn't worry about someone that resourceful. I believe that in my bones, and as you can see, I'm all bones."

Owen half smiled, but the smile left almost as soon as it arrived. "Do you have any idea why McNally would have let him go like that? He could have stopped him . . . the admiral never would've taken him if he'd just . . ."

David Owen broke off, and Black awkwardly put a hand on his shoulder.

"I do have a theory, in fact. Think about it. Your boy was granted a rare opportunity—to go aboard a Dutch yacht, to learn where they sail and how, find out more about the people and the customs of the East and how the Netherlanders deal with them. And Bren's brilliant mind would have captured it all."

"A spy?"

"Nothing so cloak-and-dagger as that," said Black. "But he must've known Bren would absorb everything he saw and heard. Of course, he couldn't guarantee Bren's safe return, but the upside more than outweighed the risk for Rand McNally."

David Owen cursed so loud some of the soldiers stopped arguing.

"Maybe we should make the best of this and get home as soon as we can," said Black. "Trust that resourceful boy of yours to survive."

Owen nodded, then said, "Say, why don't we see how well this thing works?"

Black arched an eyebrow. "A bit late for that, isn't it? McNally's already having more made to send over with the British team."

"Oh, we tested this bugger thoroughly," said Owen, "but there are no jungles in Britannia."

"I guess . . . ," said Black.

"Archibald!" said Owen in a half whisper. "I'm hatching an escape plan!"

"A what?"

"We walk off into the jungle, I distract them, and then you take off. Hide for a while, then make your way to Persia."

"Are you out of your mind? There are at least a dozen things wrong with this plan. . . ."

David Owen had already set the wheel upright and begun walking east from their camp. When Aziz heard the clicking noise, he stopped what he was doing and ran after them.

"Where are you going?" he asked.

"Just over here," said Owen. "We're testing the . . . the Waywiser." He winked at Black.

"You must not wander off!" said Aziz. "It's dangerous out there."

"We're not going far," said Owen.

"How dangerous?" said Black.

"Rebels, for one thing," said Aziz.

"Rebels? You said Akbar wanted to survey during the rainy season because the fighting would stop," said Black.

"Officially, perhaps. Still . . . there are tigers."

"Actual tigers or is that a faction of rebels?" said Owen.

"Real tigers," said Aziz. "Man-eaters!"

Black rolled his eyes. "Tigers are primarily nocturnal. They sleep most of the day."

"Come with us," said Owen. "Protect us."

Aziz looked even more fearful. "If you insist."

The Indian boy walked between the two Brits as Owen pushed the large wheel through thick undergrowth and sloppy mud. While the wheel was large, to more easily roll over bumpy terrain, it was also heavy, and they bogged down in the mud after fifty yards or so.

"Not to worry," said Owen. "We just need to keep it clean. Help me, Aziz."

They lifted the wheel and Owen made a big production of how clogged the mechanism was. While Aziz was trying to help clear the mud, Owen lifted his head at Black, encouraging him to go.

Black froze instead, then turned and tried to gingerly put his foot down, stepping noisily on a pile of twigs instead.

"It's unstuck!" said Aziz, jumping up and putting the wheel back on solid ground. Black shrugged and the three of them pressed on farther, trying to avoid the worst of the mud. Owen went out of his way to dodge a puddle, and as he did so, the large wheel rolled over a fallen tree branch, breaking it in half with a crack so loud it silenced the birds.

All three of them stopped in their tracks, startled by

the noise. In that brief moment of stillness, they heard a low growl, followed by a second, quieter *snap*. All Black saw was the orange face framed in black and white, and the heavy orange paw stepping forward on top of the now-broken twig.

"Don't panic," said Black, "but just over there is a—"

"Tiger! Tiger!" screamed Aziz, tearing off back toward camp, leaving Black and Owen standing there, too surprised to move.

The tiger sprang from hiding and crossed the distance between them in just a few lazy lopes. David Owen tried to run but found his feet sunk to the ankles in mud and promptly lost his balance. He fell backwards as the tiger leaped toward him, and he did the only thing he could—he used both hands to hoist the surveyor's wheel up in the air. The tiger's belly struck the wheel, spinning the predator off the edge and right over Owen, who still just lay there.

"Get up, David!" said Black, reaching to help Owen as the tiger collapsed into an ungraceful pile of stripes before righting itself and turning back to face its prey.

It approached more cautiously this time, unsure about this strange new weapon it was facing. Owen couldn't hold the heavy wheel up for long, so he turned it handle first to the ground, using the wheel as a shield. Black stood behind him.

The tiger charged again, swatting at the wheel, spinning

it madly and trying to clutch it with its massive paws but instead getting one paw caught in the rotating spokes. The cat howled and backed away, then leaped again, sinking its teeth into the wheel, a full-fledged attack.

"Now!" said Black. "Let's get out of here!"

They took off running back to camp while the tiger continued to maul the surveyor's wheel. It had already pulled the rim apart; broken spokes were everywhere.

They met a group of soldiers running their way—Aziz had obviously alerted them—who hurled spears at the tiger but failed to hit it. Instead the tiger left the wrecked wheel in a heap and ran off into the jungle.

Black and Owen just stared at each other, each paler than usual and breathing hard. Finally, Black started laughing.

"Maybe we should call it the Tiger Shield," he said, which got Owen laughing too.

"Good thing McNally's sending more of those," he said, clapping Black on the back as they headed back to camp with the soldiers. "And hello, one less instrument to keep up with!"

CHAPTER 20

THE DRAGON KING'S DAUGHTER

There was little conversation the next several days as Bren, Mouse, Sean, Barrett, and Yaozu crossed the land south of Lake Dongting. At first Bren had been relieved, like they all were, to be out of the mountains and forests, to be walking through wide valleys and plains of rice and tea farms, rhubarb and melon patches. But Bren couldn't easily get over the terror he'd felt, the sudden loss of faith in things he'd come to count on.

It was growing cooler, too, and they had to shelter themselves numerous times from rainstorms. With few exceptions, they found the locals welcoming, willing to open their homes and share their food, especially while Barrett still had a few pouches of poppy seeds to trade. In small villages they also met craftsmen who were selling gowns, blankets, and the most beautiful silk Bren had ever seen. Not that he had seen much—fabric like this was only available to the wealthiest classes in Britannia— but he could immediately see why the entire ancient trade network between East and West had been called the Silk Road. Silk must have been the most coveted good imaginable to Europeans used to dressing in linen, or heavy, scratchy wool. Bren had immediately taken to the local clothes Yaozu had given them, and the fabric he was seeing here was much finer.

But it wasn't just the quality of the fabric. The men and women working with it were so skilled they would have made Britannia's Italian tailors jealous. Many of the pieces were elaborately embroidered with dragons, flowers, trees, birds, and other symbolic images. And then there were the jade carvers, the first sight of which made Bren instinctively reach for the black stone around his neck.

None of the jade here was black or white, but rather a pale, soapy green, carved mostly into figurines of dogs, birds, people, temples, and of course, dragons. Bren was afraid to touch the more elaborate carvings, but he couldn't resist picking up what looked like a polished rock, rolling it around in his hand, comparing it to his own jade.

The man selling it began speaking to Bren.

"Oh, I'm sorry, I don't—"

"The boy is in perfect health," said Yaozu, taking the stone from Bren and returning it to the peddler. To Bren he explained, "He said to rub on your side. Will cure kidney stones."

"It may not have the power to heal," said Barrett, nodding to the pale green stones. "But I daresay we could resell any of these back in Britannia for a handsome profit."

Almost as unexpected as seeing goods of this quality for sale in small, rural villages was when their path took them onto what Yaozu called the Imperial Highway. Bren felt the same sense of awe as when his mother had taken him for walks along some of the original Roman roads that ran through Britannia. At times they were on a wide, stone-paved path, with trees and flowers lining both sides, so that it was like walking through a tranquil but spectacular garden. On one particularly steep portion, wide, low steps had been carved into the rocky hillside.

"Begun nearly two thousand years ago," said Yaozu. "Now said to be twenty-five thousand miles long, across the empire."

"Take a moment to appreciate what it took to make this," said Barrett, as if she was leading a tour. "The Romans had nothing on the Chinese when it came to building. Though Marco Polo never mentioned it, there is supposedly a wall that runs across the entire empire to the north. Thousands of miles long."

"Is that true?" said Mouse, to Yaozu.

"Not sure," he said. "I've heard of it, but never seen for myself."

Sean whistled. "You could wrap a road 'round Eire ten times with that."

"You can travel continuously, without stopping, even across mountains," Yaozu added.

"Not across the Forest Above the Clouds," said Bren.

Barrett reached out her right arm to pull Bren closer, and with her left arm she pulled Mouse to her other side, so that the three of them were walking side by side, through a promenade of cherry trees.

"It was very brave what you did," she said to Mouse. "Running back to make sure Bren was okay, to help him cross. You're fearless, aren't you?"

"No," said Mouse. "I wish I were, but I'm not."

When they camped that night, Yaozu consulted with the farmer who was playing host to them. From a distance it looked as if they were discussing the man's farming methods, and Bren guessed that Yaozu perhaps took a genuine interest in such things, since he came from China. But it turned out Yaozu was discussing not crops but the calendar—they had figured their journey to the tomb would take a month and a half or so. But here they were, still south of the lake, and two months had passed, apparently. The farmer said the rainy season had already begun farther north.

"Good news is, we will reach the lake in fewer steps," said Yaozu.

"Because it will have started expanding, like you explained before," said Barrett.

"Might already be twice as wide by the time we arrive."

"What's the bad news?" Sean asked.

Yaozu shrugged. "Perhaps there is no bad news? It is easier to boat a long distance than walk. More lake, more boating."

"There has to be a downside, or you wouldn't have mentioned it before," said Sean.

"I can think of two," said Barrett. "Sailing across huge lakes can be just as treacherous as sailing the open sea. Storms, in particular, if we hit the beginning of rainy season. Many men have drowned in a lake."

"And the other?"

"Foraging. The hospitality we've come to count on. Many of these provincial farmers pack up and move to dry land for the summer, then come back when the lake recedes. They take their rice and other goods and sell them elsewhere."

"Also," said Yaozu, "the land north of the lake can be

dangerous. The summer migrations Lady Barrett speaks of make people targets for thieves, or highwaymen, as they say in the West."

"It's not as if we have a choice," said Barrett. "We just need to know what we're up against, and we won't until we get there, I'm afraid."

"And how much farther from the other side of the lake to Qin's tomb site?" said Bren.

Yaozu looked at their map. "Perhaps four hundred miles? A bit more?"

Sean sat down. He seemed weary. They all did. No one said it aloud, but they were all thinking the same thing: they had barely covered more than half the distance they needed to go. It had been a difficult trek, over a longer period of time than they had planned, and more dangerous than they imagined. Bren wondered if they were really fit to travel so much farther.

▲▲▲

Their trek to the edge of Lake Dongting was a soggy one, as the group was beset by blowing rains on and off for a week. When they reached the lakeshore, Yaozu calculated how far they had come and estimated that the lake had already tripled in size because of flood runoff from the several rivers that fed into it.

Barrett turned to Yaozu. "I assume you have an idea where we might get a boat?"

"The White Crane Tower, this way," he said, leading them east.

They walked along the marshy southern rim of the lake, past small fishing villages that made charming portraits against the mist rising from the surface of the lake and the sky streaked with waterfowl. It reminded Bren of those woodcut illustrations in some of Black's books on the Far East.

"You can hear songs lifting from fishermen's boats when the moon is out," said Yaozu.

"They don't sing in the daytime?" said Sean.

"It can be strange to be on the lake at night," said Yaozu. "I believe the singing calms them."

"We call that whistling past the graveyard," said Barrett.

The number of birds seemed to multiply as they kept curving east, thousands and thousands of cranes, herons, gulls, ducks, rails, and other marsh lovers. After they had walked for an hour, Bren could see the tall white tower, tiled in gold, off in the distance. Moored below it were dozens of the shallow teak boats known as dragon boats.

"This lake is where dragon boats originated," Yaozu explained, when he saw Bren looking that way.

"Why here?" said Bren.

"The great poet Qu Yuan drowned himself here. He had been exiled south of the lake by his king during the Warring States, because the poet opposed his king's alliance with Qin. When Qin eventually conquered all, Qu Yuan fell into despair and took his own life. It was said that the villagers rowed out into the lake to recover his body, but did not succeed. The dragon boat races honor his death."

"Why do they dress the boats up like dragons?" said Bren.

"According to legend," said Yaozu, "one of the four Dragon Kings once lived at the bottom of this lake."

Bren's and Mouse's eyes went wide. Yaozu smiled. "Would you like to hear the story of the Dragon King's Daughter?"

"Yes!" they both said, along with Barrett. Sean let out a great sigh, but was ignored.

"The Dragon King had three sons, and they all lived in a crystal palace at the bottom of the lake, but the third-born was fond of going his own way. He bridled at his father's commands, and caused his family much grief. So his father ordered his brothers to never let this one out of their sight. As you can imagine, this did not sit well with the disobedient one.

"The next time they went swimming, the third-born changed himself into a carp to trick his brothers and swam off to a different part of the lake to play. But he was captured by a fisherman, who took him to market."

"Serves him right," said Sean.

"When third-born's brothers came home without him, the Dragon King was very angry, thinking the boy had run off. Lake dragons control the wind and rain, and he brought forth a great storm to scare his son into returning. When that didn't work, the king appeared above the lake in the form of a waterspout to look for his son, but again he failed. He returned to the crystal palace in despair, mourning for several days until a curious piece of news came to him: farmers and fishermen were flocking to a nearby village, where a carp that had been caught was still alive. Everyone wanted to buy this fish, believing it would make them immortal if they ate it. When the Dragon King's older sons made it to the market, the carp had just been sold for an extraordinary amount. The brothers offered the buyer more than he had paid, explaining that the carp was their brother, but this only made the buyer want the carp more.

"The first- and second-born turned to depart for the lake, devastated at the loss of their brother and terrified of having to give such news to their father, when something extraordinary happened: an eight-year-old girl pushed her way through the crowd and offered to make a trade with the buyer of the carp.

"The man laughed in her face. *What could you possibly trade me for a carp that will make me immortal?* The girl brought forth a perfectly round white jade stone. *I will give you this, which supposedly has great power. And then you will not have to eat their brother.*

"The man with the carp couldn't believe his eyes. He had been born during the time of the Ancients and knew of the Eight Immortals. He took the stone and gave her the fish.

"The two brothers were so grateful that they invited the girl back to the lake, to the crystal palace, so their father could thank her in person. The Dragon King was so grateful, he made the girl a great offer: *It is not human beings alone that know gratitude,* he told her. *Your great kindness will be repaid. A dragon's life lasts for ten thousand years, and I will share my years of life with you, my daughter.*

"They all lived happily together in the lake for some time, but their story became well known, and emperor after emperor came to the lake to discover the secret of immortality. Emperor Qin himself came here as a young man, determined to find the Dragon King, or what had happened to the white jade stone. And so the Dragon King and his three sons and one daughter left the lake, never to return, and that is why there is no longer a Dragon King at the bottom of this lake."

"What was the point of that story?" said Sean.

"Sometimes stories are just entertainment," said Yaozu. "Sometimes not. It depends much on who the listener is."

"But wait," said Bren. "A white jade stone isn't one of

the magic artifacts. Why did the man give up the carp?"

"There is a story I haven't told you—any of you—about one of the Eight Immortals," said Yaozu. "Li Tie Guai, whose instrument was the bottle gourd, could free his soul from his body and travel in both the earthly and heavenly realms. Once, while his spirit was gone, a disciple found his seemingly lifeless body and assumed he was dead. He burned Li Tie Guai's body, cutting loose his soul.

"To punish him for his carelessness, the other seven Immortals divided his soul between two stones, one black jade, the other white, the black symbolizing Li Tie Guai's heart—his passion—and the other his head, or wisdom. But his soul was trapped in the earthly realm."

They had all stopped walking, and even Sean opened his mouth to ask the question Bren blurted out: "Are you saying Mouse's stone—and mine—are the spirit of this Immortal?"

"I'm just telling a story," said Yaozu. "But there is clearly something special about them, is there not? They have exhibited powers?"

"But the catfish man—"

"Catfish man?" said Sean.

"Mouse and I may have left a couple of things out," Bren stammered. "I didn't think it was important." He took a deep breath. "This skeleton where we found the white jade . . . it was guarded by a man who looked like a catfish. He claimed to be the girl's guardian, because she was a sorceress prophesied to restore the Ancients, and when she died on the island she had transferred her spirit, and thus her power, to the stone."

"Fascinating," said Yaozu. "I don't know how to reconcile that. There are many stories, many legends. Hard to know the truth."

"That's why there are so many religions," said Barrett. "You find a story that suits you."

They resumed walking until they reached the tower, which was three tiers of white-painted wood supported by white columns. Each of the three roofs was tiled in gold and curved up at the corners like a bird in flight. Inside, there was a shallow, stony creek running through the tower front to back, the creek stones engraved with writing.

"Poetry," said Yaozu, following Bren's eyes. "No one is sure who wrote it, or how many different authors there may be, but this is the passage that gives the tower its name."

He walked them over to a large stone and began to translate:

For seven years but one he had built the wooden
forms, giving shape to the mud that would become
barrier between land and sea. Until, having labored mile

*upon mile of shore, it seemed it would take more earth
than there would be left to defend. And so, one night, he
lay down to sleep.*

*He was awakened by the sensation of flying, and
lifting his eyes, he saw that he had been carried off by
a white crane, its angular, origami shape floating above
him like a kite.*

*Fearing to look down, he shut his eyes until he felt
his feet returned to the ground, knowing not where he
had landed. When he dared look, his eyes beheld the
Great Marsh of Cloud Dream.*

"Is that what this lake is called?" said Bren. "The
Great Marsh of Cloud Dream?"

"Not that I am aware," said Yaozu. "Poetic license, I
suppose."

They walked through all three levels of the tower,
listening to Yaozu read more of the engravings while they
took in the spectacular views of the lake from the higher
levels. There was one in particular that affected Bren, at
the tower's highest point:

*The lake embraces distant hills and devours the
Yangtze, its mighty waves rolling endlessly. From
morning glow to evening light, the views change a
thousand, ten thousand times. On top of the tower the*

*mind relaxes, the heart delights. All honors and disgrace
are forgotten. What pleasure, what joy to sit here and
drink in the breeze.*

Bren was only snapped out of his trance when Sean
said, "Aye, it's a beautiful view, but we don't have the
luxury of sitting here and drinking in the breeze."

He was right, but it still irritated Bren that Sean once
again felt the need to contradict everyone.

No one lived or worked at White Crane Tower, so the
cost of a boat was this: to leave five lumps of rice wrapped
in leaves—one for each passenger—as an offering for the
drowned poet. Yaozu explained that when the villagers
failed to save the poet, they had tossed rice into the lake
to keep the fish from eating his body. Yaozu had traded for
the rice along the way and carefully wrapped each bundle
while the others waited.

It was getting dark, but the moon was waxing full, so
they set out in the dragon boat upon the dark, placid lake.
When they had been rowing for perhaps an hour, Mouse
stood up and pointed to a small island off in the distance.
"There!" she said, as if answering a question no one asked.
"That place."

Not much could be seen from this far away, even with a
near-full moon, except that the island looked unwelcoming,
with dozens of tall, sharp peaks. Bren felt sick, thinking of

the Forest Above the Clouds. He'd had just about enough of China's forbidding geography.

"That must be Junshan," said Yaozu. "There is a tomb on the island, for the two favorite consorts of Emperor Shun, who was one of the Ancients. Some even claim he was one of the Eight Immortals. Four thousand years ago, these two consorts, Ehuang and Nuying, fearing that their beloved Shun was dead, drowned themselves in the lake. Shun was not dead, but rather far away, engaged in a military battle, and when he learned of their death he had the tomb built in their honor."

Yaozu paused before continuing.

"Do you remember how I told you that the great Qin came this way to search for the secret to immortality? Well, a storm nearly destroyed his boat, and he and his attendants were stranded on this island. He consulted his geomancer to see if the storm had been caused by evil spirits, and the geomancer told him of the tomb. Convinced that these beloved consorts of one of the Ancients—the people Qin had helped destroy—were trying to kill him, Qin ordered a curse be put on the island and for five stones to be laid in front of the tomb, to seal it forever."

"Yes," said Mouse. "We have to go there."

CHAPTER 21

THE TEA OF SILVER NEEDLES

They landed the boat and pulled it up onto the island, to where a thicket of black-spotted bamboo formed a natural fence along the shore.

"Do you know where this tomb is?" said Barrett to Yaozu.

"I do not," he admitted. "I'm not even sure what to look for."

"I'll find it," said Mouse, and Bren half expected her to become a bird and fly around the island. Instead she just took the lead walking deeper into the island, as if she had no doubt she was meant to find the consorts' tomb, the way she apparently was meant to find the white jade. No one questioned her.

Eventually they came to the foot of a hill, where an area otherwise wild and undisturbed had been cleared of brush and the face of the hill was bare, but for five large stones stacked two by two by one. Sean came forward and put his hand on the top stone.

"What now, little one? Do we move them?"

Mouse shook her head. "That wouldn't work," she said, pulling out the white stone. She closed her eyes for a minute, and Bren thought he could see a slight tremble along her lips, as if she were silently reciting a spell or an enchantment. And then they waited. They were surrounded by a small forest of the strange bamboo, and the black spots made Bren feel like he was being watched by a thousand creatures peering through the pale green stalks.

Suddenly there was a rustling, and everyone but Mouse flinched as the bamboo near the tomb parted. Two women appeared, thin as wisps and plainly dressed, one in a white robe trimmed in black, the other in grey and black. Both had fair skin and black hair tied back from their face and neck. They looked at Mouse as if she were the only one there.

"I am Nuying," said the one in white. "This is my sister, Ehuang. No one has called to us in centuries. We thought that power had been lost."

Mouse held out the white stone, almost as an offering, but neither of the women reached for it. It was merely proof of what Mouse had done.

"Come," said Ehuang. "You must help us prepare tea and tell us why you are here."

Barrett, Yaozu, Sean, and Bren stood dumbstruck as Mouse followed the two women back into the bamboo. Had she really just summoned two spirits from the grave? Bren was the first to snap out of it when he saw Mouse disappear, urging the others to catch up lest they never find her again, carried off by these specters to the land of the dead.

But there she was, following the women up a gently sloping hill covered in small trees with pale green leaves. Mouse alone helped the sisters pick buds from the trees— long, narrow things that reminded Bren of green beans, each with a delicate fuzz that gave them a silvery cast. When they had collected enough, the sisters led them all to a small grotto, where they wrapped the fresh-picked buds in cloth.

"Men huan," said Nuying. "A resting period. Those will replace the leaves we brew tonight."

As she said this her sister brought forth a cloth package and set it on the floor in front of them, unwrapping it to reveal buds that had already been allowed to "rest." These had a slightly yellow color to them.

There was a well near the grotto, and Ehuang went to it and pulled up a bucket of water to brew the tea. The sisters had a tall, narrow glass vase, into which they put the prepared buds, and then they slowly poured the well water over them.

"Now, we wait for the leaves to dance," said Nuying.

The leaves had floated to the surface of the vase as Nuying had poured in the water. But as each leaf absorbed water, it sank to the bottom. Then, for mysterious reasons, the leaves began to rise to the top again. It took more than an hour for each leaf to perform this "dance," but Bren didn't care. There was something enchanting about it. Even Sean seemed mesmerized.

"This is silver needle yellow tea," said Nuying as she poured the steeped tea into small porcelain cups for each of them. "The rarest tea in the world. Drink now and tell us your dreams."

Bren put the delicate cup to his mouth, his eyes darting from Mouse to Yaozu to Barrett to Sean as he took his first sip. It wasn't like anything else he had ever tasted—far less bitter than coffee, and with some of the intoxicating sensation he had felt when sneaking some of his father's cabbage wine. It was delicious, and he took another eager sip, and another, and another, and then he remembered nothing.

They all awoke, seemingly at once, upon a hill of yellow-grey. The wind was blowing, warm and dry, and Bren could feel fine bits of sand on his lips. He looked at the others, shielding their faces from the gritty wind, and thought he saw Yaozu smile, just a bit. He had explained that Fenghou was a place where winds came charging like horses through narrow mountain passes, and where Silk Road traders could carve shelter for themselves in the porous dirt.

This had to be that place.

The five of them stood up in various postures of weariness, soreness, disbelief, and hopefulness.

"Where are we?" said Barrett, looking around at the desolate landscape.

"We're near the tomb, aren't we?" said Bren.

"I believe so," said Yaozu. "I only know for certain we are not in the middle of Lake Dongting."

"How on earth did we get here, Mouse?" said Sean.

"The tea," she said.

"I remember drinking the tea," said Bren. "Does anyone remember anything after that?"

One by one they shook their heads.

"I remember Nuying asking us to tell her our dreams," said Barrett. "And I pictured myself finding the rest of the magic artifacts, or at least, I tried to, but all of a sudden I could think of nothing but my father."

"It has been a long time since you've seen him?" said Yaozu.

"Yes, and for good reason," said Barrett. "We hate each other."

"Aye, I remember what I said—or thought," said Sean. "That I wanted to bloody get back to Britannia in one bloody piece."

"I thought the same thing," said Bren. "Maybe not with as much bloodiness."

Sean laughed. It was the first time Bren had seen him smile that broadly in a long time. But the truth was, getting home was not what Bren had thought about as he sipped the tea of silver needles. He had thought about Mouse, and how he wanted to find out what she was really after. He wanted to know how their two stones fit together, learn her whole story . . . whether she really was keeping something from him. And in doing so he might even learn why his mother had once owned a black jade stone that, according to Yaozu, might contain half the soul of one of the Eight Immortals.

"And here we all are, together," said Yaozu. "It can only mean that our various ambitions intersect and depend on one another."

Sean pulled his shirt up over his nose and mouth to deflect the wind. The rest of them gathered their meager possessions and followed Yaozu down the hill, to a dirt road barely recognizable from its windswept surroundings.

"Which way?" said Barrett.

Yaozu looked at their map again. "I'm not sure. We left the well-traveled path, you might say."

"This way," said Mouse, walking east. The rest shrugged and followed her. At this point no one doubted her instincts.

As darkness approached, they made camp in an abandoned cave. It was a relief to be out of the wind. When they had built a fire and eaten a small meal of dried fish and rice, Bren asked Yaozu, "How much do you know about the tomb itself?"

"What anyone knows comes from a book called *Records of the Grand Historian*," Yaozu explained. "The oldest history of China, from before the time of your Christ. According to the book, Qin began preparing for his death as soon as he came to the throne. Later, when he had unified the empire, nearly a million men from all over China were committed to the task. The tomb is alleged to be deep underground, filled with both treasures and dangers, and yet despite being underground the stars shine and the rivers flow, and candles made from whale fat burn and never go out. If you will permit me a page in your journal, I can draw a diagram of what I know."

Bren ripped out one of his few remaining pages and handed it and his graphite stick to Yaozu.

"It was modeled after Qin's capital, Xianyang," he said

as he began to draw. "The outer city has a wall with a perimeter of three point seven eight miles. The inner city wall has a circumference of one point five miles."

"Good heavens, that's close to twenty acres!" said Sean.

Yaozu nodded. "Not just that. The whole site is a necropolis. A city of the dead. All of Qin's consorts who had no male sons were buried there."

"Alive?" said Bren, horrified.

Yaozu nodded. "Furthermore, it was suggested that it would be a serious breach if the craftsmen who constructed the mechanical devices and knew of the tomb's treasures were to divulge those secrets. Therefore, after the funeral ceremonies were completed and the treasures hidden away, the inner passageway was blocked, and the outer gate lowered, immediately trapping all the workers and craftsmen inside. None could escape."

"He thought of everything, didn't he?" said Barrett.

Yaozu drew other chambers around the outside of the page. "Once the burial complex was sealed, any remaining officials and soldiers who might have knowledge of the site were buried in pits all around the outer wall. As you can see, the cost of secrecy was quite high."

"This Grand Historian who described all this," said Sean. "He didn't know where the tomb was?"

"Doubtful," said Yaozu. "Qin would have wanted the splendor of his tomb known, but not for it to be ransacked."

"And the tomb itself?" asked Barrett.

"A pyramid, at the southern end of the complex, within the inner wall," said Yaozu. "There I do not know what to expect to find, except traps and other defenses against pillaging."

"Fantastic," said Sean.

"Mind you, this is based on the *Records*," said Yaozu. "Things could end up looking completely different. The last thing recorded by the Grand Historian was that trees and grasses were planted on the tomb mound so that it would in time resemble nothing more than an ordinary hill. But I trust we have the resources to identify it."

Barrett started to douse their fire when Yaozu stopped her. He then did something very curious. He removed a single long scroll of parchment from inside his bag and spread it out along the ground, holding it in place with a stone at each end. The scroll was perhaps two feet long and four inches wide. He then collected a small pile of ash that had already formed in the fire, dipped his finger in it, and drew a row of stick figures from one end of the scroll to the other, side by side with their arms overlapping. Above each of their heads he wrote Chinese characters, then tore a piece from the scroll containing the first man and threw it into the fire.

This he did over and over, until each of the paper men had been incinerated.

"A prayer to your ancestors?" said Barrett.

"A summons to allies," said Yaozu, but he explained no

more than that. He spread out his bedroll and was soon fast asleep.

▲▲▲

The next morning Bren awoke to find a small army of men standing outside their cave. He grabbed Yaozu by the shoulder and shook him. "Yaozu, wake up. I think someone answered your call."

There were at least a hundred of them, all dressed in full-length gowns of blue with black trim, but no other decoration. No embroidered dragons or lotus flowers or birds. Each had a sword strapped to his waist on one side and a dagger on the other. All had dark hair, and beards and mustaches of various lengths, but Bren couldn't tell how old or young they were. None were elderly, but none were as young as him, either, or even Sean.

As the others woke up, they each reacted with alarm—Barrett grabbing her sword, Sean drawing his small dagger—but Yaozu assured them their weapons weren't necessary.

"Friends, not foes," he said.

"Where did they come from?" said Sean, reluctantly putting away his dagger.

"These are members of the Society of Paper Men," said Yaozu. "An ancient fraternity of spies. They can help us in the event of armed resistance."

"How could there be resistance?" said Sean. "If no one knows where the tomb is?"

"Not the sort of army you are thinking of," said Yaozu. "I must ask you to trust me, Sean. Perhaps assistance will not even be necessary."

Sean opened his mouth to argue but then took stock of all the men standing outside the cave and thought better of it. "We should get going," was all he managed.

The dusty road they followed passed dozens of rolling hills, little wrinkled hounds sleeping at the feet of the surrounding mountains, and Bren wondered how they would possibly find the hill they were supposedly looking for. But Mouse and Yaozu seemed to know just where they were going, and around midmorning, after the landscape had turned green again, Mouse stopped in her tracks and pointed to what looked like an ordinary mound of vegetation in the distance.

"I think that's it," she said.

When they got closer, Yaozu said, "The *Records* mention an underground entryway. But of course there will be no obvious way in. Just like there was no obvious bridge across Big Rattan Gorge. But there must be a way."

They all instinctively looked at Mouse, as if she possessed some magic key to all this. Bren had seen her pick many locks. The problem was, you had to have a locked door first. But she did have the white jade, and none of them—including Mouse—had yet figured out the limits of its power.

"Maybe there's a tree branch we pull down and a

door in the earth opens up," said Sean. "I'd believe most anything at this point. Or maybe your magic mirror can unlock this, too."

"I wish it were so," said Yaozu, slowly scanning the area, his face pained with concentration. "As I explained, I've tried the jade tablet, too, but either knowledge of the tomb doesn't exist to be divined, or perhaps counter-magic is blocking access."

"Or there is no knowledge because there is no tomb," said Bren. "Couldn't that be it?"

"Mr. Graham's been a bad influence," said Barrett. "Yaozu, what about your friends there?"

The Society of Paper Men had been noticeably silent since appearing at their cave.

"I think I can find the entrance," said Mouse.

"How?" said Bren.

"A mole or an earthworm might know," she said.

Bren pulled her aside and whispered, "Mouse, have you ever traveled into a creature that lives underground? If you were afraid of becoming a fish, or a bird, I don't know if this is a good idea."

"I have to try something," she said. "We've come this far."

"I don't want you to do it," said Bren.

"Do what?" said Barrett.

Mouse told the others her plan. Yaozu and Barrett were willing to let her try. Bren and Sean weren't.

"The truth comes out," said Sean, glaring at Barrett. "You don't care at all about these children."

"Mouse is the one leading this mission now, as far as I'm concerned," said Barrett. "I'm not forcing her to do anything, and I don't believe any of us has the power to stop her, do you?"

Sean didn't answer, but Bren knew Barrett was right. Mouse was on a mission, whether he understood it or not.

"How can I help, Mouse?" said Bren.

"Find me a worm," she said.

He dropped to his knees and began digging into the soft dirt with his bare hands. He kept at it until he had turned enough soil for a four-inch-long worm to wriggle to the surface. He picked it up and held it gently between his fingers. "Will this do?"

"I'll try," she said, and she sat down next to Bren and closed her eyes. When she appeared to lose consciousness, Bren put the worm down and watched it tunnel its way back through the dirt.

There was nothing to do but wait, and that was the worst part—there was nothing Bren could do to make sure Mouse was okay. After what felt like hours, a worm wriggled back to the surface and Mouse opened her eyes. They all crowded around her.

"I know where the entrance is," she said.

CHAPTER 22

THE ARMIES OF
PAPER AND CLAY

She led them to a spot north of the hill and pointed to the ground. "Dig here."

"With what?" said Sean. "Do either you or Yaozu have a magic shovel?"

"Before shovels came hands," said Yaozu, turning to the Paper Men. "They will dig for us."

Without a word one of the men dropped to his knees and began to dig through the grass and weeds with his hands. Several others joined him, forming a circle around the hole they were making.

"Mouse, does something seem funny about them?" Bren whispered.

"Yes," she whispered back. "I don't know what, though."

It took a dozen of them two hours before the bottom of the hole they were digging gave way, the loose dirt falling into a large open pit below. It wasn't too deep, and Mouse led the way, sliding down the edge of the hole and dropping feetfirst to the bottom.

She motioned for them to follow, and one by one they did, into the pit and down a set of stone stairs to a tunnel, or hallway, that went on forever, Bren thought. When they finally emerged, what he saw astonished him—it was as if all of London's Hyde Park had been buried underground. There was a large, open lawn with an enormous pond at the center, populated with bronze cranes, swans, and ducks. Except the lawn was moss or some sort of algae, and the metallic taste in Bren's mouth told him that the pond wasn't water, but quicksilver. All of it was lit with glowing lanterns hung from the roof, as if they had come upon the park at night, just before a celebration. A river cut through the far end of the park, also quicksilver, Bren assumed.

"Absolutely astonishing," said Barrett. "More amazing than I even imagined."

"Just the beginning, if the stories are true," said Yaozu.

"Did anyone notice those?" said Sean, pointing up to

the lanterns. "Someone must come here to tend to them. They couldn't have remained lit from the time the tomb was sealed."

"Remember what it says in the *Records of the Grand Historian*," said Barrett. "Candles were made from whale fat, to burn forever."

Sean smirked. "Literally?"

"I appreciate your skepticism," said Barrett. "But by now I should have thought you'd quite believe the Chinese could have kept a light burning for a couple of millennia."

Bren had wondered how the five of them and the hundred or so members of Yaozu's secret society would ever cram themselves underground, but they had plenty of room to roam around the park, examining the bronze animals and other artifacts, like a small boat on the "pond" and stone benches surrounding the shore. Across the water they discovered a band of bronze musicians, along with jugglers and acrobats and strongmen posed in various athletic postures.

"Entertainment for the emperor?" Barrett asked.

Yaozu shook his head. "Not sure. Why would they not be within the tomb?"

"Maybe acrobats and strongmen were bodyguards back then?" said Bren.

"And musicians, too?" said Sean.

Bren thought about it. "A girl in my grammar school

hit me in the head with her flute once. It hurt."

Sean laughed. "I've no doubt you deserved it, yeah?"

Barrett turned to Yaozu. "There must be an exit from the park to the outer city."

He consulted his diagram again. "This way."

Mouse took the lead again, finding the exit tunnel opposite of where they had come in, but for once her uncanny instincts failed her. The passageway turned out to be a dead end.

"It's a maze," said Sean. "I only hope there's no Minotaur waiting at the end."

Mouse walked up to the rammed earth wall, putting her hand against it.

"No," she said. "This is the way," and she moved to where the two walls met and began to brush away dust and loose dirt until the rest of them could see the seam of a doorway.

"Mouse, have I told you how much I love you?" said Barrett.

"Door still doesn't open," said Yaozu.

"Trust me, I've never seen a lock Mouse can't pick," said Bren.

Yaozu leaned forward, studying the door intently. "Do you see a lock?"

"Maybe it goes up and down," said Sean. "Like a castle gate."

Yaozu turned and said something in Chinese to the Society, and two of them disappeared back down the passageway toward the park. When they returned, they had a long bronze rod—the leg from one of the bronze cranes, in fact.

"Eureka!" said Bren, smiling. The others gave him a funny look. "Oh, come on," he said. "Eureka? Archimedes? Discovered the lever? That's what you're going to use that for, right?"

"He discovered the lever *for Westerners*," said Yaozu.

"I beg your pardon," said Barrett. "Who discovered the lever for your people?"

"I do not know," Yaozu admitted. "But I am sure it was long before some Greek man."

"Merciful heavens!" Sean blurted out. "I joined the navy so I could drop out of school. Can we just wedge this thing open and get on with it?"

They cleared room for two members of the Society to wedge the bronze leg under the door, while four more then depressed the lever, causing a slow, grinding movement along the seams.

"It's working!" said Bren.

When the door was just high enough, another group of Paper Men squatted beneath it, using brute strength to push the door the rest of the way up.

"Will it stay?" Bren wondered aloud.

"Perhaps," said Yaozu. "Perhaps not. Bring the lever to this side, in case."

When they were all safely through, the men holding the door moved from beneath it, and the door stayed put. Bren breathed a sigh of relief and then turned to behold an open courtyard of sorts, about half the size of the town square in Map. Opposite the door was another wall, this one with two doors spaced evenly across. He took one step forward and tripped.

Bren landed with a great clatter on a pile of rocks, or sticks, he wasn't sure. He just knew it hurt. He held up a stick poking him in the ribs and realized it was a bone. He threw it aside and scrambled to his feet, stumbling and flailing.

"Are those human bones?" he said.

"This is a tomb," said Barrett, picking her way through what were the remains of at least twenty skeletons. "Remember that the histories say the workers were sealed inside?"

Bren did remember. "Yaozu said almost a million people helped build this place. Are we really going to find that many skeletons down here?"

Yaozu was shaking his head. "The tomb took thirty years to finish. Made mostly by prisoners and debtors, who would have died during their hard labors, or been executed or imprisoned when they were done. The crafts-men—those who finished whatever mechanical devices or other secrets—were many fewer, and were supposedly sealed inside the inner tomb. These men here I suppose were among the last, and tried to escape."

"That must be the inner city wall, then," said Bren, and he began walking past the pile of bones, across the open space.

"No!" said Yaozu, and immediately one of the Paper Men leaped ahead of Bren, blocking his way and swiveling his head left and right, as if he'd heard something.

"There is a reason for our friends to be here," said Yaozu. "They will take the lead."

"Sorry," said Bren. "I forgot."

"Do you really think the place is booby-trapped, or was all that written to scare potential grave robbers?" Sean asked.

"The latter is possible," Yaozu agreed. "But as you have seen, the emperor took his burial seriously. He believed in the need for a properly equipped tomb, so I would not assume otherwise."

The shuddering thud of a door slamming shut made the whole group spin around. The gate of the outer wall had closed, but that's not what made Bren's heart drop into his stomach. Standing there was a siege of larger-than-life-size bronze cranes, the upper and lower parts of their long, sharp bills scraping against each other. The one in front was missing a leg.

"Go open the door to the inner city," said Yaozu, his expression set. "We will deal with this."

"Which door?" said Sean, looking from one to the other. "Is one a trap?"

"What does it matter?" Yaozu replied harshly. "We have already sprung a trap."

"They're just birds," said Sean. "Probably a mechanical trick. Meant to scare—"

Before he could finish, one of the cranes stretched its wings like a pair of rusty hinges and flew directly at Yaozu. A Paper Man lunged in front of Yaozu just as the crane attacked . . . the bronze bird jabbed at the man's face as if it were spearing a toad from a pond, plucking an eyeball right out of the man's head.

Sean didn't have to be told twice.

"Pick a door! Pick a door!"

They rushed forward to the inner wall, toward the door on the left, dragging Mouse along while the eerie sounds of brass cranes fighting Chinese spies roiled behind them. In a matter of seconds Mouse had unlocked the door and they were pushing their way through.

All except for Barrett. She had drawn her sword and held it out, half brandishing it like a normal sword, half holding it up like a wizard's wand. It seemed to have no effect on the fighting that was going on behind them, but Bren did see the one-legged crane stretch its wings enough to glide over to where Barrett was standing.

The crane landed with a clank and stood there for a moment, tilting its head one way, then the other, as if examining the sword. And then it lashed out, clutching the blade in its bill and wrenching it out of Barrett's hands.

"Let's go," said Yaozu, grabbing Barrett's arm as he ran toward the open door. The Paper Men did their best to fight off the violent metal birds, and eventually they all made it to the other side, except for perhaps a half dozen of the spies, who either couldn't make it or felt bound by duty to hold off the birds so the others could retreat inside.

"I guess the Tamer of Beasts doesn't work on magical animals," said Barrett, leaning against the now-shut door and breathing heavily. "Sort of ironic, when you think about it."

"Where are we?" said Sean. The room they were in was dimly lit by the same ever-burning lamps or whatever had lighted the park and the courtyard. It was the length of a ballroom, and along the walls were swords, spears, battle-axes, scimitars, shields, crossbows, dagger-axes, and halberds.

"An armory," said Barrett.

"For what soldiers?" said Bren, who began to feel tiny legs of fear crawl along his arms. He stopped before a jagged, three-foot-long shield. The wood showed no rot, and its surface was painted a brilliant red, green, and white that had not faded. Nearby was a military drum with a leather head and fine red lines painted around the body. There were also silk and linen textiles folded neatly on a stone seat, looking as if they had been woven only yesterday.

"Do you think some of the Eight Immortals might be in here?" said Bren.

"Possibly," Barrett replied, "although except for the sword, none of the artifacts resembles a weapon."

Bren went to the opposite wall, where he stood before a large crossbow. He had read of crossbows being used in ancient Greece and Rome, but he was still amazed to see evidence of one so old. It even appeared to be in working order. As with the shield, the wood was not rotted, and the bowstring was intact and unworn. He couldn't resist: he reached up and lifted the device off the wall, nearly dropping it. He couldn't believe how heavy it was.

"Yaozu, did the Chinese actually use crossbows this size? Or is this just for show?" He braced the bow with his foot and pulled the string back with both hands. It cocked beautifully. "Don't worry, it's not loaded," he said, when he saw the horrified look on Yaozu's face. "I don't even know where the bolts are."

Yaozu turned his head toward the eastern wall, as if listening for something. Then Bren heard it too—the scrabbling of boots on hard stone.

"Where is that coming from?" said Sean.

"Beyond the outer wall," said Yaozu. "We must have triggered an alarm."

"Everyone grab a weapon!" said Barrett.

The Paper Men obeyed immediately, and though Bren had a crossbow at his feet, he knew it was too heavy for him, so he dropped it and took a saber from the wall. Yaozu chose a halberd—sort of a cross between a spear and a battle-axe—Sean, a pair of dagger-axes, and Barrett another sword, to replace the one that had been plucked from her hands. Only Mouse chose the shield, which was nearly as tall as she was, though Bren had no idea how she planned to carry it.

"The tomb chamber should be on the far side of this armory," said Barrett. "They must be planning to cut us off, and they'll likely surround the inner city as well. Even if we make it to the tomb, we'll still have to fight our way out."

There was another screeching of stone, and a door they hadn't noticed opened at the end of the long room. Soldiers began to file in two by two, dressed in purple tunics with reddish leather armor over their torsos, each carrying a heavy bronze sword. Behind them were more purple-clad warriors carrying spears and scimitars, and others with weapons of brute force: clubs and hammers.

But these weren't like any soldiers Bren had ever seen. Their faces were expressionless. Their black eyebrows and facial hair stood out in stark contrast to their pale pink faces, but there was no movement. It was as if they were all wearing masks, and this was just some eerie form of theater. Except this wasn't playacting, and the Paper Men did not wait for anyone's orders—they attacked at once, charging at the soldiers, weapons forward. The Chinese army met them with force, and the armory was suddenly filled with the clashing of bronze and iron swords and axes. One of the Paper Men stood with his back to Bren, who jumped back in horror as the sharp point of a spear came through the man. Bren forgot he was holding the saber— he felt helpless watching the chaos of two hundred men entwined in the fury of battle.

Mouse had crouched down behind her shield, but not from cowardice. She was holding the jade eye in the palm of her hand, and her lips were moving silently.

"Mouse, what are you doing?" said Bren.

He had broken the spell, if that's what it was. She looked up at him. "Trying to call the dragon. You saw the silver river back there."

He nodded and looked up just in time to see a soldier charging straight for him. His first instinct was to duck, which he did, but remembering a story he'd read, he dove to the side and swung his saber as hard as he could at the man's shins.

What happened next Bren wouldn't have believed if he hadn't seen it himself.

His bronze saber struck the man's legs with a crack, and they shattered into a dozen pieces, one hitting Bren square in the face. The soldier immediately pitched forward, and when he did, his nose struck the hard dirt floor and smashed to pieces like a dropped vase.

"What the . . . ," said Bren, but he couldn't finish, the acid taste of fear and confusion coming up his throat. He queasily picked up one of the pieces, expecting to see bloody bone and flesh; instead he realized it wasn't bone, it was clay! A shard of reddish brown terra-cotta with a man's nose and right eye painted on one side.

Bren rushed to where he had dropped the crossbow, frantically looking for a bolt. He found a quiver of them, loaded one into the crossbow, and using all his strength, he took aim and fired. The brass bolt shot with stunning force toward one of the Chinese soldiers, striking him in the chest. There was a thunderous crack, and the soldier fell to pieces.

"They're made of clay!" Bren shouted. "We have to smash them."

He loaded another bolt into the crossbow, but his excitement got the better of him. His aim was off, and his heart sank as he saw one of the Paper Men move in front of a Chinese soldier just as Bren fired. The bolt struck the Paper Man in the back, stopping him in his tracks, and seizing the advantage, the clay soldier swung his scimitar at the man's head, taking it off clean at the neck.

That's when Bren got another serious shock: the Paper Man's headless body hit the floor, the crossbow bolt sticking out of his back, but there was no blood. His head lay five feet from him, but there was no blood there or at the neck, either. Only confetti and feathers.

"Yaozu," said Bren, but he knew it wasn't loud enough for Yaozu to hear him. Everyone else was discovering for themselves what was going on, and the room was filled not only with the sound of clashing weapons but of clay smashing against stone.

Bren fumbled with another bolt and clumsily loaded the crossbow again. This time he steadied himself, taking aim at a clay soldier who was hoisting a huge battle-axe over his head. Bren fired. The brass bolt struck him square in the chest . . . his torso shattered, his raised arms fell to the floor, breaking to pieces, sending the battle-axe sliding across the floor . . . his bodiless legs teetered there a moment before tipping over and adding to the pile of shards.

"Bren, look out!"

Bren turned in time to see a scimitar coming right at him. He ducked, and the curved sword struck the dirt wall, wedging there. Before the clay soldier could react, Bren summoned all his strength and swung the crossbow at him, smashing him against the wall.

He turned back to the battle, where the terra-cotta

warriors and Paper Men were going at each other. Bren could see Barrett and Sean slowly coming to the same realization—these "men" Yaozu had summoned weren't men at all, but some sort of animated illusion. He watched as a clay soldier thrust a spear through the gut of a Paper Man, only for the weapon to shred right through and plunge into the back of another clay warrior, shattering its back. This happened over and over, the clay army slashing and spearing at the paper one, only to destroy themselves. Meanwhile Bren and company could shield themselves and attack from behind. Yaozu had summoned the ultimate army—bloodless drones who absorbed the enemy's attacks and tricked them into attacking themselves.

The problem was, the clay warriors kept coming. Yaozu had said there were rumors of thousands buried nearby. They didn't have enough Paper Men to stave them off.

"We have to block that door!" said Barrett.

"We can't!" said Sean. And he was right. They couldn't fight their way to a passageway that was filled a mile deep with fresh warriors. They had to either leave the way they came in or find the door to the inner tomb. And fast.

CHAPTER 23

THE TOMB
OF QIN

Either there was no exit from this room, other than the door where they came in or the one the clay soldiers were marching through, or the door was hidden. And based on what little he had seen of the burial complex, Bren guessed it was the latter.

He dragged Mouse to the south wall—the direction the actual tomb should lie if Yaozu and Barrett were correct—and the two of them began to check for any signs of a secret mechanism. A crack, a seam, a lever . . . anything. But their frantic scrabbling against floor and wall gave back nothing but dirt.

"Bren, we've got to go back!"

It was Barrett, and apparently they were out of time to find a secret way into the tomb. Bren spun around to see Barrett, Yaozu, and Sean all retreating toward the door to the outer city. There were few Paper Men still standing, on a floor littered with shards of pottery and shredded tissue, and clay warriors were beginning to surround them now, flowing out into the room like bees from a hive.

Bren didn't think he and Mouse could make it to the other door in time. They were trapped.

He tried to get Mouse's attention, but she was staring into the mass of warriors, apparently paralyzed with fear. At least, that's what Bren assumed just before she pointed into the crowd and said, "Him. Kill *him*."

From across the room Barrett, Yaozu, and Sean exchanged looks with Bren. He looked away from them and tried to follow where Mouse was pointing.

"That one," she said again, and Bren suddenly realized who she meant: a figure no taller or shorter than the others, with the same purple robe and leather-brown tunic, but with a headdress different from the rest: a red piece tied up like the swooping horns of an antelope.

Before he could think about how foolish he was, Bren picked up his saber and ran straight for him, charging into the throng of warriors. He bulled right into two of the remaining Paper Men, pushing them into the wall of warriors like a battering ram, and then when he was close enough, he thrust the saber through the back of one, impaling him but also striking the one Mouse wanted square in the breastplate.

The warrior didn't shatter. In fact, he didn't even crack. The saber tip had only chipped the surface of the clay, and Bren was surrounded by warriors about to strike.

Something darted between Bren's legs. Suddenly Mouse was between him and the warrior, holding one of the bronze crossbow bolts in her fist. She struck at the warrior's abdomen as hard as she could.

Bren thought he heard a crack . . . for a moment everything went fuzzy, as if time had both stopped and sped up somehow, and then he saw the spidering fissures radiate across the front of the warrior's body.

The battle-axe he was holding clattered to the ground. Others followed . . . weapons of all kinds suddenly dropping from the hands of the warriors to the floor. The wounded warrior's painted eyes remained fixed and lifeless, and yet Bren thought he could see something like fear there, and the warrior's hands went to his fracturing chest, vainly grasping for the falling pieces.

When his body hit the floor and broke, the sound that followed was like a building collapsing. Every clay warrior in the room toppled to the ground, until Bren and the rest were standing in a garbage heap of red clay. For a moment Bren thought he heard someone just behind him, but then he realized he was just hearing his own panting breath. He tried to calm himself, but his nerves had run away from him, and when another piece of clay slipped from the pile and crashed onto the floor, Bren nearly jumped out of his skin.

For a moment there was nothing in the room but a haunting silence, just before Barrett, Sean, and Yaozu began trudging through the shards of clay toward Bren and Mouse.

Mouse reached down into the broken head of the warrior she had targeted and pulled out a small gold worm, slowly wriggling in her grasp.

"What is that?" said Bren.

"A silkworm?" said Barrett, taking the live thing in her hand. "Is it real, or enchanted, like the cranes?"

"Ingenious," said Yaozu, taking the worm from Barrett and holding it up, so that they all could see that its surface was metallic. "A mechanical brain, controlling the others."

Barrett looked around at the wreckage. "Mouse, how did you know?"

"It was the headdress, wasn't it?" said Bren. "This one was different."

She shook her head. "I'm not sure. He seemed more alive than the others."

"Unreal," said Sean. "And you can take that any way you like."

"Now what?" said Bren. "We still don't know how to reach the tomb."

Barrett grabbed one of the bronze crossbow bolts and began drawing a crude map of the tomb in the dirt. "We came in here," she began, indicating the underground park and the tunnel to the outer wall. "We then chose this door, which we now know dead-ends to the south, but has a door toward the east, here." She looked toward the door, where clay warriors had fallen higgledy-piggledy when their thread of life was snapped. "Probably pointless trying that direction . . . could be thousands more choking the way."

"There is supposedly a western gate, here," said Yaozu. "We just need to go back into the outer city and walk around."

"And hope the worm of life or whatever you call it was animating those big birds," said Sean.

"Indeed," said Yaozu, "but just in case . . ." He chose a weapon from the pile—a scimitar—and silently encouraged the rest of them to do the same.

When they reentered the outer city, they could see the aftermath of the battle they had left behind. There was nothing left of the Paper Men save for scraps of paper and feathers. The cranes were all toppled, and there were piles of clay warriors here, too. Bren realized they must have been waiting outside in case the group had tried to retreat—there truly would have been no escape if Mouse hadn't saved them.

Barrett picked her way among the pile until she found

what she was looking for: the sword the crane had snatched from her hand. Then she led them to the gate, some two hundred yards south along the inner wall, passing more construction relics, bronze tools, and other devices Bren had never seen before. And near these craftsman's tools were more skeletons of the men who had been buried alive to protect the tomb's secrets.

They passed a burial pit full of chariots and horses, and a massive kiln where the clay figures must've been fired. The gate itself was nothing special, at least on the surface. Just a pair of wide, wooden doors, unpainted and unadorned. Bren knew it had to be a trap.

But it wasn't. The doors were locked, but Mouse quickly fixed that, and then Barrett and Sean pushed open the heavy doors to reveal what at first seemed to be a vast, open space with a twinkling night sky. Even the air was cooler, as if they had entered a different realm altogether.

"We're in," said Barrett, struggling to control her enthusiasm.

"It can't be this easy," said Bren.

"Maybe they never expected anyone to get this far," said Sean. "We certainly wouldn't have . . . not without Yaozu's Paper Men, and of course, our Mouse."

For his part, Yaozu was saying nothing, which wasn't unusual, but in this case it made Bren a little nervous. Part of that, however, was all that Bren had seen since they entered the burial complex. The Paper Men, being the mere illusion of men . . . was Yaozu like them? Bren tried to suppress the same feeling of fear and mistrust that had infected him after what had happened with Mouse back on the Vanishing Island. The feeling that someone you had grown close to was something else entirely.

As they went deeper into the chamber, they began to see the stunning level of detail inside. Just as the *Records of the Grand Historian* had promised, there were mercury rivers coursing through the ground, and above them was a constellation-filled sky, as vast and brilliant as if they were standing atop a lonely mountain in the dead of night.

"Look at that sky," said Bren.

The rest looked up. "I wonder if those really are pearls, like the Grand Historian claimed," said Barrett.

"Figure out a way to boost me up there and I'll tell you," said Sean. "Might as well come out of all this with my pockets full."

"That's not what I'm talking about," said Bren. "Look— the position of those two constellations, and what must be the planet Venus."

"What are you getting at?" said Barrett.

"They are almost identical to the sky I saw the last night we were aboveground, just before I fell asleep," said Bren.

"I still don't get it, little brother," said Sean.

"Either the ceiling of Qin's tomb was built around the exact date, two thousand years ago, that we happen to be here . . ."

"Or the sky is moving," said Barrett.

Bren nodded. There was a wealthy earl back in Britannia who had taken a fancy to astronomy and hired an Italian named Galileo to build him a mechanical model of the solar system, one that reflected the notion that the earth revolved around the sun, not the other way around. The model, which operated on some principle Bren couldn't fathom, supposedly took up a whole room in the earl's castle and never needed winding. But this was something else entirely.

"Impressive," said Yaozu.

Bren found himself moving away from the mercury rivers. "This way?"

"Lead on," said Barrett.

They crossed the cavernous room, which was like a miniature landscape—rivers, sand, hills, trees, and even pools of mercury that Bren assumed might be oceans. It was as if the entire tomb were a topographical map, and at the far end sat an enormous step-sided pyramid. Qin's tomb.

On their meandering path to the pyramid they saw nothing that looked like any of the Eight Immortals, no fan or flute or gourd, but those could be inside Qin's coffin. They circled the base of the pyramid, which Bren guessed must've been an acre, based on the time he had had to walk Old Man Spenser's farm picking up acorns. All that space to bury one man.

"Where would they have put the entrance, Yaozu?" said Barrett, her eyes darting all around the stepped face of the pyramid. They had seen nothing resembling a door around the base.

Yaozu tilted his head for a better look at the top. "Probably higher up. One reason the sides are stepped."

Barrett nodded and began to climb. The steps themselves were as tall as Mouse, so she had to boost herself up and onto each one as if she were climbing a fence. Bren was about to hoist himself up when he noticed that Mouse was a ways behind them, standing over one of the pools of mercury. He went to her and noticed that it wasn't mercury at all, but water. Actual water.

"Must be groundwater," said Bren. He tasted it. "It's clean. Cold. Come on, now, we could use your help to find out how to get into this bloody thing."

She just stood there, saying nothing. Bren went over and stood next to her, trying to see what she was looking at. All he saw was the watery reflection of a tall, still-thin boy, now looking much older than thirteen, his brown hair long and dirty, his eyes marred with dark circles, his face smudged. But more than that, he looked weary, and sad.

He looked at Mouse's reflection. He had been with

her every day for a year now, and what struck him was how much she hadn't changed. A girl of eight, or however old she was, should have grown over the past months. Her hair should have been much longer, her face aged with struggle, like Bren's. Like all of them. But the other thing he noticed looking at her reflection was her eyes, still large and black and fathomless, and yet alive with intelligence . . . searching.

"Mouse, Bren! We need you up here!" It was Barrett, shouting down at them from halfway up the side of the pyramid. Sean and Yaozu were close behind.

"Come on," said Bren, grabbing Mouse by the hand and pulling her away from the pool. She didn't want to come away, but she did, and together they slowly scaled the stone tower until they reached the others.

Barrett pointed to the outline of a small door—more of a hatch, really—in the horizontal part of one of the steps, and nodded at Mouse. But after looking it over, she turned back to them and said, "It's not locked. It's not really a door."

"Clever," said Yaozu. "When you want no one to enter, don't leave a door."

"Meaning what?" said Sean.

"When the workers finished with the inner tomb," said Barrett, "they just came out of this hole and dropped this one last stone in place, to rest here forever."

"And then discovered they had been buried alive for all their hard work," said Bren.

Barrett laughed. "Rather cruel, isn't it? But what's holding this piece in place?"

Yaozu was stroking his beard. "Must be braced from behind, probably wood or leather straps."

"Which have been exposed to moisture for two millennia," said Sean.

They all looked at each other, and then Sean delivered the first blow, stomping down on the hatch with all his might. The others joined in.

"Careful," said Barrett. "We don't want one of us following this block to the bottom."

They applied their collective force around the edges, which they reasoned would be the weak point anyway, and after perhaps half an hour of exhausting effort, they heard a crack, followed by a snap, and finally, slowly, the stone began to fall inward.

"Back up, everyone, back up!" said Barrett. "Mouse, come here."

Barrett grabbed Mouse by the arms and dangled her over the now-crooked block. "Kick the living daylights out of it, Mouse." She did, slamming both her feet down, over and over, while Barrett held her from above, until with a final cracking and snapping and grinding the square of stone fell away into the tomb, Mouse's legs dangling over the dark hole left behind before Barrett snatched her back.

"Well done, little one," said Sean, giving her a hug. "You can kick like my granny's mule."

"So how do we get down there?" said Bren, peering into the black hole.

"Take the stairs," said Yaozu, and he fetched one of the whale-fat lamps and used it to show them a zigzagging wooden stair the workers must've built to get themselves into and out of the pyramid. The only problem was, Bren and company had broken off the end of it when they kicked the stone through.

"Yikes. How sturdy do you think that is?" said Bren.

"Sturdier than jumping," said Barrett, and she took the lead, dropping herself legs first through the hole and then grabbing one of the leather straps Yaozu correctly predicted had been bracing the stone, hanging just for a moment before swinging herself over to the top of the stair. "Easy as English," she said.

Bren and Mouse went next, and Bren was relieved that it was too dark to see how far up they were. Sean and Yaozu also made it with no complications.

The staircase itself wobbled and creaked beneath them, but it seemed sturdy enough after all these hundreds of years.

"Greenheart wood," said Yaozu, as if reading Bren's mind. "Impervious to weather; immortal as the gods."

If he ever returned to Map, thought Bren, what won-ders he would have to tell of the Far East at the Gooey Duck. The sailors he had eavesdropped on over the years didn't know the half of it.

If he ever returned to Map.

Bren had to remind himself he was on the other side of the world, inside a two-thousand-year-old booby-trapped tomb.

As they got near the bottom, the burial chamber grew brighter, lit by hundreds more of the mysterious lamps. In the center of the floor was a raised stone platform, and atop that was a gold coffin, rectangular in shape but curved along the top. Barrett and Yaozu reverently walked around the coffin, running their hands over the surface.

"Can you believe we're standing next to the tomb of China's first emperor," said Barrett to no one in particular. "People have searched for this, wondered about the legends, for almost two thousand years."

"The coffin alone must be worth a fortune," said Bren. "Though I suppose you'd have a hard time getting it out of here."

"What about all this?" said Sean, who was walking around the main floor of the tomb, picking up treasures made of gold, silver, bronze, jade, and lacquer as if he were rummaging through an old curiosity shop. The oth-ers joined him and found everything from carved animals to kitchen utensils like cauldrons, wine vessels, cups, and pitchers. More decorative pottery and lacquer boxes were everywhere as well.

"There must be thousands of items in here," said Bren. "Tens of thousands! The other six Immortals could be buried under any of these piles."

"Let's check the coffin before we rummage through all this," said Barrett. "Many a king, pharaoh, and emperor has been buried with his goodies within arm's reach."

They all ascended the stone platform again and surrounded the emperor's coffin—large enough from the outside to hold a giant, which gave them some hope the emperor might have been buried with artifacts.

"Is there some Chinese phrase we can say, for good luck?" said Barrett.

"No luck needed," said Yaozu. "At this point the magic objects are either inside here or they are not."

Barrett nodded and all five of them pushed on the coffin lid from the same side, barely budging it at first, but finally getting it to slide away from its base.

"Not too far, if we can help it," said Barrett. "I'd hate for the lid to crash to the floor and become damaged."

"Says the grave robber," said Sean, straining to help move the lid.

They didn't move it far, but they did move it enough to see what was inside. Bren had been expecting a skeleton, or at least a mummy, but instead there was a life-size suit of armor made of green tiles.

"A jade burial suit!" said Yaozu, growing excited. "Another rumor that had not, before now, been proven true."

They slid the coffin lid away just enough so that they could lift the body out and set it on the stone platform. It was lighter than Bren expected. Then again, there were three adults and Mouse helping lift it.

Yaozu and Barrett both turned back to the coffin, hoping to find more, but there was nothing else. They could see that the inside of the coffin was lacquered and exquisitely made, but that didn't change the fact that it was empty. There were no magic artifacts.

"I don't understand," said Yaozu. "I was so sure . . ."

"Maybe someone else beat us to them," said Sean.

Barrett shook her head. "It's obvious no one's been in here."

Yaozu was already off the stone pedestal, going through the mounds of treasure on the floor of the pyramid.

"You and Yaozu said that might be the case," Bren reminded her. "You may just have to keep looking."

"There may not be time!" Barrett said, more loudly than she'd intended. "I just mean, we don't want them to fall into the wrong hands."

"Are the wrong hands anyone's but yours?" said Sean.

Barrett turned on him like she was ready to strike, but Sean threw up his hands and said, "Sorry, Lady Barrett. My apologies. But honestly, have you not looked around you? At the wealth of treasure in here? You're an antiquary who's just unearthed one of the most sought-after tombs in history! Bloody hell, I bet this jade suit alone would set you up for life. . . ."

Sean kicked at the suit, not hard, but harder than he'd intended. His boot hit the right shoulder, caving in several of the jade tiles and leaving a gaping hole.

"Oops."

"You idiot!" said Barrett, but when she knelt down to examine the damage, her jaw dropped.

"What is it?" said Bren.

"The suit," said Barrett. "It's empty."

"What?" said Yaozu, coming over to kneel next to her, examining the hole Sean had made. They all took a turn looking, and finally took the suit apart entirely, still not believing their eyes.

"Could the body have disintegrated after all this time?" said Sean.

"Not without a trace, I don't believe," said Barrett.

"So someone took the trouble to pretend to bury Emperor Qin inside the biggest, most expensive funeral complex ever?" said Bren.

"It would appear so," said Barrett.

"Unless . . . ," said Yaozu, stroking his straggle of a beard.

"Unless he found the secret to becoming immortal?" said Mouse.

"That is what I was thinking," said Yaozu. "Qin's obsession with eternal life was well known."

That's when Bren noticed that the wall directly behind the coffin had begun to sweat. Little beads of perspiration, as if the chamber had suddenly become as humid as a greenhouse. Except it hadn't. If anything, Bren felt cold, probably from fear but also from being so far underground. And it was only that one wall.

The beads became bigger, and to Bren's horror, they weren't beads of water at all. A minute later the wall began to weep metallic tears, heavy globes of quicksilver that poured down from cracks in the pyramid steps, puddling on the ground, then gradually rolling together in wobbly silver balls.

"What . . . is . . . happening," said Sean.

Bren was almost too scared to speak, but he reminded himself that he had been through this before, and he calmed his nerves by telling himself that Mouse knew what she was doing.

"Mouse, is this necessary?" When she didn't answer, he asked again, more firmly, "What's going on?"

She tore her eyes away from the wall and looked at

Bren. "It's not my dragon," she said.

Bren's heart stopped.

He turned to the others and screamed, "Run! Back up the stairs!"

Sean ran for the staircase, followed closely by Barrett and Yaozu. Bren tried to push Mouse along next, but she seemed mesmerized by the mercury dragon forming around her. Already several pools had melded and mutated into the dragon's spine, a long, gleaming row of silver spikes. Bren could see the outline of a mouth and teeth and nostrils on the far side of the chamber, and the beginnings of a tail, a shiny liquid whip.

The others were halfway to the top by the time Bren and Mouse made the bottom step. When they reached the first turn in the staircase, Barrett was already to the top and leaped onto the dangling leather straps, hauling herself up and out of the hatch. Sean was next, and once Barrett had helped reel him in they made sure Yaozu made it out safely, too.

Except they weren't safe, Bren realized as he and Mouse made the second turn, which would take them to the catwalk across the top of the pyramid. He had seen the mercury dragon throw itself after the admiral in the cavern. It was both solid and liquid at the same time, and despite how small the hatch was it could just pour itself through and re-form.

No sooner had Bren thought this than the dragon, fully formed, sprang from the floor, metal jaws snapping, aiming for the catwalk just ahead of where Bren and Mouse were running.

The massive jaws with their massive teeth came together like a clashing of swords, but they missed the catwalk, and the dragon plunged back to the floor like a kite that had suddenly lost wind. For the first time Bren felt himself breathe . . . they actually had a chance to get out of here if there was a limit to how high the dragon could go.

"Come on, Mouse," he said, pushing her forward. They had both frozen in their tracks when the dragon leaped. But the dragon had a backup plan. Bren looked down in time to see the silver tail slash at the wooden stair, shattering part of the bottom section.

Bren and Mouse stopped again, which was a mistake. The second swipe from the dragon's tail took out the rest of the bottom, and the whole ragged staircase began to fail.

"Hurry!" Barrett screamed. She and Sean had both wedged themselves halfway through the hatch, their arms extended. Mouse ran and jumped, not even going for the leather straps, and Barrett and Sean caught her and pulled her through. Bren had to pause until they reappeared, and when they did he ran and leaped toward their arms as well.

Except the thrashing dragon had swiped at what was left of the stair, collapsing the whole scaffold, so that Bren pushed off against loose wood falling the other way. He felt himself falling through space, the bottom of the closest leather strap seemingly a mile away . . .

His hand caught leather, somehow, and when he looked up he saw that Barrett was hanging almost all the way through the hatch while the others held her. She had ripped loose one of the leather straps so that Bren was able to catch it lower.

"We've got you, son," she said, slowly hauling him in while the others pulled her back up. Bren's heart was so quick with terror that he could barely think or breathe, but one clear thought did manage to cross his mind—the dragon could jump this high.

He told himself not to look down, but his eyes disobeyed, and when he saw the gaping metal jaws rising to his legs he lost his grip on the leather strap.

But he didn't fall. Barrett had his arms now, and when the dragon's jaws clanged shut, Bren's legs were safely away, and a moment later he was being pulled out of the hatch to the outside of the pyramid.

The five of them collapsed on the nearest step, but Bren forced himself to stand up again and said to the others, "We have to keep going." He led them down the steps of the pyramid until they reached the bottom. Bren turned to make sure Mouse was with them, and when he did, he saw tiny blobs of mercury oozing through the seams of the pyramid. The dragon had found another way out.

"Once that thing re-forms, we have no hope of outrunning it," said Bren. "Trust me."

"I believe you, lad," said Sean. "So now what?"

He looked for Mouse and found her standing over the pool of water again. "Mouse, we have to get out of here!" He tried to pull her away, but she held fast and said, "Look—show me the Bridge Across the Sky."

The water clouded and then came back into focus, and Bren's heart jumped into his throat. It was as if Mouse had turned a telescope to the south and they were now looking at the stone bridge where Bren had nearly lost his life.

"Show me the Dragon's Gate," she said.

The Bridge Across the Sky faded from view, and in its place was a mountain range towering above a shabby village. There was nothing like a gate there, much less a dragon.

"Mouse, we need a way out," said Bren, turning away from the pool and watching the mercury dragon slowly take shape.

"Show me the way to the Dragon's Gate," she said. This time the pool showed no reflection, not even their own. Bren couldn't make sense of it.

"Mouse . . ."

"Here," said Mouse. "In here."

She pulled her hand away from Bren and jumped into

the pool, disappearing below the surface. When she didn't come up after a few seconds, Bren began to panic. The dragon was forming, but he couldn't leave her . . . he stuck his arm in the pool, fishing for her, but there was nothing there. He plunged his head into the water and opened his eyes. The water stung but it was clear. He pulled his head back and looked for the others. "Over here!" Bren cried. "I think Mouse found our way out."

CHAPTER 24

THE OLD WOMAN
OF THE MOUNTAIN

B ren had the sensation of swimming, but not like a boy
swims. Rather he felt himself shooting instinctively
through the water like a fish, able to see and breathe normally. And then suddenly he needed to be out, to breathe
air again, so he leaped from the water onto a stone floor
and lay there, dripping wet.

He sat up and noticed he was in a small, circular
room that looked as if it hadn't been occupied in ages.
In the middle of the floor was an opening—a well, he
guessed—and along the walls were four arched doorways.

Mouse appeared in one of them.

"Where are the others?" he said.

Before she could answer, Yaozu, Barrett, and Sean each sprang from the well onto the floor. From the looks on their faces Bren could tell they had no more idea how they got here than he did.

"Did I just become a fish?" said Sean.

"All I know is that I'm wet," said Barrett.

"Mouse, do you know where we are?" Bren asked.

"Yes," she said. "I believe we are near a place called Khotan. Follow me."

Still dripping, the group followed Mouse out of the room, down a corridor to a wooden ladder that disappeared through a hole above. They climbed up into another circular room, but this time the four archways were admitting daylight. When he stepped outside, Bren could see desert in all directions, and a tumbledown village in the distance, at the foot of a mountain range. Mouse was heading that way.

▲▲▲

The walk to the village took about an hour, plenty of time for them all to dry as they walked across the sand in the warm sun. Despite the look of the village, it was bustling. The main streets were packed with canvas-covered stalls offering all manner of food and goods—fruits and vegetables; piles of fish; clothing, uncut fabric, rugs; musical instruments; and vendors selling hot food, including

kebabs of meat and boiled sheep's lung. Camels and donkeys crowded the stone streets, as did men and women
dressed in colorful clothes.

There was an entire section of the market devoted to
animals—ducks, geese, and chickens hanging by their feet;
goats, cows, donkeys, sheep, horses, and camels either being
bought, sold, or led to slaughter. Bren had to look away
when he saw men openly killing and dismembering these
beasts, even though he knew very well he would happily
accept a large leg of lamb or pork shoulder for dinner if it
were offered to him. Elsewhere was a village apothecary of
sorts, selling dried frogs, animal gallbladders, rhino horns,
and dried sea creatures for medicinal purposes.

Bren gravitated to a group of artisans working with
jade and silver. Many vendors were simply selling polished
stones, which they sprinkled with water to make them
appear more lustrous. Others had carved totems similar to
the ones Bren had seen during their journey. The metal-
workers were selling finely wrought pieces of silver, and, in
some cases, tin—teapots, urns, dishes, wind chimes, snuff-
boxes, candlesticks, horse collars, and more, all precisely
shaped and inlaid with complicated designs, mostly religious
motifs, on all surfaces.

But what made Bren stop in his tracks were the houses
in the center of the village, once they had finished wandering through the vast bazaar. The homes were made of

adobe, and along their fronts were massive wooden plank doors, all of them adorned with script. And some of the script had been struck through with a line.

"Yaozu, what is that?" said Bren, pointing to one of the wood doors.

"In olden days, this was how villages conducted their census," Yaozu explained. "The names of every person living in the house were written upon the door. If someone died, they were struck through. If someone new had come, they were added at the bottom."

Bren immediately thought of the recurring dream he had had back on the Vanishing Island—seeing a door with his name and his parents' names, then his mother's name struck, with Black's added, and then Mouse's, and finally, everyone's name crossed out except his mother's.

"You know this place?" Yaozu asked.

"No," said Bren, not really knowing how to explain to Yaozu that he'd dreamed of a place he never knew existed. "I don't think so."

"I promised to take you to the Dragon's Gate, Mouse, but it would seem you have taken me instead. The mountain where the Black and White Jade Rivers meet is this way."

They rejoined Barrett and Sean and the five of them followed the Khotan River to where it divided, at the foot of the Angry Mountain from Yaozu's story about how the rivers split. Except it was more than a mountain. It was three overlapping hills, which to Bren's eye looked like they could be three arches of a magnificent gate . . . or in his wildest imagination, the serpentine body of a Chinese dragon.

"What are we looking at?" said Sean.

"The Dragon's Gate," said Bren. "Isn't that right, Mouse?"

She nodded.

"Can you open it?" said Yaozu.

"What are you talking about?" said Sean. "I don't see a bloomin' gate."

Yaozu kept his eyes fixed on Mouse. "Can you?"

Mouse slowly shook her head. "No. The bones didn't tell me that."

If Yaozu was disappointed, he didn't show it. "I've asked around . . . apparently there is an old woman up the mountain whom people seek out for advice and fortune-telling. She may know."

"How do we find her?" said Barrett.

"She lives next to a tree that bears every kind of fruit."

Sean raised an eyebrow, but apparently he had given up questioning Yaozu's stories.

"Lead the way," said Barrett.

▲▲▲

As Yaozu led them along a path up the first of the three hills, Mouse grabbed Bren's hand and motioned for him to slow down. When there was enough distance between them and the others, she said to him, "I know how to open the gate."

Bren stopped altogether. "Then why did you say you didn't?"

"Because the gate mustn't be opened," she said. "They aren't here for the right reasons."

"Mouse, how do you know . . ."

"You two coming?" Sean called to them.

They hurried to catch up, and Bren and Mouse said nothing more as they continued to climb, until finally Yaozu stopped and pointed to something away from the path.

"There," he said, and Bren saw it too. A tree, heavy with fruit—gold, red, orange, and pink. Hundreds of pieces, no two seemingly alike. Near it was a small stone house with a wooden door and a stone chimney. There was a garden planted along the side, and a fire pit in front. Before they could approach, a woman came out of the house carrying a straw basket. She was the oldest person Bren had ever seen, her face so creased with lines you almost couldn't tell which was her mouth. But her eyes were black and bright.

She started at the sight of the five strangers, but then her eyes landed on Mouse and she dropped the basket.

"I've been waiting for you for a long, long time," she croaked, motioning to Mouse with a hand so withered it was almost a nub. Mouse went to her.

"My friends have questions for you," said Mouse, and

the woman's beady eyes darted in the direction of Yaozu and Barrett.

"You can each ask me one thing."

Yaozu went first: "Did Emperor Qin pass through the Dragon's Gate?"

The old woman replied, "He did."

"Are the Eight Immortals behind the Dragon's Gate?" Barrett asked. "The demigods themselves, I mean."

The old woman replied, "They are."

She looked at Sean. "Do you have a question?"

Sean was taken off guard. "Me?" He thought for a moment before asking, "Can you tell me how to get these two children home safely?"

"Yes and no," she said. "The Black Jade River crosses the mountain and passes through a corridor. Your kind are there, you and the boy. As for the girl, she is home now."

To Bren she said, "And you, young son?"

A million thoughts flooded Bren's mind . . . so many he couldn't think straight. There was so much he wanted to know but he didn't know where to start . . . or if he even knew the right questions to ask to get the answers he sought. Finally, he took two halting steps forward and asked, "Is there a way to see my mother again?"

His hands began to sweat and his mouth filled with a bitter taste as he awaited her reply.

"Yes, there is a way," she said. "Open the Dragon's Gate."

He turned to Mouse, who avoided his eyes. "Mouse . . ."

The old woman held up her hand. "She must come with me."

"No!" Bren almost shouted. "I have to know!"

But the woman was pulling Mouse into the house. "She will be back, you have my word," she said, just before the two of them disappeared.

Bren tried to run after them, but Yaozu stopped him.

"I'm with Bren," said Sean. "The old woman could be dangerous!"

"No," said Yaozu. "Mouse will be back."

Bren forced himself to sit and wait with the others, when all he wanted to do was kick the door in, to ask Mouse whether she would open the gate now that she knew there was a way for Bren to see his mother again. Or maybe Mouse already knew that.

Finally, after close to an hour, the door opened, and Mouse came outside, alone.

The whole group rushed toward her, but she stopped. "No, just Bren," she said, and she took him up the hill, away from the others, behind the Tree of Every Fruit, and held his hands with hers.

"Are you really not coming with us?" he asked.

"This is where I am meant to be," she said, her eyes as opaque as ever. When Bren tried to argue, she cut him off: "There's something you need to know about the cavern, and the girl there. She was never a sorceress, or an heir to anything. She was a pawn of the magician, Anqi Sheng—the catfish man. Anqi Sheng helped Qin defeat the Ancients because he thought they had lost their way. It was he who wrote the prophecy that one day an heir would be born to restore the Ancients to power. When Kublai Khan's star reader revealed the prophecy, Anqi Sheng feared the emperor, or those who succeeded him, wouldn't rest until the heir was found, so he sacrificed Sun."

"Mouse—"

"Just listen," she said. "We don't have much time. I was the true heir, Bren, born much later, of course, but still long ago. Long before you. Anqi Sheng decided to exile Sun so he could keep the white jade far away from everyone, until I could find it. His decision fated me not to grow up until I made it to the Vanishing Island. He also needed to buy time—centuries, millennia, whatever it took—for the black jade stone, which had been lost through the ages, to reappear."

She reached up to touch the black stone around Bren's neck. "It's the two stones together where true power lies."

"Mouse, I don't understand. The power to do what?"

"Open the Dragon's Gate," she said. "The power of the artifacts alone is but a shadow, enhanced by you and me, without our knowing it, because of the soul of Li Tie Guai trapped within our stones. Yet he is but one of eight, and divided at that. That's what Anqi Sheng wanted—to open the gate and release the full power of the Immortals back into the world. But I refuse to honor the prophecy."

"Did the old woman tell you all this?" said Bren.

"Some of it. She also told me she could give me my name, a real name, something I have always wanted. But the cost would be dear. I would become my true age before the sun set. I want you to know I'm okay with that. I'm ready. I don't want to be a child forever."

She grabbed Bren's hands, and he saw that hers had changed. They were beginning to wrinkle. At first he thought it was just because she was gripping him so tightly, but that wasn't it. They were aging . . . Mouse was aging.

"Mouse, what's happening?"

"My white stone and your black one," she said. "They represent a wound as old as time. They are the key to the gate, Bren, but you mustn't open it!"

"Mouse, the old woman said I could find my mother. . . ." He choked on his words. Mouse's eyes had begun to change, too. They were no longer black and opaque, but more of a cloudy, translucent grey. And they were no longer emotionless. They were full of sadness.

"There is only one way for you to be reunited with your mother, Bren."

Her hair was turning grey before Bren's eyes. Her face was changing, too, pruning and shrinking. He looked down at his hands—they were in the grip of an old woman's hands, her fingers thin, brittle sticks.

Bren was crying now.

Mouse pressed her white jade stone into Bren's hand. The stone was cold in his hands, and Mouse's hands were cold around his. She was older now than the woman in the house. Her skin was shrinking against her frail skeleton, her skull now showing through her thin hair.

"I've been alive for hundreds of years," she continued, her voice becoming weak and hoarse. "The Ancients lost power for a reason, and are no more deserving than Qin, or Kublai Khan, or the Netherlanders, or any of the religions that have tried to lay hold to the East. Whoever comes to power, there will no doubt be a prophecy about their downfall, and another child stolen from a family, or some other atrocity by those hoping to make it so."

"Then why did you tell me how to open the gate?" Bren cried.

"Because you must make this decision for yourself," she said. "Just like I did. You must know what you are capable of, and make your own choices."

"Mouse, please don't leave me."

She stepped forward and threw her arms around Bren, and he hugged her back harder than he had ever hugged anyone in his life. It was as if he thought he could hold her tight enough that she would never be able to leave. She whispered in his ear, but the words became wind, and as he was squeezing her, pressing her against him, he felt her body becoming light . . . insubstantial. He closed his fists and heard the crunching of leaves. He clenched his arms tighter but there was almost nothing there, just a swirling mass of dried leaves and bare twigs, and then a great wind blew down the mountain, scattering the leaves and twigs, and Bren stood there, alone, his arms empty.

CHAPTER 25

THE DRAGON'S
GATE

The next thing Bren knew he was being helped up from the ground by Barrett and Sean. He wasn't crying anymore, but his eyes were puffy and his vision blurry. He tried looking around for Mouse, hoping it had all been a dream, or a trick, but all he saw was the old woman standing there between her house and the Tree of Every Fruit.

"Lad, what happened?" said Sean. "Where is Mouse?"

He had to fight the urge to cry again. "I don't . . . she's gone."

"Gone?" said Barrett. "Gone where?"

Bren was shaking his head. "Just . . . gone."

Yaozu met them and helped lead Bren back down the mountain, where they found a place to stay overnight in the village. They took him to a room, where he realized he was clutching something in his right fist. He opened it and saw the white jade resting there.

"Is that her stone?" said Yaozu.

Bren nodded. "She left it with me. She told me how to open the Dragon's Gate."

He could almost hear Barrett and Yaozu catch their breath. Neither seemed willing to ask him about it right now. Instead, Barrett put her arm through Bren's and said, "Lie down, son. I think you need rest. We all do."

Bren obeyed and was soon asleep. At some point during the night he could have sworn an old woman was standing over him, her crabbed hand around the collar of his robe. When he did awake, early in the morning, Barrett was sitting at the foot of his bed, holding the white jade stone.

"Put that down," said Bren, more harshly than he had intended. It was the only thing he had now of Mouse, and he didn't want anyone else to touch it.

"I'm sorry about Mouse," said Barrett. "I wish I knew what had happened."

"I know what happened," said Bren, taking back the white jade. He knew what was coming next.

"You said Mouse told you how to open the Dragon's Gate. But she told you not to open it, didn't she?"

"How did you guess?" he said.

She patted Bren gently on the leg. "Yaozu will be very disappointed."

"But not you?" said Bren.

She didn't answer at first. "You're right, Bren. I wanted the artifacts for more than just their historical value. There are people who are powerless in this world who deserve better. The Eight Immortals could do a lot of good."

"Is that what Yaozu believes?" said Bren. "Does he fancy himself some sort of messiah?"

"You'll have to ask him," said Barrett. "But I don't believe he's an evil man."

Bren didn't dispute that. "I dreamed the old woman sneaked in here last night, to take both stones. Or maybe it wasn't a dream. In any case it probably isn't safe for us to stay here any longer."

Barrett stood up. "I'll tell the others. But let me ask you something first, Bren. Are you sure this is the right decision? That old woman told you that opening the gate might bring you and your mother together again. And it was your mother who gave you that stone around your neck. Don't you think you were meant to use it? It's just a question I might ask myself."

Barrett left him, and Bren was alone for the next two

hours, except for a young girl who brought him something to eat and drink. It reminded him of when he first met Mouse, when he thought it was a young boy bringing him broth when he first boarded the *Albatross* and was seasick for days.

As soon as the girl left, he wept.

▲▲▲

Bren didn't wait for the others, nor did he pack his things. He headed for the mountain between the rivers alone, the black stone in his left hand, the white stone in his right, carrying them as if they were the scales of justice.

"Bren!" Sean called to him, half running to catch up. "Lad, what are you doing?"

"Opening the Dragon's Gate," he said. "It's what everyone wants."

"Mouse didn't want it. She told you so."

Bren tried to show no emotion, but his voice was cracking. "What difference does it make what she wants now? She had a choice to stay with us, and she chose to leave."

"Mouse must've believed it was dangerous to do this, Bren. A lot of people could die. *You* could die."

"Maybe that's not such a bad thing," said Bren, and he kept walking. Or tried to—Sean had grabbed his arm.

"Your father wouldn't agree with that," said Sean. "Neither would I."

Bren saw Barrett and Yaozu running to catch up with

them. He laughed. "They want me to open it." He pulled away from Sean and kept walking until he was standing at the fork in the river at the base of the mountain.

"Before she left, Mouse told me that to open the gate, the white and black jade stones had to be returned to their rivers at the same time by the same person."

He closed his hands around each stone and waded into the Khotan River, until he could reach forth his arms and touch the waters of the Black Jade with his left and the White Jade with his right. He sank his fists below the surface, and as he did so he felt the stones come alive in his grip, thrumming against his fingers and palms. He closed his eyes, took a deep breath, and opened both hands together.

Nothing happened right away. The mountain didn't explode and the earth didn't open up to swallow them. Still, Bren was afraid to open his eyes. Then he felt something, a slow rumbling along the bed of the river through the soles of his shoes, which had been worn thin as parchment. Slowly the vibration grew in power.

Bren opened his eyes and turned to the shore to find Sean, but as the quaking amplified, his body began to tremble uncontrollably, his teeth clattering and his vision going blurry. He could see none of the others and suddenly began to panic, the ground sending shock waves through his heart.

And then the shaking stopped.

Bren dragged himself from the shallow river and collapsed on the shore in relief. He looked around for the others, but they were no longer there. No one was. He was alone.

A bird landed nearby. It was a crow. Bren looked closer at the blackish bird, its black eyes, and then it blinked and its eyes were blue. Bren cried out, or tried to, but his voice was mute, and the bird blinked again and its eyes were black.

Bren dropped his head, not wanting to look. He grabbed a rock and threw it at the crow, chasing the bird away.

Did you know a group of crows is called a murder?

"Who said that?" said Bren, wobbling to his feet and looking around.

Well, did you?

"No."

I thought surely I must have taught you that up at the lakes. There were so many crows there.

He stumbled toward the Dragon's Gate, and there, sitting on a rock next to the Black Jade River, was a woman with dark brown hair tied up upon her head, wearing a homespun grey sleeping gown and slippers. It was exactly how she had looked the last time Bren saw her, lying in bed on top of the blankets. Her hair had been pulled away from her face because she had been sweating so.

So the stone I gave you came from here, she said, dipping her fingers in the river. *I had no idea.*

"It saved my life," said Bren.

Did it? I have my doubts.

"What do you mean?"

You're a resourceful boy, Bren. Both in imagination and spirit. It's the thing I love most about you. But I'm glad it meant something to you. That makes me happy.

"Is it really you?" he said, and he took several more steps toward her, not quite willing to believe it was true. But his mother stopped him.

Don't come any closer, Bren.

"What? Why not?"

This is no place for you right now. If you didn't believe Mouse, believe me. Please.

"Mom, I don't understand. . . ."

Take this back, she said, holding out her fist, then opening it to show him the black stone. *If you take it back now, you can close the gate before more damage is done.*

He tried to argue but he choked on his words. His mother stepped closer and gently lifted his hand from his side, folding it over the stone. Her touch nearly killed him, and he had to shut his eyes to stop the tears from flooding out. He didn't want his mother to see him cry. When he was able to open them again, she was gone.

"No! Mom!" he called, terrified that he had missed his

chance. His heart was beating against his chest, so hard and fast Bren didn't realize the ground had started shaking again. He looked at the mountain, and there in the center of the three hills a huge seam had opened up from the ground to nearly the top.

"Bren, come on!" It was Sean, grabbing him by the collar and pulling him away from the river. The mountain had begun to shed rock as the quaking grew more violent. A tumbling boulder just missed them, landing right in front of them. Sean and Bren used it for cover as more went bounding by. And then, almost as suddenly as it had begun, it stopped.

"Aye, lad, you really do have a death wish," said Sean, breathing hard. When they felt it was safe to move, they carefully stood and looked around. The ground was cracked and fallen rock was everywhere. It looked as if the whole village had been destroyed.

Bren looked up at the Dragon's Gate. It was no longer open, if it ever had been. The long vertical crack he thought he had seen was filled with rock. He realized the hand his mother had touched was still clenched, and when he opened it, there sat the black stone.

"Sean, what have I done?"

"You've survived, lad," said Sean. "You've survived. I know that's not what you meant, but that'll have to do for now."

Bren nodded, looking back at the mountain and the Black Jade River and to what was left, if anything, of the village. Then he threw his arms around Sean and hugged him, not letting go for a very long time.

A WORLD APART

"Are we even in India anymore?" said Archibald Black as he and the rest of the Second Regiment of the Indian Royal Survey crested yet another bleak hill over-looking another bleak valley.

"Anything the great Akbar puts on a map of India is part of India," said Aziz.

David Owen planted the theodolite on its tripod and surveyed the valley. "I can't quite get the angle on this one," he said. "The sun's too bright."

"First it's too rainy, then it's too sunny," barked Hasan. "You Brits need to toughen up! No wonder you're a second-rate empire."

"An up-and-coming second-rate empire," said Black.

A bit later, when they stopped for lunch, Owen pulled Black aside. "I'm beginning to feel like an indentured servant."

"You're just now getting that feeling?"

"Maybe we can send a letter back to McNally."

Black gave him a withering look. "And how do you propose to do that?"

"I'm thinking," said Owen.

Black choked down the rest of his dried camel meat. "Wasn't McNally supposed to come out here for the christening, or whatever you call the big show Akbar put on in Agra?"

Owen shook his head. "After Whitehall, he's decided he doesn't like to travel. A bit ironic for a mapmaker, don't you think?"

"His world revolves around him, I suppose," said Black.

Owen gripped a piece of camel jerky in his teeth and pulled. When the strip separated, his hand sprang out and hit Black in the arm.

"Ow!"

"Sorry. Maybe we could just make a run for it?"

"That worked well last time, didn't it?"

"There are no tigers out here," said Owen. "Anyway, I drew a map of this part of the world once for McNally. There's a disputed region northeast of here, not far from where we are now, actually."

"How can you tell?" said Black. "Everything looks the same."

"Not to a mapmaker," said Owen.

Black sighed and sat down on the case concealing the Gutenberg Bible. "Fair enough. But that doesn't really help us get away from our regiment, does it? We'd need a miracle."

Owen finished his jerky and was halfway into his waterskin when they felt the first rumblings.

"Oh dear God, more elephants?" said Black.

"I don't think so, Archibald."

It felt like a herd of wild horses at first, a collective trampling of the ground that made Black and Owen tremble where they sat. But it soon became obvious that it was the ground itself that was trembling, from some unseen force.

"Earthquake!" screamed Aziz, running around frantically. "Run for your lives!"

"No one move!" Hasan ordered. "Store the equipment and we'll ride it out!"

No one did move, or store the equipment—they were stricken with panic. Hasan, their regiment leader, obviously felt he had to do something.

"We're on high ground," he said, his voice being swallowed by the growing tremors. "We have nothing to worry about!"

No sooner had he said it than the hill they were on calved, sending two great chunks of rock sliding down toward the valley. One carried the weight of almost the entire second regiment, the other Archibald Black and David Owen.

The chunk carrying Black and Owen broke off cleanly, sliding down the mountain in one great mass like a ship being launched. It started gradually, then picked up terrible speed, causing both passengers to rapidly make amends with their creator, just before the chunk splashed into a large lake on the eastern end of the valley.

"Archibald!"

"David!"

"Archibald!"

"David!"

Each had fallen into the water—Owen clinging to the slowly sinking rock, and Black to his valuable trunk. They called to each other over and over until finally Black had pulled Owen onto the trunk with him. They dog-paddled to safety, and when it was shallow enough to walk, they pulled the trunk onto the shore and plopped down beside it. They watched together as the giant rock slipped under the water.

"Is it over?" said Black.

He was answered by another trembling of the earth, a long and steady one, but not nearly as severe.

"If I weren't already a religious man . . . ," said Owen, slapping the trunk. He and Black both laughed, but it was a brief moment of levity.

"I wonder about the others," said Black.

"Should we try to find them?"

Black shook his head. "I don't know the right answer to that, David. Morally, perhaps. But we have a chance to get free of here. I think we should take it."

Owen nodded slowly.

"The disputed territory is that way," he said, pointing to the northeast. "A valley at the foot of the Himalayas. When I mapped it for McNally, the region was called Cashmere."

Black struggled to his feet, his clothes covered in dirt and full of holes. He opened the trunk, took out the Bible, and then shoved the empty trunk into the lake. "Lead the way, David. Perhaps we can get a bath and a change of clothes there."

▲▲▲

Bren and Sean looked for Barrett and Yaozu for days after the earthquake. They never found them. They climbed the mountain where the old woman and the Tree of Every Fruit had been, but her small house had been demolished and the tree uprooted. They couldn't find the woman, either.

The damage to the village, both in lives and property, had been severe. They could only wonder at how far away the earthquake had been felt, how widespread the damage. Bren felt sure he would never get over this.

Sean did his best to keep both their spirits up and to plan their next move. "The old woman of the mountain said I could get you home safely if we follow the Black Jade River over the mountain, through a corridor. How does that sound?"

Bren nodded.

"And hey, I went to the inn where we'd stayed. It was a mess, but I found some of our things."

Sean opened his rucksack and pulled out Bren's journal.

"Remember when I said I grabbed this from the *Albatross* 'cause I thought it might bring good luck in finding you? Well, let's consider it our lucky charm in getting home, yeah?"

Lucky charm. Bren reached for the necklace around his neck, but there was nothing there. Old habits. He pressed his hand against his jacket pocket and felt a lump, and with his heart nearly racing out of his chest he reached in and pulled out the black stone—the stone his mother had given back to him on the mountain. But that wasn't possible, was it? He quickly put the stone away and turned away from Sean, afraid he might burst into tears again.

That night the two of them camped in an orchard miles to the west, on their way toward the towering mountains of China's western border. Bren pulled out his journal, but he couldn't make himself write. All he could think about were his last moments with Mouse, and what she had whispered to him, just before she left.

She had said, "Those who seek immortality find only death. There are greater rewards elsewhere, if you keep looking."

Bren put his journal away and slept.

TURN THE PAGE FOR A SNEAK PEEK AT

THE
SEA OF THE
DEAD

Being the **THIRD**
and **FINAL VOLUME** *of*
THE CHRONICLES OF
THE BLACK TULIP

THE JEWEL
OF CASHMERE

The Minister of Wit fussed with his clothes and beard for an hour before leaving his house, changing his trousers, tying and retying his jama, picking out just the right turban, and grooming his beard with cola nut oil until it shined like a brand-new rupee.

As if he wouldn't be dead before the night was over.

He shrugged on his choga, an expensive, heavily brocaded silk coat that always reminded him of a sofa cushion, and took a good look in the mirror. His wife caught him admiring himself and teased him. "You will make a fine nawab of Cashmere, Mullah," she said. "Everyone knows the primary requirement is vanity."

"Pshaw," said the minister, kissing his wife good night and turning to leave.

"Where are you going, fatso? The front door is that way."

"I'm going out the back," he said, flustered. "I want to check on the garden."

"It's still there," his wife said.

"Yes, yes," he said, hurrying out before she teased the beard right off his face.

The garden was fragrant with spring blooms, jasmine and hyacinth and poppy, and the overwhelming aroma calmed him. He took in every scent and buzz of insect, touched the leathery leaves of a rubber tree, moistened the tips of his fingers with the stray drops of a recent summer rain.

And then, a shock: he opened the garden gate onto the pitiful scene of a young girl slumped against the wall across the alley, petting a rat.

"Urchins!" he said, disgusted. "Be gone from here!"

The girl raised her eyes to him, and he received another shock—they were pale green. Not the irises, but the eyeballs themselves, cupping a pair of huge brown pupils, like an avocado sliced in half. She just stared at him and continued to stroke the rat, and the Minister of Wit felt sure he would lose his nerve and run back inside. But then he thought of having to explain to his wife that he was frightened of a little orphan, and so he stamped his foot in the alley and shouted, "Be gone, I say! Are you deaf?"

The girl turned to set the rat aside and slowly stood up. When she wobbled a few steps toward the garden gate, the minister felt his ample stomach clench. What if she tried to lay hands on him? But to his relief she turned and shuffled up the alley into the darkness.

The minister let out a great gust of air and turned the opposite way, following the alley to Dhari Street and then walking briskly through the heart of Jammu until he saw the sign for the Broken Camel.

The man he knew only as Lord Thursday was waiting for him, his white hair like a boll of cotton and his white eyebrows a pair of billowing clouds. Despite being dressed in a wool jacket and trousers and wearing a tweed cape, he had picked out a spot near the fireplace and apparently made the owner start a fire. That was a Brit for you—always fearing a chill, even in India. And was he drinking hot cider in June?

"Grab a seat, Minister," said Lord Thursday, offering his hand but not bothering to get up. "You're looking splendid as usual. Everything in Cashmere looks splendid, come to think of it. The streets, the gardens, the temples . . ."

"Yes, the great Akbar is quite the aesthete," said the minister, eager to avoid chitchat.

"So what it is you wanted to see me—"

The minister slapped his hand down on the table before Lord Thursday could finish his question. If the Brit was startled, or offended, he didn't show it. The minister peeled his hand away, leaving behind a small piece of paper, neatly folded. "Go ahead, read it."

Thursday picked up the paper, studiously unfolded it, and read. The wind seemed to catch his eyebrows.

"A poem?"

The minister nodded. "They've been left all over Cashmere, allegedly by a woman known only as Habba Khatoon."

"A lady poet?" said Thursday, astonished.

"I'm sure you have lady writers in Britannia," said the minister.

Lord Thursday thought about it for a minute, becoming distracted.

"*Anyway,*" said the minister, "the problem is obvious."

"Is it?" said Thursday, marshaling his eyebrows toward the paper again, looking for clues. He mumbled aloud:

Where now is the day's delight?
And where the night's romance?
In garden paths the cobras sleep,
In flowered beds the widows weep
And the nightingale sings of revenge.

Our mourning dress shall be woven air and evening
   dew;
We pluck out our eyes and
Replace them with gemstones.
In henna I have dyed my hands;
In blood I will dye yours.

Thursday's lips kept moving as he read and reread the poem to himself, until the minister realized that the problem was *not* obvious. "Khatoon is known as the nightingale, you see, and the revenge she speaks of is for the Mogul takeover of Cashmere, which many feel was accomplished with deceit."

"Ah, yes," said Thursday, waving a hand at the poem. "The cobras and such."

"'Woven air' and 'evening dew' describe two different kinds of muslin used in Mogul clothing, suggesting that the aggrieved shall mourn by taking back from us."

"And this bit about plucking out their eyes?" said Thursday.

The minister sighed. Was this really a member of British intelligence he was sitting across from? "Akbar's nine ministers, of which I am one, are known as his navaratnas—his nine gems."

Suddenly Lord Thursday's eyebrows leaped upward like a pair of startled cats. "You mean all this talk about a conspiracy to steal the nine gems . . . it's not a jewel heist?"

"No," said the minister. "It's an assassination plot."

All Lord Thursday could do was shake his head. "Dear me, dear me. What can we do?"

"Prevent it?" said the minister. "Just an idea."

"But how?"

The minister stared at Lord Thursday, wondering how much pain he could inflict by plucking out his eyebrows one hair at a time. "The other ministers and I might have dismissed all this as mere poetry, but then I got wind of something called the Lapwing Conspiracy. I have it on good authority that this is the group planning to turn the nightingale's songs of revenge into action."

"Nightingales, lapwings," said Lord Thursday. "Why the preoccupation with small birds?"

"Is that really important?" said the minister, struggling to remain polite.

"Perhaps it's a clue!"

"I assume they take their name from a speech Akbar made a few months ago," the minister explained. "He described the protests against Mogul rule in Cashmere as the screeching of so many lapwings. Regardless," he added quickly, before Lord Thursday could get off track again, "we're all on guard until the identities of these people can be ferreted out. I myself am afraid to show my face in public. Akbar says he can't spare extra security right now, but he's offered the help of the British, per his arrangement with Queen Adeline."

"Well, you're in good hands," said Lord Thursday. "Tell me everything you know, and I can assure you that the Britannic Secret Service will do the rest."

The minister decided not to ask why the BSS didn't *already* know everything, and proceeded to spend the next hour giving Lord Thursday a detailed rundown of the situation. He was so frustrated by the time he left that he marched straight home by the main roads and walked right up to the front of his house, lapwings be damned. He was going to enter *his* house by the front door.

His sudden bravery didn't stop him from stealing glances up and down the street before unlocking the door, or from closing and locking the door behind him as quickly as possible.

"You wouldn't believe the night I've had, Wife," said the minister, shambling back to his bedroom as he unwrapped his choga and tossed his turban aside. "Britannia will forever be stuck in the Middle Ages if this ancient dimwit they sent to me is supposed to be one of the queen's finest."

The minister filled his wash basin with the pitcher of water and washed his face. He looked in the mirror and noticed how quiet the house was. "Where are you, Wife? Shveta?"

"Here I am, Mullah," she said, coming into the bedroom

and wrapping her arms around her husband from behind.

"And what did you get up to tonight?" said the minister.

"I just sat here and thought about how much I worship you," came her reply.

"Funny. Perhaps *you* should be the Minister of Wit."

"Perhaps," she said, moving her hands up his back and gently massaging his shoulders. The minister closed his eyes, the tension from his meeting melting away. "The neck, Wife, the neck. Ah, yes."

Her agile fingers worked her husband's long neck with the skill of one playing a musical instrument. In fact, the minister never realized he was having trouble breathing until he began to feel lightheaded and wobbly, his legs going out from under him. And perhaps, before darkness overtook him, he was able to catch a glimpse of the slight smile on his wife's lips as he collapsed to the floor, sputtering his last words: "Deceitful cow."

The creak of a wooden door made Shveta Do-Piyaza look up.

"Is he dead?" said the girl with the avocado eyes.

"As a doornail," Shveta replied.

READ THEM ALL!

"Fans will wait with bated breath for
the third book in the trilogy."

—*Kirkus Reviews* (starred review)